"I am not very experienced with men, you know."

"I deserve that reminder." He stood, looking down at the evidence of her undressing that night: the pearl earrings and necklace discarded on the dressing table, a scatter of orange blossom on the boards, one silk stocking. He stooped and picked it up, letting it hang from his fingers. "If you weren't so sheltered, so innocent...."

"I might be sheltered and inexperienced," Hebe observed tartly, "but I am hardly innocent. I understand exactly what the matter is: my inexperience means that I do not know what to do about it."

That made him laugh, a sudden gasp of amusement. "I wish I could show you."

"So do I." It was out before she realized she was going to say it. Her hands flew to her mouth and her gray eyes stared at him aghast over the shield of her fingers.

* * *

The Earl's Intended Wife
Harlequin® Historical #793 – March 2006

THE EARL'S INTENDED WIFE

*is Louise Allen's stirring debut novel
in Harlequin® Historical*

Louise Allen
The Earl's Intended Wife

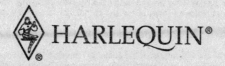

TORONTO • NEW YORK • LONDON
AMSTERDAM • PARIS • SYDNEY • HAMBURG
STOCKHOLM • ATHENS • TOKYO • MILAN • MADRID
PRAGUE • WARSAW • BUDAPEST • AUCKLAND

ISBN 0-373-29393-3

THE EARL'S INTENDED WIFE

Copyright © 2004 by Louise Allen

First North American publication 2006

This edition published by arrangement with Harlequin Books S.A.

www.eHarlequin.com

Printed in U.S.A.

Available from Harlequin® Historical and
LOUISE ALLEN

The Earl's Intended Wife #793

Look for the next great read from Louise Allen

THE SOCIETY CATCH

Coming July 2006

Chapter One

It was an ordinary day when Hebe Carlton first set eyes upon the handsomest man in Malta and took an instant dislike to him. Up until that Wednesday, life had seemed to consist mainly of ordinary days: after it, looking back, she could recall few that were.

Hebe's reaction to the stranger was not, as she would have readily admitted, because she was impervious to good looks in a man, or to the appeal of a smart military uniform. Nor was she a young lady given to making instant judgements about people—experience had taught her that they were usually far more interesting than one thought at first sight. But there was something about this man that she could not quite pin down yet which disturbed her, and she watched intently as he strolled towards their house on the shady side of the square in company with Commodore Sir Richard Latham.

The Commodore, the intended of Hebe's widowed stepmama, was dropping in for luncheon as was his habit when he could escape from the demands of squadron headquarters down at the dockside, and he was already somewhat later in arriving than was usual.

The two men were deep in conversation, but paused

before crossing the road, which gave Hebe the opportunity for a more careful scrutiny of the stranger. She then decided that she liked him even less than at first sight, for an expression of severity and utter seriousness sat austerely on regular, tanned features. Hebe indulged the fantasy that he was one of the dispossessed Knights of St John, exiled from their island only a few years before by Napoleon, and still negotiating their return with the new English overlords.

An interest in hellfire, celibacy and the writings of the more rigorous early Church Fathers would suit him, she decided, curling up more snugly in her eyrie and enjoying her fantasy. The graceful whitewashed house with its green shutters and curving iron balconies possessed a number of deeply embrasured windows, each with its seat, and Hebe was often to be found curled up in one with a book, or watching with lively curiosity the passing scene below.

'Hee…bee!' her stepmama called impatiently from the foot of the stairs. 'Is the Commodore coming or not?' She had dispatched Hebe to keep a lookout ten minutes ago, at the usual time for his arrival, so that she could ensure that Cook put the final touches to luncheon at exactly the right moment. Mrs Carlton was a firm believer in the maxim that a lady could not be too careful when attaching the interest of a gentleman, and attention to his every comfort was of prime importance.

'Yes, Mama.' Hebe uncurled herself and ran to the landing to deliver the news. 'He is on the other side of the square with an army officer—it looks as though they are both coming this way.'

Mrs Carlton's uptilted face became thoughtful. 'A *young* officer?' she enquired.

'Umm.' Hebe thought about it. 'Late twenties, perhaps thirty.'

She was not surprised when Mrs Carlton, with a toss of her blonde curls, picked up a pair of snips from the hall table and opened the door. 'Perhaps a flower or two for the table,' she said casually, stepping outside.

Hebe sighed and made her way back to the window. Any new officer upon the scene—naval or army—attracted her mama's interest, and provoked concentrated efforts to make Hebe behave in such a way that he would instantly perceive what an eligible catch she was. The monk, for that was how she was beginning to think of him, was about to be subjected to Mrs Carlton's skills. Hebe rather suspected she had met her match with this man.

The Commodore and the severe stranger were still on the other side of the street. It appeared to Hebe that they were discussing business, for the army man had a leather portfolio under his arm, which he offered to the senior officer.

At that point Sir Richard became aware of Mrs Carlton. Without leaning out Hebe could not see her, but she was sure she was making a show of clipping bougainvillea blossoms while posing decoratively against the climbers that framed the doorway. The Commodore removed his cocked hat and made a little bow and the other man did likewise.

With his hat off Hebe had a much better view of a dark head, classically perfect features, a strong chin and a severe, well-modelled mouth. Definitely a monk, she decided. Most men on sighting Mrs Sara Carlton for the first time allowed an expression of appreciation to cross their faces, but not this one. At that moment he abruptly looked up, as though he had sensed he was being watched.

The upward glance was rapid, but Hebe started back as though he had touched her. The impression that she was looking at a priest vanished entirely: this was a hunting bird, a hawk who knew he was being observed and was poised to strike whether the watcher was prey or enemy. She added the confused impression of piercing blue eyes and dark brows to her mental picture as she backed away from the glass. No wonder he had made her feel uneasy at first sight. Why, she felt like a sparrow who had just seen the falcon stoop to the kill! Hebe spent a moment calming her breathing, which was suddenly short, wondering at herself for such a reaction.

He could not possibly have seen her she reassured herself, hastily running a comb through her hair and twitching her hem straight. Mama would not be at all pleased if she came down to luncheon looking less than pin neat.

Mrs Carlton had long since reconciled herself to the fact that her stepdaughter was not a beauty, nor even pretty. She was even resigned to the fact that Hebe stubbornly refused to compensate for this disaster by employing wiles to intrigue, or displays of domestic virtue to attract older men who might be looking for a conformable wife to make them comfortable. However, Mrs Carlton was still fighting the battle to make Hebe look and behave like a young lady at all times. Sometimes she succeeded, and just now Hebe felt not the slightest desire to appear in any way out of the ordinary and attract that hard stare.

She ran down the stairs then slowed, hesitating on the wide polished boards of the hall to hear what was being said in the elegant sea-green reception room. 'We are always prepared for Sir Richard to take potluck with us at luncheon,' Mrs Carlton was saying. 'It is not the slightest imposition, Major. I would be delighted if you would stay.'

'In that case, ma'am,' a deep, cool voice replied, 'I would be very pleased to accept your kind invitation.'

Hardly an unseemly show of enthusiasm, Hebe decided. Still, he was polite enough, if chilly. Doubtless the Commodore had already said something that alerted the other man to the fact that Mrs Carlton was his intended wife, so the monk was presumably feeling safe enough, even in the company of a voluptuous blonde who could well pass for the thirty-three years she admitted to. *Let us see what he makes of the plain single daughter*, she thought with a wry twist of her lips.

'There you are, Hebe dear,' Mrs Carlton cried as she hesitated in the doorway. 'My stepdaughter Hebe, Major,' she added.

Just in case, Hebe thought resignedly, *he thinks she is old enough to be my mother, or that she is responsible for such an ordinary-looking girl.* She was very fond of Sara Carlton, but sometimes she could…

She disciplined her face and allowed the introduction to continue. 'This is Major the Honourable Alex Beresford, Hebe.'

Hebe dropped a neat little curtsy and observed the elegant bow she received in return.

'Miss Carlton.' Again that cool, deep voice and expressionless face, although now she was close to him she realised that his eyes were startlingly blue and that it was the hawk, not the monk, who was watching her through them.

She was piqued both by his indifference and by her own sudden surge of curiosity about Major Beresford. Not, of course, that she was attracted to him, although

the effect of his voice was to send a strange tingle down
her spine. No, it was simply that the army officers of her
acquaintance were generally a friendly, gregarious body
of men. Occasionally one met a shy or awkward one, or
a rake best avoided by a single girl, but on the whole
they mingled cheerfully with the resident English community, pleased to be invited into private homes and
ready to partake fully in local society.

'Shall we go through to the dining room?' Mrs Carlton
asked, taking Sir Richard's arm and making her way to
the door, thus neatly leaving Major Beresford little option
but to offer his arm to Hebe.

He escorted her efficiently, and silently, to the place
indicated by his hostess, pulled out her chair and took
his own place by her side. After the first flurry of dishes
being passed, Mrs Carlton addressed a question about a
recently widowed lady of their acquaintance directly to
the Commodore. Hebe waited with some amusement to
see whether the Major was going to fulfil his social ob-
ligations and talk to her.

'You have been living on the island long, Miss
Carlton?' It was perfectly polite and a reasonable question in the circumstances. There was not a hint of bore-
dom in his voice, but Hebe sensed he was deeply impa-
tient at finding himself trapped in this situation.

Her stepmother, when making one of her frequent lists
of Hebe's faults, placed curiosity a close second after
harum-scarum behaviour. Hebe failed to understand why
this was frowned upon. People intrigued her. She had a
deep concern for the affairs of their servants, her friends
knew they could confide in her and find someone who
entered into their every feeling—even if she asked an
awful lot of questions in the process—and watching complete strangers was an abiding fascination. She did not

gossip, she never pried, she simply watched and listened and asked questions, then followed with interest as events unfolded, helping if she was offered the opportunity, rejoicing or agonising as the case may be if she were not.

So why was this officer so reticent, so cold? Thinking of him as an interesting mystery, rather than a severe, rather frightening man, made sitting next to him easier. She offered him a plate of bread and butter as she answered his question. 'I have been here three years—since my father was posted to Malta with his squadron. My mother died ten years ago and he married again four years later. Where circumstances allowed my stepmama and I followed him from naval base to naval base. Then he died two years ago of a fever and we have remained here ever since.'

There, she thought, *that's a nice full answer with lots of dates, now you say something.*

'Indeed?'

'Possibly we will return to England after Mama marries Sir Richard, our plans are not yet certain. So much depends on the disposition of the squadron.' Silence. 'It will be interesting to see England again after so long.'

'I am sure it will.'

He cut his bread and Hebe found herself watching his hand on the knife. Long, tanned fingers that looked as if they were more used to gripping a sword hilt, strong tendons showing sharp against the skin, a long-healed scar across the knuckles, white against the tan.

'And has your regiment been long on the island, Major? I was not aware of any new troop landings.' She could not place his uniform at all.

He answered her question with one of his own. 'Do you always take such a close interest in troop movements, Miss Carlton?' One dark brow rose slightly and the corner of his mouth curved in what, if his eyes had shown any warmth, she might have read as a smile.

So, he thought she was one of those giddy girls who hankered after any man in a uniform, did he? Hebe bit the inside of her lip to stop herself making a brisk retort and instead smiled brightly back at him, wishing she had the nerve to tell him he need not worry, he was the last man on Malta whose interest she would wish to attach.

'Why, no more than anyone else with reasonable powers of observation, sir. All of us exiles from England know which warships have docked, which regiments have landed, who has left, who has arrived. These comings and goings control the arrival of news from home, the mails, the company we ask to dinner or meet at parties.'

Major Beresford was helping himself to cold fish, apparently unmoved by her smile. 'A somewhat restricted social life on such a small island.'

Hebe ploughed on, all too aware that Mrs Carlton was watching her from the corner of her eye. 'I should imagine it is no more restricted than that experienced by the residents of a resort such as Brighton or Harrogate. Would you be so kind as to pass me the butter, Major?'

He did so, unfortunately raising his eyes in time to intercept an encouraging nod of approval from Sara Carlton to her stepdaughter. Hebe considered feigning a sudden headache and fleeing the table, but that nagging curiosity kept her there, despite a growing feeling of frustration. She was going to get a straight answer, or at least a genuine smile, out of him before they rose from the dining table if it was the last thing she did.

'Will you be staying long on Malta, Major Beresford?'

'That will depend.' She found herself watching those long fingers again as they curled around the bowl of his glass. They were drinking lemonade, cold from the pitcher's long immersion in the fountain, and condensation beaded the outside of the goblet. His little finger ran up and down, leaving a track through the moisture, and Hebe watched as though mesmerised.

'Upon what?' she asked abruptly, pulling herself together.

'Upon my orders,' he responded frostily.

'Ah. Well, of course I will ask no more, Major.' Like all of the English community, Hebe was well aware of the need for complete discretion about orders, for however careful the authorities were, there were bound to be French spies all over the island.

'Will you not?' He half-turned in his chair to regard her with that piercing blue gaze. Hebe had the sudden fantasy that he was about to demand that she confess all, when he added, 'And what will we talk about if you are resolved to stop interrogating me, Miss Carlton?'

Taken aback, she met his hard stare with her own; grey eyes wide with anger. 'I am sure, Major,' she said, keeping her voice too low for the other couple to hear her, 'I am sure you must find it an intolerable bore to be expected to make small talk with a young lady. Could I suggest that you consider whether the young lady concerned is also finding the experience somewhat tiresome?'

That did, at least, provoke a reaction. She still kept her eyes locked with his and something stirred in the blue depths: anger, heat and, she saw with a sudden sense of shame at her own behaviour, exhaustion. Now she was looking at him properly she could see that the skin beneath his eyes was white under the tan and realised that his excessive coldness was simply a device to keep him on his feet and conscious, able to respond to this unwelcome luncheon party into which Sir Richard had pitch-forked him.

She glanced at his plate, feeling the moment when she broke away from his gaze as something almost physical. He had eaten hardly anything.

'Miss Carlton,' he began.

'Oh, dear,' Hebe said shakily, but loudly enough to attract the attention of Mrs Carlton and Sir Richard. 'Oh, dear, I feel quite faint all of a sudden. Major, please could you help me into the garden?' He got to his feet swiftly, one hand under her arm and she let herself lean a little on to the support. 'No, no, Mama, I will be quite all right if the Major does not mind. I will just sit in the shade…'

Mrs Carlton took a swift look at Hebe's face, which was indeed somewhat pale, and decided that this was as good a way as any of throwing her and this attractive, and doubtless eligible, man together. The small back garden was always busy with the servants passing to and fro—Hebe would be well enough chaperoned. 'If you do not mind, Major, I would be grateful.'

As soon as they were outside the door Hebe freed his arm, casting him an anxious look. 'I am sorry about that, but I think you ought to rest and the garden is the coolest place.' She was steering him towards the open door at the end of the hall, towards the green arbour in the little courtyard and the soft sound of water trickling from the fountains.

'*I* should rest?' He looked down at her frowningly. 'But you said you were…'

'Faint, yes, I know. It was a fib, but I do not expect you want Sir Richard to know you are not feeling quite yourself,' she replied briskly. A maid popped her head out of the door as they passed and Hebe added, 'A pitcher of lemonade, please, Maria, and two glasses.' Major

Beresford allowed himself to be directed through the door, stooping under a tangle of hanging climber and into the deep shade of a little paved area. A lionhead fountain burbled gently against the wall, and two fringed white hammocks hung companionably side by side.

'There, lie down,' Hebe ordered firmly, plumping up pillows. 'If you drink at least one more glass of lemonade and then sleep for half an hour, you will feel somewhat better when you wake.'

The Major was obviously unused to taking order from débutantes, but the novelty appeared to be sufficient to secure at least compliance. He sat on the hammock, long legs over the side, and watched her with the beginnings of a genuine smile catching at the corners of his mouth.

'I think you should take your coat off as well,' she added. 'You will sleep much better.'

'I should imagine your mama will be out here any minute to see exactly what is going on!' he retorted, making no effort to start unbuttoning the row of shining buttons.

'Oh, no,' Hebe said, curling up in the opposite hammock and setting it swinging to and fro. She pushed up the pillows behind her and looked at him. 'Go on, take it off, we are quite safe for at least half an hour. Mama will enjoy talking to Sir Richard without me there and she will be delighted to think we are in the garden indulging in a little genteel flirtation.'

'Is that what we are doing?' He started to open the jacket, his eyes on her face.

'Of course not! But you are exhausted, and you will be able to carry on with your business with the Commodore much more efficiently after a little rest. Here, give me that jacket and I will put it on this stool.'

She looked at him critically as he poured the lemonade

and tossed back half the glass in one gulp. In the white
shirt Alex Beresford looked far less like a bird of prey,
and not at all like a monk. She studied the line of his
throat as he swallowed, the width of his shoulders as he
lay back against the pile of pillows and the length of his
legs, elegant in tight overall trousers and black boots as
he swung them up into the hammock.

He leaned out to put down the glass and met her gaze.
'What told you I was tired? I did not think I was so easy
to read.'

'Your eyes, and the skin under them. And you hardly
ate anything.'

'And I was very rude to you.' Hebe twinkled back as
he pulled a sudden, rueful face. 'You know, Miss
Carlton, tired as I am, I think I would rather flirt than
sleep.'

She could see his lids were beginning to droop. 'I
never flirt, Major.'

He opened his eyes at that and turned his head on the
pillows. 'What, *never*? You really are an extraordinary
young lady, Miss Carlton.'

'Oh, no,' Hebe corrected. 'A very ordinary one.' But
his eyes were closed, the sweep of dark lashes feathering
the skin. Alex Beresford was asleep.

Chapter Two

Hebe's prediction of the amount of time she and Major Beresford would be left alone together proved accurate. She had noticed the hall clock standing at five past the hour as they passed it: when it chimed the half-hour she climbed carefully out of her hammock, filled up the major's glass with lemonade and shook out his uniform jacket.

It seemed a pity to wake him. He had fallen at once into a deep, still sleep. His long body lay with the utter relaxation she had noticed in cats, only the slight movement of his lids suggested that perhaps he was dreaming. Hebe had found him very relaxing to watch as she swung gently to and fro in her hammock, thinking of nothing very much except how pleasant it was in the warm shade with the sound of water and the scent of flowers.

Hebe stretched out a tentative hand, hesitating about how to wake the Major. A lock of black hair had fallen across his forehead and her fingers hovered, almost stroked it back, then were snatched away. What was she thinking of? She touched his shoulder, only lightly, but instantly he was awake, his body tensed under her flattened fingers.

Meeting the Major's eyes, she realised that he truly was totally and immediately awake. Despite his strange surroundings he knew where he was without having to think about it, swinging his legs down and getting to his feet in one swift movement. Hebe handed him his jacket and he shrugged it on as the sound of voices from the hall reached them.

'Here, take this.' Hebe thrust the glass of lemonade into his hand, then propelled him firmly along one of the paths between the troughs of plants before taking her seat demurely on the stool. She picked up the piece of embroidery which she had carried out there that morning and began to ply her needle.

'Hebe, dearest!' Mrs Carlton emerged into the garden with just the slightest expression of anxiety on her pretty face. She had not realised how the time had sped by as she had sat chatting to the Commodore in the dining room. Had she perhaps been unwise to leave Hebe alone with a total stranger? It had seemed such a good idea on the spur of the moment... Her face relaxed at the sight of her stepdaughter, perfectly composed and, by some miracle, carrying on a charming, ladylike activity.

'Are you feeling better, Hebe dearest?' she cooed, fluttering over and allowing the Commodore a delightful picture of pretty maternal attention. 'Where is the Major?'

'Here, ma'am,' Major Beresford rounded the corner, ducking under a bamboo. 'I have been admiring your lovely garden: what a peaceful haven. Might I guess that yours is the designing hand here?'

Behind his back Hebe raised her eyebrows. Unless flattery was second nature to him, Alex Beresford certainly appeared to have recovered from any fatigue he had been suffering. She waited in silent amusement to hear whether Mrs Carlton was going to accept his praise for the garden, which was already beautifully laid out and planted when they took the house.

Her stepmother dodged the question with a pretty laugh. 'You are flattering me, Major! Now, tell me: do you stay long on the island?'

'Possibly two or three weeks, ma'am. I am bound for Gibraltar and must wait for a convenient ship.'

'So you are not with your regiment then?' Sara Carlton persisted.

'No, ma'am. I have been in the Ionian islands, delivering dispatches.'

Mrs Carlton was too busy calculating whether two or three weeks would allow her enough time to squeeze in at least one supper party and a small soirée to notice that it was most unusual for an army officer to be wandering around the Mediterranean detached from his regiment and delivering dispatches, a task normally fulfilled by the smaller vessels from the fleet. The fact that he was by himself she merely noted as being helpful: how much more likely it was that he would rely on others to entertain him if he was separated from his brother officers.

Hebe, however, did mark the evasion, as, she could tell from the Commodore's expressionless face, did he. Then she realised he must know exactly what Alex Beresford was about. Hebe would never speculate aloud about such matters, but her brain was busy with the puzzle. A detached officer, newly arrived from the Ionian islands and bone weary—the most likely explanation was that the Major was an intelligence officer. She regarded him with even more interest: what a fascinating role...

'I must thank you for your hospitality, ma'am,' the major was saying, bowing over Sara Carlton's hand. 'Miss Carlton.' Hebe put down her embroidery and came to shake hands. 'I do hope you will feel much more yourself soon.'

'I feel better already; doubtless it was a little too much sun earlier,' she replied composedly. 'Thank you for your company just now.'

Major Beresford regarded her quizzically, then smiled. 'No, thank *you*, Miss Carlton.'

Hebe felt warm inside. When he smiled like that, directly into her eyes, she could see neither the monk nor the hunting falcon, simply a very attractive man who appeared to enjoy her company. And suddenly she felt a deep concern that he should continue to feel like that about her.

The front door had no sooner closed behind the two officers before Sara Carlton turned a look of glowing approval on her stepdaughter. 'My dear Hebe! I had not thought you could be so adroit in attaching the Major. Why, I declare the man is already half in love with you.'

Hebe flushed. 'I beg you will not talk so nonsensically, Mama. Major Beresford was merely acting as any gentleman would under the circumstances, and I most certainly was not trying to *attach* him in any way. No doubt he has already put out of his mind a rather ordinary young lady whom he was obliged to assist for a few minutes. Why should such a man pay me any attention?'

This realistic appraisal was certainly enough to dampen Hebe's own spirits, even as she spoke the words, but Mrs Carlton merely smiled indulgently and pushed her towards the stairs. 'Have more confidence in yourself, Hebe. You are unused to having a success with gentlemen—largely as a result of your own attitude, I might say—but we have an excellent beginning to build upon here. Now, where is Maria?' She continued to urge Hebe up the stairs. 'We must review your wardrobe this minute while I consider the best way to approach this. Bother the girl—Maria!'

Hebe perched on the edge of her bed, allowing the bustle created by Mrs Carlton and Maria turning out every gown she possessed to pass over her head. Mama had obviously decided, on the flimsiest of evidence, that Major Beresford was not only an eligible suitor—which he most certainly was—but was inclined by some miracle to favour her stepdaughter.

Hebe, on the other hand, had a very realistic understanding of what sort of young lady was likely to attract extremely handsome, aristocratic, military officers. She thought that he might have been amused by her unconventional behaviour and grateful for the opportunity she had afforded him to rest, but could not believe that he would harbour any of the feelings that Mrs Carlton was intent on attributing to him. Which was a pity, but she was not going to delude herself. Men, in her experience, were quite likely to pour out their troubles of the heart to her as a good friend, but she had no expectation that she was going to cause anyone's heart to ache in her own right.

'Yes, of course, Mama,' she said, suddenly aware that Mrs Carlton had been speaking to her for several minutes. Agreement was usually the wisest course.

'Hebe, really! I declare you have not been listening to a word I have said.' However, this familiar scold did not continue as usual. 'It is a little early to be indulging in too many fond daydreams, my dear. The time to do that is when the gentleman concerned has been securely attached. No, this is the moment in our campaign for planning, then action. You will need three new gowns...'

'*Three?*' Hebe squeaked. 'Whatever for?'

'And two—no, three pairs of new slippers, a gauze scarf, some long gloves...' Mrs Carlton finally registered her stepdaughter's surprise. 'Why, I will start with an invitation to a soirée next Tuesday evening, and your primrose silk really will no longer do for best. Then I will suggest to Mrs Forrester that the Major should be invited to her ball in ten days' time: she will be only too glad to add another new man to her list and for that we must make every push to present you at your best.'

'And the third gown?' Hebe enquired faintly.

'Just a day dress, something suitable for the promenade, I think. Major Beresford must see you to advantage in every setting.' She paused and looked fixedly at Hebe. 'And your hair. This time you *must* allow Monsieur Faubert to do something with it. Perhaps a new crop?'

'No!' Hebe clapped her hands to the sides of her head as if to ward off the threatening scissors. The refugee French coiffeur might find a willing subject in her stepmother, but she had no intention of letting him near her with scissors and hot tongs. 'No, Mama, I do not want to cut off my hair.' It might be an unsatisfactory brown, but Hebe secretly thought the mass of unruly curls were her only beauty. Although who else was going to admire their romantic tumble when she only let them loose at night in the privacy of her own bedchamber, she could not say.

'Oh, very well then.' Mrs Carlton was not going to waste her energy on a fruitless battle. 'Maria, please see that all of Miss Hebe's gowns are well aired and pressed and that she has sufficient silk stockings.'

As the maid began to gather up the gowns that had been tossed on to the bed, her brown eyes sparkling with vicarious excitement, Hebe said, 'I suppose Major Beresford *is* unmarried, Mama.'

'Oh, my goodness, never say such a thing!' Mrs Carlton hurried from the room, her face a picture of alarm. 'Thank goodness Sir Richard gave us an up-to-date copy of the *Peerage* last month…' Her voice could be heard faintly as she disappeared into her own room. 'Here it is. Now…Abbotsford, Avery, Bottley, Brandon…'

The little Maltese maid turned to Hebe, her arms full of muslins and Hebe's two silk gowns. 'Oh, Miss Hebe! You are going to marry that man who looks like a beautiful, fierce saint?'

'Certainly not!' Hebe retorted firmly. Fierce saint, indeed!

'Beresford,' came the echo of Mrs Carlton's voice, gaining in volume as she walked back along the landing, reading aloud as she came. 'Here we are. George Beresford, third Earl of Tasborough, married Emilia… Has issue eldest son William, Viscount Broadwood, also Major the Honourable Alexander Hugh Beresford. The major is not married, thank goodness.'

'He may have been since that was published,' Hebe said repressively. 'Or he may be affianced to be married.'

'We must find out,' Mrs Carlton said firmly. 'Off you go, Maria. Now, be careful not to scorch anything.'

'Well, I am certainly not going to ask him,' Hebe said, jumping off the bed and walking to the window where she lingered, looking out longingly. What a beautiful day for a walk. A proper walk, not the sort of dawdling stroll, pausing every few moments to gaze into a shop or gossip with an acquaintance, which Mrs Carlton favoured.

'Goodness, no, that would be fatal,' Mrs Carlton agreed, shocked at the very thought. 'I will ask Sir Richard to ascertain the position. In fact, I will write a note at once. The sooner we know where we stand, the better, for Major Beresford will be sure to call in the next day or two.'

But three days passed without sight, or word, of the Major. Mrs Carlton was cast down, and inclined to be cross with Sir Richard who, when closely quizzed, would only say vaguely that he was sure Major Beresford was busy somewhere about the island.

Hebe, who was not at all surprised, maintained an air of utter indifference, which infuriated her stepmother and hid a little ache of regret. It had been ridiculous to entertain any sort of hope that Alex Beresford would want to pursue their brief acquaintance, but she had foolishly allowed herself to be carried away by Sara Carlton's enthusiasm and led into the sort of daydreams which could only end in disappointment.

She felt she had some excuse, for the Major was, it had to be said, very attractive when he smiled. And it would utterly overthrow the conceit of every young lady of Hebe's acquaintance if he showed any sign of interest in her, the Plain Jane of Valetta society.

On the fourth morning after Sir Richard had brought the Major for luncheon Hebe slipped out of the house while Mrs Carlton was still propped up against her pillows, yawning over her morning chocolate and fretfully complaining that her curl papers had been twisted too tight the night before and she had hardly slept a wink.

The Carlton ladies enjoyed a respectable competence thanks to the careful provision of Hebe's late papa, who had received his fair share of naval prize money, and to Mrs Carlton's own modest portion. But Mrs Carlton's ideas of elegance, and the accompanying niceties of life which were essential to maintain that state, kept their budget under constant tension.

Hebe had become an essential part of their domestic economy, for she found it both easy and enjoyable to hunt for bargains in the markets, barter over purchases and keep the household supplied at a cost that no servant would have bothered to achieve. Mrs Carlton might bewail the necessity of Hebe's daily expeditions with her big basket, but she could not deny the quality and quantity of the food that graced their table, bringing a smile of satisfaction to Sir Richard's face or earning a look of envy from less-adept hostesses when she gave a dinner.

And Hebe, with her regrettable enthusiasm for making friends with anyone and everyone, was consequently an infallible source of the cheapest crochet lace work, the latest arrival of scented almond oil soap from the North African coast or the news of a wonderful dressmaker who could copy a London fashion plate at dagger-cheap prices.

So her marketing trips were tolerated and Mrs Carlton shut her eyes to the fact that a simple trip to buy tomatoes, lemons and lamb cutlets and to place an order for fresh flowers could last most of the morning.

That morning Hebe was early, for she was intent on fish for dinner. Sir Richard was coming and fish of any kind was his declared favourite dish. She made her way down through the streets, already busy, cutting confidently through back alleys and tiny squares and running lightly down the long flights of steps to emerge at last through the great encircling wall overlooking Barriera Wharf.

She stopped there, as she always did, to look out over the blue of the Grand Harbour to the Three Cities, as the small towns on the opposite shore were so grandly known. The jumble of houses, walls, watchtowers and church towers, all in golden stone, glowed in the morning light, divided by the long fingers of water which penetrated deeply between them. In Dockyard Creek she could see the tops of the forest of masts that marked the English frigates and sloops clustered there, and across the water came the shrill call of a bosun's whistle, cutting cleanly through the competing noises.

The scene never failed to hold her for several minutes, but eventually she tore herself away and walked down the paved slope to the waterside where the main fish market was held.

But its stalls proved disappointing for once and, after buying some shallots, six lemons and a large bunch of herbs, she turned her steps along the harbour wall to stroll in the direction of the mouth of the harbour and the defending bulk of Fort St Elmo. Small fishermen often berthed alongside here under the towering protection of the cannon-battered St Lazarus curtain wall. Usually they only landed enough fish for their extended families' needs, but occasionally there was something interesting that they would be willing to part with for a fair price.

But the long wharfside was almost deserted as she rounded the angle of the bastion. A few of the brightly coloured boats bobbed at the end of their mooring ropes, sails furled, empty, the painted eyes watching silently from each prow. Perhaps the weather out to sea had been unfavourable. Hebe supposed it would be sensible to go back and look at the meat stalls in the long covered alleyways where the butchers congregated, but it was early still and she was disinclined for the bustle of the streets and the smell of the newly butchered meat.

Settling her basket more comfortably in the crook of her arm she began to wander slowly along, feeling pleasantly invisible in her plain gown, her wide-brimmed straw hat in the local style and her handwoven shawl draped simply around her shoulders. She looked like any of the local girls out marketing, which was exactly the appearance she intended to give. Despite her desire to preserve appearances, even Mrs Carlton had to admit that, surprisingly, in this cosmopolitan harbour city with its naval ships, trading vessels and polyglot population, any respectable young woman could walk unattended in perfect safety, let alone Hebe who, besides having a grasp of several languages, was widely known and liked.

Hebe walked on for some time, eventually coming to rest almost at the St Lazarus Bastion. She leaned against the bulk of an ancient cannon, dragged up on to the harbour wall many years ago after some great battle and left to rust slowly into oblivion, and wondered what the hour was. It was probably time to turn back, she realised, discovering that her feet were more than a little sore, for she had foolishly put on light shoes and the waterside cobbles pressed painfully through the thin soles.

As she turned she saw a small fishing boat, its sail flapping as it was tacked to and fro to catch the light wind. It had the distinctive high prow of the traditional luzzas, and was banded brightly in blue and yellow, although something about it was not quite the same as the local boats; it was a variant from Gozo, perhaps. It appeared to be heading for her part of the wharfside. As she watched it a small boy of eight or nine years of age, who had been sitting with his feet dangling over the edge tossing pebbles at the minnows, got up and began to stroll towards her, a wide wicker fish basket in his arms.

Meeting his father, she deduced. Perhaps it would be worth waiting and seeing what the fisherman had caught and if he was willing to part with some of his catch. She curled up in an embrasure beside the cannon and waited, watched by a tiny green lizard who flicked away as she sat, then settled again, an emerald jewel on a sun-warmed ledge of crumbling stone.

The little boat came on, dancing over the small waves, and glided neatly to a halt against the wharf only a few feet from Hebe's perch. The fisherman was obscured by the sail and she waited patiently while he freed it and caught the tumbling canvas, bundling it up to stow away.

As soon as he straightened up Hebe realised this was no Maltese fisherman, however authentic his clothing might be. The tall, dark-haired, unshaven figure in its coarse linen shirt and canvas trousers, feet bare on the wet boards, was unmistakably Major Alex Beresford.

Chapter Three

Instinct kept Hebe in her place. She did not want to spy, but something told her that intelligence officers were hardly likely to wish to be seen by chance acquaintances under such circumstances. The Major could simply have been out fishing, or he might have had quite another purpose.

The boy called out a greeting, *'Bongourno!'* and came to kneel on the edge of the quayside, holding out his basket ready for the catch.

Alex Beresford grinned up at him, a startling white flash of teeth against tanned and stubble-darkened skin. *'Bongourno, Pauli. Kif int?'*

The lad started to reply in Maltese, then caught himself and said carefully in English, 'I am very well, I thank you, Signor Alex. That was good, no? Mama says I must practise if I am to find workings…work for the English.'

'Very good indeed, Pauli. Hold the basket steady now, I have had a good catch.'

Alex Beresford began to toss the mixed collection of fish into the waiting basket, then suddenly his focus changed from his task and his head came up as he scanned the harbour wall. It was the same piercing bird-of-prey stare that had so startled Hebe when she first saw him. Was he so sensitive to anyone watching him, or was there something about her gaze which touched him? She held her breath.

'Who is there?' he called out sharply in Maltese.

'It is only me,' Hebe replied composedly in English, sliding down from her niche and out of the shadow. 'Good morning, Major. Your Maltese is very good.'

'Good morning, Miss Carlton. I have about six phrases and twenty words, all the rest is a mixture of Greek, French and Italian, but it seems to suffice. But what the d—how did you come to be here so early?'

'I am out marketing; looking for fish, in fact, but the catch this morning was very dull. You seem to have done better, though. Will your young friend sell me any, do you think?'

Pauli, who had been following the exchange with bright-eyed interest, jumped forward, his basket of fish held out for her inspection. '*Ghal bejgh*…all for sale, Madonna.'

'*Kemm?*' Hebe asked. Not to bargain would be to be taken for a fool.

'*Irhis hafna.*' Pauli named an ambitious sum.

'That is not cheap,' Hebe protested, looking shocked. 'I only want a few—that one, that one and those red snappers.'

Frowning with the effort of mathematics, Pauli adjusted his price down.

'*Gholi wisq!*' Hebe gasped in apparent horror, with a fair imitation of the Maltese matrons bargaining in the market. Never, her expression said, never had she heard of such an outrageous price for fish.

They wrangled amiably some more, then Hebe handed over a sum that was roughly double what she would have paid in the market, let him put the fish in amongst the palm leaves with which she had lined her basket and smiled as the boy skipped off with a wave and a jaunty, '*Sahha!*'

'*Sahha!*' Alex called in response, turning back to Hebe. 'You paid him well, his mother and little sisters will be proud of him.'

She smiled down at him as he stood, bare feet braced on the wet bottom boards of the boat. 'He looks as though he works hard.'

'He does. He approached me as soon as he saw me sail into harbour and offered to do any odd jobs for me in return for what fish I catch. He runs errands, takes messages—and eats anything he can lay his hands on.'

Questions were crowding into Hebe's brain, clamouring to be asked, but she bit her tongue. So few days had passed since the Major had arrived in Malta, surely he could not have had time to purchase a boat, and the more she looked at it, the more she was convinced that it was not a local boat. Could he have arrived in this little vessel all the way from the Ionian islands? No wonder he had looked so exhausted.

'Are you going to moor her here now?' she asked casually, swinging her basket.

'I was,' he replied, eyeing her with some amusement. 'It is considerably less crowded than it is nearer the fish market. Why? Do you wish to be conveyed to somewhere?'

'Well, yes,' Hebe admitted. 'I have walked much further than I intended, and in quite the wrong shoes, and my feet hurt.'

'Do you mean to say you walked here all the way from your house? Where is your maid?'

'I rarely trouble with a maid,' she explained. 'And I like to walk. Malta is very safe, you know.'

'What, no impudent officers to ogle you?' he teased, pulling on the mooring rope to bring the boat tight against the quayside. 'Come on, I will take you wherever you want. Give me the basket first.'

Hebe handed it down, then, wrapping her skirts tight around her, sat on the edge and reached out a hand. It was a drop of several feet to the bottom of the boat, but she felt no qualms about jumping.

'No, keep still,' the Major ordered. He reached up, took her firmly round the waist with both hands and lifted her bodily down into the boat. Hebe gasped at the ease with which he held her, for she was slightly above average height and by no means the ethereally slender sylph that Mrs Carlton considered to be the ideal.

The little vessel rocked, but Alex Beresford seemed perfectly balanced. He set her down on the bottom boards, but did not at once release his hold and Hebe was suddenly aware not just of his strength but of the warmth of his hands through the cotton of her gown and the nearness of his body. His shirt was open at the neck, baring several inches of tanned chest, and her eyes seemed fixed on the curl of dark hair that showed there.

Then she was free and he was helping her to sit. 'Your feet are going to get wet, I'm afraid,' he said, matter of factly, apparently untouched by their closeness, which had left her breathless and disconcerted.

Hebe swallowed. *For goodness' sake*, she scolded herself, *pull yourself together! You are simply not used to being held like that, nothing more.* 'It does not matter,' she replied, managing to sound no more than slightly breathless. 'They are an old, worn pair—which is why I have such sore feet.'

Alex Beresford paused with one hand on the sail. 'Where would you like me to take you?'

'Just round to the fish market, if you would be so kind, Major Beresford.'

'Will you not call me Alex?' he asked, his eyes crinkling into that sudden smile which transformed his face. 'I have, after all, slept in your hammock—I think that justifies some degree of informality.'

Hebe, with the fleeting thought that for once Mama would not scold her for her impetuous friendships, smiled back. 'Very well, but only if you will call me Hebe.'

It seemed a long moment passed while Alex Beresford stood looking down into her upturned face, then he said, 'I would be delighted, although perhaps Circe would be more appropriate.' Hebe sought desperately through her rather sketchy memories of Greek myths for the reference and failed to find it before he added, 'But is your house not on the far side of Palace Square, near the Archbishop's Palace? I am still getting myself lost in the streets here, but I think I am right about that.'

'Umm…yes,' she agreed, still puzzling over who Circe was.

'Then unless you have any more business near the fish market, would it not be closer if I took you round to St Elmo Bay? It must hardly be more than a few minutes' walk up from the sea gate there.' He was unfurling the sail as he spoke, shaking it out, then hauling it up with strong, skilled hands.

'That is right around the Point,' Hebe protested, but her eyes were sparkling at the thought of the sail, however short.

Alex cast off the mooring rope, pushed them away from the side with an oar and coaxed the sail round to catch the breeze. 'Do you mind that? Will you be sea-sick?'

'Certainly not!' she protested. 'I just did not want to take you so far out of your way.' In reply he only smiled. They sailed for a minute or two in silence while Alex tacked three or four times to find the wind to take them out of the harbour. Hebe watched him, noting again the growth of stubble on his chin and the faint tiredness around his eyes. He had been out for more than a night's fishing, that was certain.

'Do you not have to report back?' she asked innocently.

'What?' He looked at her quizzically, although she noticed his gaze had sharpened. 'After a night out fishing?'

Before she could think about what she was doing, Hebe said, 'More than one night, surely? Three, perhaps. And for that length of time, not a very good catch. I would hazard a guess that you did not have your mind on it.'

Alex was silent for a moment while he adjusted the tiller to keep clear of a larger boat heading into the docks. 'And what makes you think I have been away for three nights?' His voice was perfectly pleasant, but Hebe felt a sudden tingle of apprehension. 'The fact that I have not called?'

'Certainly not! But I cannot believe you have gone without shaving for only one night,' she said tartly, suppressing the internal voice which was saying *Careful!* 'And your eyes look tired again—although not like they did the other day. But then you had had a much longer voyage, had you not?'

This time there was no mistaking the hardness in the look he bent on her. 'And what do you deduce from that?'

'That it would be better if you shave before anyone else sees you and draws the same conclusion.'

'I would suggest that you do not treat this as a joke, Miss Carlton.' His blue eyes searched her face and she felt herself colouring. 'Perhaps I am a French spy and will simply continue out to sea where I can drop you neatly over the side with no one to see me.'

So chilly was his voice, and so sinister the threat, that Hebe found herself looking round rather wildly. They were now clear of the harbour and she could see the bulk of Dragutt Point far out to their left. In this freshening breeze they would indeed be well out to sea in only a little while longer.

Then she pulled herself together. 'What nonsense! I know perfectly well that you are an English intelligence officer.'

'And how do you know that?'

'Because I am not a brainless little débutante. I observe things, and I am quite capable of putting two and two together and making four. And,' she added, becoming quite heated as his expression became positively sardonic, 'I guessed the other day and I have not mentioned it to anyone else, nor will I, so you can stop looking like a Spanish Inquisitor.'

'Like a *what*?' His attention caught, he let the tiller come over and the sail flapped. With a soft curse under his breath he regained control.

'An Inquisitor, or at least, a very disapproving and sinister monk.'

Alex Beresford appeared to beyond speech, so Hebe added maliciously, 'Maria, my maid, says you look like a beautiful, fierce saint.'

'I suppose I am expected to be flattered by the "beautiful"?' he began darkly, then suddenly began to laugh, clutching the tiller while his shoulders shook. 'No, do not answer that, I beg you: for heaven's sake, Hebe, spare me any more blows to my self-esteem.' He mopped his eyes on his sleeve and grinned at her.

Hebe grinned back. They were in open sea now, the waves beginning to increase, but she had no intention of pointing this out just yet: suddenly she was enjoying herself very much indeed.

'Do you not want to look fierce and sinister?' she teased.

'Certainly not, I want to look like a perfectly ordinary English officer with nothing more on his mind than drilling his troops and when the next party is going to be held.' He watched her steadily. 'Are you not going to ask me what I am doing on Malta?'

'No!' Hebe was shocked. 'I would never dream of asking such a thing. However careful one is, there is always the danger that one might say something out of place, and the island is a perfect hotbed of French spies. Or so one is led to believe.'

'Possibly not a hotbed, but I suspect there are more than a few. Good grief, look at how far out we are—next stop Sicily at this rate. I am going to be in serious trouble with your mama, which is an alarming thought. Hold tight while I put about.'

Hebe did as she was told, happily ignoring the splashes that spotted her skirts as they came round and headed back. The sunlight sparkled off the wave crests, the gulls swooped and screamed overhead and the sea was dotted with sails. It was a perfect scene, and she knew she was going to remember this moment for ever.

'What did you mean just now,' Alex asked suddenly, 'when you said you were not a "brainless little débutante"'?

'Did I say that?' Hebe looked conscience-stricken. 'I should not have done so, it was a horrid thing to say. And most of them are very nice girls.'

'Most of *them*? You do not count yourself amongst them, then?' The Major's blue eyes focused for a moment on something over her shoulder. He adjusted his steering, and looked back at her.

'Oh, no,' Hebe said cheerfully. 'I am too old to be a débutante. I am out, of course, but I have never been *brought* out—launched, as it were. When we might have returned to England for that, Mama had just met Sir Richard, so we stayed here instead.'

'That seems rather unfair on you.'

She shrugged. 'I know everyone here, I go to all the dances and parties.' She did not add that her mama was just as anxious as the hopeful mama of any fresh seventeen-year-old at Almack's to catch her an eligible husband. It was just that she had to achieve it in the more limited society of the island, and with the unpromising material that Hebe represented.

'And you have numerous beaux?' Alex's eyes narrowed as he began to steer into St Elmo's Bay. They were almost back. 'A fiancé, perhaps, who will call me to account for taking you out to sea unchaperoned in a little boat?'

Hebe's answering gurgle of frank amusement made him raise his dark brows. 'I have numerous friends,' Hebe said, still smiling at the thought of a crowd of beaux all laying siege to her. 'But no admirers, and certainly no fiancé.'

'Why is that so amusing? So many officers, both naval and army... Mind your hand on the side, we will be alongside the wall in a moment.'

'And so many pretty girls to entertain them.' The boat

bumped on the wall. Alex picked up the coil of mooring rope in one hand but made no move to reach for the stanchion.

'And you?' he asked, in such a matter-of-fact manner that Hebe was betrayed out of her light, uncaring manner into revealing something of what she really felt.

'As you may observe, and as Mama frequently laments, I am not a beauty.'

'No,' he agreed.

Although she always told herself that she despised empty flattery, Hebe was nettled by this honesty. 'And not pretty, either,' she went on, determined to heap up the coals of misery now she had begun.

'Certainly not pretty.' Alex finally got to his feet to tie up the boat. Through a haze of hurt tears, Hebe could still admire the easy way he moved about the small vessel, the strength with which he pulled on the rope to bring it tight against the harbour side.

He leaned over to take her hand and help her to her feet and she tried to turn the awkward conversation into a joke. 'How ungallant of you, Major! You are supposed to protest that I am the epitome of prettiness: neither of us need believe it.'

'Ah, but I would rather say something that is true and which we can both believe.' He kept her hand trapped in one of his as she came to her feet and she found herself standing very close indeed to him. The little boat, rocking gently at its mooring, suddenly became an enclosed, private world. Somewhere she was aware of the salt smell of the sea mixed with the more pungent odours of the harbour, somewhere sea gulls were calling harshly and further along, under the curtain wall, children were playing, but they all seemed distant, as though on the other side of a window.

'You are not beautiful, Hebe,' Alex said quietly, 'but then few people truly are.'

You are, she thought, looking up at him.

'And you are not pretty, which is very fleeting and usually turns to a sad disappointment in middle age—no, Hebe, you are something far better, and much more dangerous.'

It was strangely difficult to breathe. 'What…what am I?'

Alex released her hand and brought up both his to cup her face. His fingers traced lightly across her cheekbones and she dropped her gaze in confusion, not realising that her lashes brushed his fingertips. 'You are enchanting.'

'Enchanting?' Her eyes opened wide and she stared into his face in amazement. 'Enchanting? Me?'

He released her and turned to lift her basket on to the quayside. 'Surely you have been told that before?'

'No, I have not been told that before, but then, I do not flirt, Major.' Hebe stepped carefully over a tangle of net on the bottom boards, wondering if her shaky legs were going to support her as far as solid land.

'Yes, I remember you saying so. But I am not trying to flirt with you.' He caught her hand. 'If you just step here on the side, and then put your other hand on the edge there. Just so…'

Hebe found herself standing on the harbour wall looking down into the boat and into Alex's upturned face. 'Thank you for taking me sailing,' she managed to say. 'I hope I have not delayed you too long from your duties.'

He smiled at her. 'Not at all, it was a pleasure. Could you just throw down the rope again and I will be off. And I will take your advice.'

'What advice?' Hebe paused with the loop of coarse

rope in her hand. She was very aware of the rough prickle of hemp: she seemed almost painfully aware of everything around her.

'To take my shaving tackle with me when I am away for more than one night. Has anyone ever told you that you are very observant, Hebe?'

'Observant? Oh, yes,' she said with a sudden, genuine, laugh. 'They tell me that all the time, only Mama calls it unladylike curiosity. Goodbye, Alex.'

'Goodbye, Circe.'

She picked up her basket and turned to walk up towards the sally port through the thick walls, her mind a jumble of impressions and sensations. She did not look back until she was into the shadow cast by the arch of the gate, and when she did the boat was already well out into the bay, heading back round the point on its return to the Grand Harbour.

Her feet found their own way home up the steep street. Apparently she must have crossed lanes safely, avoided the laden donkeys and the porters with vast bundles held by straps around their foreheads, who thrust their way along wide avenue and narrow alley with equal unconcern for everyone else. Hebe arrived on the doorstep, absently acknowledged the greeting of the maid who took the basket from her, and hurried upstairs.

With her bedroom door safely closed she threw off her straw hat and sat down at the dressing table. The mirror reflected back the same Hebe who had left that morning, the plain mouse with the friendly smile.

Or did it? She leaned closer. Alex Beresford had seen something else—somebody else. Someone *enchanting*. Dangerous.

'Enchanting.' She said it out loud. Was he teasing her? Flirting with her? But he said he was not, and she was inclined to trust him. What had he seen then? Boring brown hair bundled into a net, revealing none of its exuberance. Grey eyes with long lashes. Hebe frowned, not seeing the sparkle that others saw when she laughed. Cheekbones rather too wide. The memory of Alex's fingers tracing along them made her shiver. Nose: Hebe wrinkled it at her reflection. Nose, very ordinary, with freckles, despite Mama's best efforts with lemon juice. Mouth: too wide, although her teeth were even and white, which was a good point.

No, nothing there to justify *enchanting*. Perhaps he meant that she had a nice personality. That was what everyone said who wanted to be nice to girls who were plump, or too tall or just plain like her. *What a lovely personality dear Hebe has…* And what a pity she is so ordinary.

Hebe in the mirror frowned back at the real Hebe. But still, he had called her…

'Mama.' Hebe ran out onto the landing. 'Are you still in your chamber, Mama? Who was Circe?'

Chapter Four

'Circe?' Mrs Carlton regarded her stepdaughter with mild astonishment as she burst through the door of her chamber. 'Do not rush about so dear, it is most unladylike. Now, did you say Circe? A nymph, was she not, or was she that girl who was turned into a bulrush? Goodness, I do not know.' She put down the hairbrush with which she was attempting, with Maria's aid, to copy the intricate coiffure on a model in the fashion journal propped up against the mirror.

'There was a book of Greek myths somewhere in your papa's study, dear, but I have not seen it for months. But why do you want to know?' she called as Hebe whisked out of the door again. 'Oh, I do hope you are not becoming *bookish*, my dear.' But her stepdaughter had vanished.

After a dusty rummage through the books piled on the study shelf, Hebe found the volume at last and began to skim through it, for once not sidetracked by Minotaurs, men trying to fly or Zeus's amorous endeavours.

Eventually she found her quarry in the chapters devoted to Odysseus and his wanderings. 'Circe,' she read out loud, perched on the edge of the desk. 'Daughter of

Helios, the sun god, and Perse, a sea nymph… An enchantress, mistress of the island of Aeaea, who had the power to turn men into wolves, lions or swine.' She broke off, frowning at the book. That did not sound a very desirable comparison: Circe appeared to be more of a witch than anything else. 'She turned all of Odysseus's crew into swine, but he forced her to turn them back and he stayed on her island with her for one year before continuing his voyage.'

So, Alex compared her to an enchantress and one who had had such power over the great hero that he had remained on her island for an entire year. Was the Major saying that she was enchanting him into staying on *her* island of Malta?

But that was ridiculous, for he was not his own master in this, but must go where the army commanded. She was still musing on the conundrum when Sara Carlton appeared in the door, having apparently given up the struggle with the new hair style, for her blonde curls were simply knotted on top of her head. 'Did you find what you were looking for, Hebe? Oh, mind that dusty book on your skirts; why, you are the most harum-scarum girl sometimes!'

'Sorry, Mama. Yes, Circe was an enchantress.' Hebe put down the book of myths and hopped off the desk. 'I found some excellent fish for dinner,' she added, following Sara into the passage.

'Well done, dear, Sir Richard will appreciate that. But why did you want to know about this Circe? I am not sure you should be reading these Greek myths in any case, everyone in them appears to have led the most irregular lives.'

Hebe sighed inwardly. She had very much hoped she was not going to be asked that question, for, try as she might, she could think of no convincing evasion. 'Major Beresford mentioned her,' she admitted baldly.

'Major Beresford? You have seen him this morning?'

'Yes, I met him near the fish market.'

'Provoking man!' Sara swept into the sitting room and sat down in a swirl of periwinkle-blue skirts. 'He comes nowhere near this house for three days and then has to meet you in the fish market with you looking like a local maid out marketing.'

'He has been out of Valetta, Mama,' Hebe said in an attempt to placate her wrath.

'Oh? Well, in that case I forgive him. But there is no time to lose, we must send out the cards for our soirée on Tuesday. I had done nothing about it because I was so cast down by his failure to call.'

'But, Mama, that is only two days away. Will people not think it odd that we should give such short notice of a party?'

'I shall not regard that,' Mrs Carlton said with the airy confidence of a successful hostess. 'I shall say it is just an informal little gathering because I had a sudden whim.'

'Should we not wait until you discover from Sir Richard this evening whether the Major is married?' Hebe asked. 'It will be a dreadful waste of gilt-edged cards if he is.'

Her stepmother did not appear to notice her satirical tone and replied seriously, 'If he is married, then how much more we will need a party to cheer us up! But we must not despair. Now come along, let us draw up a list.'

Hebe spent the rest of the day writing cards of invitation, composing a long shopping list and daydreaming about Alex Beresford. Was he married? He should not be telling young ladies they were enchanting if he was, but then, men were inclined to flirt, she had observed, and none more than the scarlet-coated army officers.

It would be best, she decided, realising that she had spent the half-hour after luncheon gazing into space and nibbling the end of her quill, if Sir Richard told them that evening that the Major had a wife and large family. Then she could forget all about him, which would be much more comfortable. But she found she did not want that sort of comfort. It was disturbing, but also rather pleasant, to feel the butterflies in her stomach and to have a vague feeling of expectation and excitement.

The sensation was new, but she had no trouble attributing a cause to it. Was this why débutantes enjoyed flirting so much? No one ever tried to flirt with Hebe, for they were usually much too busy telling her about their problems. Or they were cheerfully taking her for granted as one of the people invited along to lend countenance to the prettier young ladies on any expedition.

Hebe dipped her pen in the standish and addressed an envelope, then another, but her mind kept wandering. Was whatever this strange relationship that seemed to be developing with Alex Beresford a flirtation? Perhaps he simply liked her and found her amusing, if unconventional, company. And, in any case, what did she want to happen? At this point Hebe's imagination refused to help her. All she was sure of was that whatever Alex had in mind, it was certainly not making a proposal of marriage to a plain, very ordinary young lady on Malta, whatever her mama might think!

By the time the Commodore had arrived for dinner and had settled comfortably at the dinner table on Mrs

Carlton's right hand, Hebe was in a fair way to being in a dither of nerves.

His fiancée was far too skilful to pounce on Sir Richard with demands for information before he had drunk his first glass of claret and had sampled the excellent baked fish, removed with a timbale of rice and sweetbreads and a savoury omelette. She waited until he had put down his knife and fork and announced, 'A most excellent dinner, Mrs Carlton,' before responding demurely,

'I am so glad it meets with your approval, Sir Richard,' then added, as if it was a sudden recollection, 'By the by, I have decided to hold a small soirée next Tuesday. I do hope you will be able to attend.'

The Commodore expressed himself both free, and delighted, to attend. 'A sudden whim, my dear?' he asked, a decided twinkle in his eye. Sara Carlton was firmly convinced that she managed Sir Richard without his having the slightest notion of it. Hebe was of the opinion that he saw through her wiles with perfect clarity, but rather enjoyed the experience of being wound around a pretty woman's finger. He was more than capable of putting his foot down when he wanted to.

'Exactly that,' Mrs Carlton agreed. 'A whim. Just an informal gathering of our particular friends. Tell me,' she added, casually, 'do you think Major Beresford would care to attend?'

The twinkle intensified as Sir Richard caught Hebe's eye. She blushed and his eyelid drooped into the hint of a wink. 'I cannot speak for his engagements that evening, of course, but I am sure he would be most pleased to attend if he is free.'

'It must be so difficult for him—indeed, for so many officers—to be so far from their wives and families,' Sara

Carlton said, in a voice of soft sympathy that failed to
deceive either of her companions.

'Yes, indeed,' the Commodore agreed. 'Hebe, my dear,
would you be so good as to pass me the parsley sauce?
Thank you.'

Normally Hebe would have enjoyed the sight of Sir
Richard gently teasing her stepmother. He knew exactly
why Mrs Carlton was fishing and would soon put her out
of her misery with an answer. Tonight Hebe was every
bit as anxious for his reply as Sara was. She fixed her
eyes on her plate and waited.

'Not that Major Beresford is married,' Sir Richard said
as he replaced the spoon in the sauce dish. 'Now, is he
engaged? There *was* something I heard…no, I must have
the wrong man, for now I think of it, our conversation
only the other day showed him to be quite unattached.
What were we talking of? Oh, yes, we were discussing
the lot in life of younger sons and he remarked that his
father was anxious that his elder brother marry, and that
as it was, neither son was showing any signs of matri-
mony, which caused his lordship some disquiet.'

'Ah!' said Sara Carlton softly.

Hebe started breathing again. Which was better? To
have been disappointed here and now, or to continue with
the flirtation—or whatever it was she was having with
Alex—and have the inevitable pain of seeing him pass
on eventually to a prettier girl when the novelty wore
off?

She looked up and caught Sir Richard's kindly gaze
on her and suddenly something inside her revolted. Why
should she give up like this? Why shouldn't Hebe Carlton
attract young men as much as any débutante? *Experience*,
an inner voice jibed at her. *Even Mama, who has every*

reason to wish you well, despairs of your looks and your behaviour. Everyone likes you, nobody desires you...

Hebe's chin came up and a decidedly martial light entered her eyes. Well, Alex Beresford apparently felt something more than liking. But he was not going to continue to feel like that if she was such a mouse. Sometimes she had wondered that this or that débutante had such a reputation for beauty and charm when she appeared quite ordinary to Hebe's friendly, but critical, gaze. Yet such young women either believed in their own charms, or pretended they did, and somehow that put an aura around them. It was worth trying.

I am enchanting, she told herself firmly. *I remind men of the daughter of a Greek nymph...* She felt better already, then was jerked out of her reverie by Mrs Carlton saying sharply,

'Hebe, dear! Your plate.' The footman was trying to clear and replace the dishes with the next course. A family dinner was obviously not the place to practise enchantment. Hebe's sense of the ridiculous got the better of her and she concentrated instead on the tale the Commodore was telling of a mishap with the flagship's cook, a crate of chickens and the Rear Admiral's wife.

The invitations for the party were duly sent out, and the Carlton ladies received back a gratifying number of acceptances, including a polite note from Major Beresford who expressed himself delighted to attend. Sara bewailed the fact that she had invited quite half a dozen rival débutantes, but she knew perfectly well that if she appeared to snub them their mamas would cut Hebe off their invitation lists and that would be fatal.

But everything else about the party gave her total satisfaction, even, to her amazement, the conformable behaviour of her stepdaughter. Hebe accepted without demur her new gown for the evening, even taking an interest in such trifles as which gloves to wear and whether she should dress her hair with flowers, twisted ribbons or gauze net. Her only act of rebellion was her stubborn refusal to cut her hair, but even that was forgiven when she meekly submitted to a dusting of rice powder over her freckles and the merest touch of rouge on her lips.

Mrs Carlton found herself in such charity with her that she let her wear her own topaz set, which was a far prettier match for Hebe's new gown of deep cream silk with a trim of deep amber ribbons at the hem, puff sleeves and neckline, than Hebe's own modest pearls.

Hebe spent the day of the party in a flurry of activity, helping clear the long salon that would act as the main reception room, set out small tables in the breakfast room for those who would wish to play cards and dress the dining table just so with sun-bleached linen and fresh flowers for the buffet.

As she worked she had continued repeating her silent charm, *I am enchanting, I am an enchantress, Alex Beresford likes me, Alex Beresford will think I look lovely tonight…*

When she finally stood up and regarded her reflection in the mirror it suddenly seemed that perhaps she was not utterly deceiving herself, for the young lady who stared back appeared tall, elegant and, if not exactly pretty, well…

'Very nice,' said Sara Carlton, unwittingly plunging Hebe into gloom. But she soon recovered her confidence as the first guests began to arrive. She was so focused on the words she was repeating silently, and so alert for the first sign of the Major's arrival, that she seemed a very different girl from the eager, friendly, uncontrived Hebe everyone was used to and took for granted.

Even the most self-obsessed débutante noticed the difference as they were greeted by a cool, calm, slightly distant Hebe in a gown that was all the crack and a set of topazes which made every brunette present quite green with envy.

As for the gentlemen, they were surprised not to be greeted with Hebe's usual warm smile and anxious enquiry about whatever problem or affair of the heart that they had confided last time they had met her. She was very pleasant of course, but somehow none of them felt they were the centre of her attention.

That was an accurate perception, for Hebe hardly saw any of the faces that passed before her, although she said all the right things, bobbed curtsies to the more senior ladies, shook hands and generally acted as the daughter of the house should.

Then the clock struck nine and Major Beresford appeared in the doorway. Hebe swallowed convulsively, instantly convinced she was making a complete fool of herself and that he had not the slightest interest in her.

He shook hands with Mrs Carlton and exchanged a few words before giving way to the formidable figures of the Misses Andrews, two spinsters rumoured to be the richest women on Malta.

Hebe forced herself to look up and hold out her hand to him. He took it and said, 'Miss Carlton, good evening.' Then he lifted her hand and for one moment Hebe thought he was about to kiss it, an unconventional thing to be doing in this setting. Instead he turned it in his grasp and touched the inside of her wrist to his cheek. 'A close enough shave?' he asked, low-voiced.

The colour spread up Hebe's cheeks but she left her

hand in his until he lowered it. 'Ye—yes,' was all she could find to say, but it was an effort of will to clasp her hands in front of her and not reach out to touch again.

Mrs Carlton's acute chaperon's instinct made her turn, but all she saw was Hebe's heightened colour and Major Beresford regarding her with a quizzical eye. 'Major?'

'I beg your pardon, Mrs Carlton, I am holding up the line. I was merely assuring Miss Carlton that I had taken the advice she gave me the other morning.' With a slight bow he took himself off into the salon, leaving Hebe breathless and blushing.

There was a lull in the arrivals, for the rooms were almost full and Mrs Carlton would have the ultimate satisfaction of knowing that her party was a complete squeeze.

'Hebe,' she hissed, 'I despair, I really do. Not only do you convince the man you are a bluestocking by discussing classical mythology with him, but now I find you have been giving him advice! It is a wonder if he does not consider you a bookish, managing girl.' Hebe made no response, so, with a sigh, she turned towards the salon. 'I think that most of our guests have arrived, let us go in and see how we can undo the damage you have wrought.'

Hebe took a deep breath and meekly followed her stepmother's elegantly-gowned back into the reception room, a small, secret smile lighting up her face. Even the sight of Alex Beresford making small talk with a group of very pretty débutantes did not shake her inner confidence.

Unseen, her right hand crept up to touch her own cheek. The smell of limes and sandalwood reached her nostrils and she realised it was the cologne Alex was wearing. Through the gaps between the buttons of her long gloves his cheek had been so cool, so smooth, yet with the merest frisson from the stubble the razor must have cut through only a while before. Suddenly she shivered with a new, sensual awareness: but for Hebe the evening's new experiences were only just beginning.

Chapter Five

'I say, Hebe...I mean, Miss Carlton.'

Hebe turned to find Jack Forrester at her elbow, two of his friends by his side. Jack was the elder son of the Mrs Forrester to whose ball Mrs Carlton was angling to have Alex Beresford invited. He was a popular young man with both sexes, and although he knew Hebe very well from her friendship with his sisters, he had never sought her out before.

'Good evening, Jack. Hello, Paul, William.'

Jack Forrester turned a shoulder as if to exclude his two friends. 'Hebe, you are coming to Mama's ball, are you not?'

'Why, yes, I am looking forward to it.' Now, what did Jack want? She scoured her memory, but could not recall that he had seemed very interested in any of her particular friends, so he probably was not hoping for her help to be alone with someone...

'Will you dance a waltz with me?' He misinterpreted Hebe's startled expression. 'Yes, I know. Dashing of Mama, is it not? She said some of the older ladies might not like it, but she was not going to have a dowdy ball for anyone. You do waltz, don't you, Hebe?'

As it happened Hebe did, and had been carefully instructed in the dashing new dance. But no one had ever asked her to perform it with them. 'Why, thank you, Jack, of course I will.'

Mr Forrester's two companions succeeded in gaining her side. 'Now let another fellow get a word in, Jack!' William Smithson demanded. 'I say, Miss Carlton, you'll give us a waltz each, won't you?'

'Well...yes, yes, of course,' Hebe stammered. She caught a glimpse of herself in the long glass over the mantleshelf: a tall girl in a pretty gown, surrounded by young men. She could not believe it.

Alex Beresford was across the other side of the room, talking to Mrs Forrester, Sara Carlton at his side. Mama must have lost no time in hinting her friend towards this eligible guest for the ball. Would he accept? Hebe resolved to listen to no more requests from partners until she knew. How awful to give away all the waltzes before he could ask her! Then the improbability of finding that she, nice, ordinary Hebe Carlton, was worrying about keeping her dance card clear, struck her and she almost laughed out loud.

Mrs Carlton had lifted the lid of the piano and was urging the older Miss Smithson to play. The clear notes of an English country tune rippled through the buzz of conversation and, while several people strolled over to listen more closely, Alex Beresford made his way to Hebe's side.

She introduced the young men. The Major exchanged a few words with them perfectly pleasantly, but somehow they appeared to be picking up an unspoken message and within a minute all three made their excuses and melted back into the crowd.

'Nice lads,' Alex remarked.

'Yes.' Hebe was glad of a neutral topic of conversation, for now she was by his side she felt flustered. 'You were talking to Jack Forrester's mother just now.' She realised it was the first time she had been with Alex in a crowd of people: it felt as though everyone's eyes were on them.

'The fashionable matron who invited me to her ball, making quite sure I knew there would be plenty of waltzing?'

'Yes, I believe she is determined it will be very dashing. Will you be attending?'

'Only if you give me the first waltz, Circe.' He took her arm and steered her gently in the direction of the long table where drinks were being set out. 'A glass of ratafia?'

Hebe said demurely, 'Yes, please.' She took the glass and watched him over the rim as she took a sip. 'I have already promised three waltzes. I do not know how many Mrs Forrester will order.'

'Dance the first with me, then your young admirer and his friends will have to ask his mama to add on more if they feel cut out.' He regarded her with challenging blue eyes. 'I suppose you will tell me that you will not be allowed to dance more than one waltz with me?'

'Indeed, yes, Mama would not like it. But a country dance would be perfectly eligible.' Was it her new confidence? Was it simply his presence? Hebe did not know, but suddenly talking to Alex was easy. She smiled up at his suddenly serious face. 'What is wrong? Are country dances beneath the interest of senior officers?'

'Not at all, and if that is all you will permit me, I must accept it and be grateful. But do not blame me for being disappointed with only one waltz.'

'Oh, now you are flattering me, to pretend to be cast

down!' She gestured round the room. 'Look, there are half a dozen young ladies here who will all be at the ball, and every one, I warrant, will be happy to dance with you.'

'Circe...'

'And that is another thing,' she continued, letting him guide her back towards the centre of the room. 'I am not at all sure I am flattered to be compared to someone who turns men into swine. Mama, when she found me looking Circe up in a book of mythology, said I should not be reading such things, for everyone in the Greek myths led sadly irregular lives.'

Alex gave a choke of laughter. 'What can she mean?'

'Well, she would say that Circe was the product of a most unfortunate liaison, Zeus's...er...friendships with young women she would not mention at all, and can you just imagine her, lecturing the Minotaur on his bad habit of eating people?'

Alex was having trouble controlling his expression. He swallowed hard and suggested, 'Perhaps a Society for the Suppression of Vice in Mythology? There seems to be a society for the suppression of just about everything else.'

'Oh, no, if you eliminate all the irregular behaviour, there would be no stories left!' Hebe was trying so hard to control her giggles that they almost bumped into Miss Dyson, who regarded her with surprised eyes that held more than a hint of irritation.

Charlotte Dyson was the acknowledged beauty of Malta society that year and was used to attracting the undivided attention of all the most eligible and attractive men at any function. Her father was an Admiral, her portion was known to be large, and her blonde hair, large blue eyes and willowy figure were much admired. She affected a style of calm elegance, and was never seen expressing any violent emotion. This cool front drove most of the men who came into contact with her wild with the desire to be the one to disturb her perfect composure.

Her cool blue gaze surveyed Hebe's animated face and sparkling eyes and noted the fact that her hand was resting on the arm of this most attractive officer. Miss Dyson was not used to handsome men failing to hover around her, waiting to be introduced. She was equally unused to seeing plain Miss Carlton with any of the beaux she had come to regard as hers by right.

'Miss Carlton, a charming party.'

'I am so glad you are enjoying it, Charlotte. May I present Major the Honourable Alex Beresford? Major Beresford, Miss Dyson.'

Miss Dyson inclined her head with the studied grace that allowed the elegant curve of her throat to be seen to its best advantage. 'Are you newly arrived on Malta, Major?' Now he would fall in by her side and follow her as she drifted gracefully across the room.

'I have been here a few days only, Miss Dyson. A most pleasant island. Excuse me, but I believe that gentleman with the red hair is attempting to attract your attention.' He bowed and strolled off, Hebe still on his arm, leaving a fulminating Miss Dyson face to face with Horace Philpott, a gauche young gentleman of small fortune who adored her with a hopeless passion.

'That was wicked,' Hebe hissed, trying not to feel triumphant, and failing utterly. She had suffered too many patronising remarks from Charlotte in the past: this tiny vengeance was sweet.

'I am sorry.' Alex sounded not the slightest bit repentant. 'Is she a particular friend of yours? Have I dragged you away?'

'No, she is not,' Hebe said with some force. 'But she expected you to stay with her.'

'And leave you. Yes, I noticed. Just because she is pretty...'

'Pretty? Why, Charlotte is the acknowledged beauty this season.'

Alex looked down at her, a wicked twinkle in his blue eyes. 'I will give you a hint. Next time you are asked to admire a beautiful woman, ask yourself what she is going to look like when she is forty—better still, look at her mother—and think again.' He glanced around. 'Now I think I had better circulate or I will be in trouble with my hostess for being a bad guest. May I take you into supper later?'

Hebe, who knew that Sara Carlton must be watching them with unalloyed delight, blushed and nodded. 'Yes, please. Now, to whom shall I introduce you?'

Hebe left Alex with a boisterous circle of naval officers, who soon absorbed him into a discussion of the best way to handicap a race between a goat and a sheep that someone had proposed, and began to circulate amongst the guests.

Normally Hebe enjoyed parties, even ones like this one where she had to worry about whether there were accidents in the kitchen, the wine had run out or an ancient dowager was neglected and in need of someone to talk to. There were always people to watch, stories and problems would be confided to her and she might even indulge in a little quiet matchmaking.

Now she found herself an object of interest. She was aware people were watching her and suspected that they were talking also. Were her friends jealous because of the attention Alex Beresford had paid her? Were they laughing to see Miss Carlton all dressed up with powder on her face? It did not occur to her that while the young ladies were indeed jealous, and curious, the older matrons—unless they had daughters of their own to puff off—were pleased to see how dear Hebe had emerged from her shell. And the young gentlemen were startled to see good old Hebe not as a sympathetic honorary older sister, but an uncommonly taking young lady.

But the object of their attention realised none of this until she heard Lady Ordleigh remark to Mrs Winston, 'Whatever has happened to little Hebe? Why, the child has suddenly blossomed.'

Hebe, unseen behind them, held her breath. 'Indeed she has. I would never have thought to describe her as pretty, but she is tonight: look at the young men watching her. Now, what has caused this, I wonder?'

The object of their speculation crept away in amazement. She found a small group who were chatting together and with an effort joined in the conversation. Without Alex to talk to she was feeling strangely flustered, almost panicky. Any moment now someone would see she was an impostor and say…

'Would you like to have supper now, Hebe?' She gave a little start, turning from the small knot of people with whom she had been talking. It was Alex Beresford, smiling at her. He was half a head taller than any of the other men in the group, his scarlet coat a startling contrast to the blue uniform of the naval officers, his saturnine dark looks almost sinister against their weatherbeaten, cheerful faces.

'Oh! Major…yes, please. Will you excuse me?' She smiled at the others. 'I had best eat now in case Mama needs any help.' She took Alex's arm, but as soon as they reached the hall he steered her, not into the dining room which was already resounding with the sound of clinking cutlery and animated talk, but out into the garden.

Hebe protested faintly, but was inexorably borne into the depths of the shrubbery until they were quite out of sight.

'What is the matter, Circe?' Alex turned her so he could see her face in the light of the lanterns which lit the winding paths. 'You are as white as a sheet and I do believe there are tears in your eyes. Has one of those little cats been spiteful?'

'No, everyone has been very kind. It is just that I am not used…' Her voice failed her. It was ridiculous, she *was* going to cry.

'Not used to parties? Surely not? You are such a good hostess.' His hands were resting lightly on her shoulders and his touch felt warm and reassuring.

'Not used to being…pretty. People are looking at me.' She dropped her gaze. Now she had said it she felt ridiculous. Now he would laugh at her.

But Major Beresford shook his head reprovingly. 'You were not attending to me the other day, Hebe. Not pretty—*enchanting*. You have always been enchanting, it is just that you have never cared to exercise the enchantment. No wonder you feel so shaky, releasing all that power.'

Now he was laughing at her, but Hebe did not mind. She smiled at him, blinking back the tears. 'Is that what it is? No, you are teasing me.'

'Only a little bit. Now, what would make you feel better?'

'A glass of wine?' Hebe suggested. She rarely drank any, but it felt like a good idea now.

Alex's blue eyes remained thoughtfully on her. 'Per-

haps, in a moment, but first, I think…' And he gathered
her to him and kissed her.

Hebe had never been kissed before. She had never met
anyone she wanted to kiss, for it always looked an embarrassing and rather uncomfortable process.

Now she felt neither embarrassed nor the slightest bit
uncomfortable. But it was all very strange. Alex's mouth
was gentle on hers, both firm and warm. It seemed to be
asking her questions in a silent language she did not understand, but which she very much wanted to speak too.
His hands held her securely to him and she could feel
the heat of him against her skin, the beat of his heart
where her hand rested against his chest. He smelled wonderful: citrus and sandalwood and an indefinably male
scent all of his own.

Her body was reacting in entirely new ways, giving
her incomprehensible messages, telling her to move
against him. She felt too shy to obey the urge, but if he
kept on kissing her she surely would…

Alex raised his head and looked down at her closed
eyes. 'Hebe?'

'Hmm?'

'Open your eyes.' She did so, blinking, and looked
directly into his blue gaze, which held an expression that
was quite unfamiliar but which made her mouth go dry.
'Now, will you forget about being pretty?'

'And concentrate on being Circe?' She smiled at him
trustingly, wondering if her heart was going to stop thudding.

'I do not know what you have turned me into,' Alex
said ruefully, turning her within the circle of his arms
until she was held lightly against his side. She could not
see his face.

'Not a swine,' Hebe assured him, wishing he had not stopped kissing her.

'Probably a wolf,' Alex retorted. 'That is what your mama would say if she could see us now. Come along, back inside and tempt me with lobster patties.'

'How do you know there are any?' Hebe challenged him as they stepped back through the door and he dropped his arm from her shoulders.

'I took the precaution of looking at the buffet earlier. Always scout ahead is a good military maxim.' They reached the door of the dining room and as they passed through a young woman with rich chestnut hair caught up on top of her head passed the far end of the table, her back to them. Alex stopped dead as though he had hit a barrier.

'Major?' Hebe looked at him in surprise, but his face revealed nothing.

'I am sorry, Miss Carlton, a sudden cramp in the calf.' Then the moment passed and they were in the room, exchanging conversation with other guests, helping themselves from the temping platters of food.

But Hebe's forehead was creased by a small line. Had she imagined it, or had Alex whispered 'Clarissa!' in the moment when he had halted so abruptly?

He seemed to recover his composure the moment they were inside the room, and Hebe wondered if she had been imagining things. She took care to introduce him to the red-headed young woman at the earliest opportunity, but his face gave nothing away and he chatted to her and her escort, an officer of Dragoons, for quite five minutes without displaying the slightest concern.

After supper Alex took her back into the salon and gave her a gentle push. 'Now go on, practise enchantment on that poor Captain of Marines over there. He looks miserable having to talk to the chaplain.'

Hebe did not think him serious, but before she knew what she was about the Captain was asking if she would be at Mrs Forrester's ball and the chaplain was enquiring if he might have the honour of a country dance. 'For I hardly care to waltz, Miss Carlton.'

'Oh, indeed not, Dr Paulin,' she agreed earnestly. 'I am sure you are right: someone in your position must set an example. But I would be delighted to join a measure with you.'

Alex passed at that moment, apparently talking to Miss Smithson about the best place in London to have a harp restrung, but he glanced up, caught Hebe's eye and his own creased in an encouraging smile. Hebe smiled back, all her earlier awkwardness and butterflies forgotten, except for that puzzling moment in the dining room. Who was Clarissa?

But she forgot the incident as the evening continued and at last the guests called for their carriages, chairs and linkboys, and vanished into the warm night.

The two Carlton ladies slowly climbed the stairs, arm in arm, sank down on the daybed in Sara's room, eased off their shoes and sighed happily in unison.

'My dear Hebe,' Mrs Carlton declared, 'I swear I have never been in such charity with you! What an evening: you were so admired, even that old pussy Mrs Winston complimented me upon you. And as for Major Beresford, why, he is positively smitten.'

'Everyone was very kind,' Hebe conceded, certain that the fact she had received her first kiss must be blazoned across her forehead.

'Well, I will not say any more, for I expect you are feeling quite strange after such an evening,' her stepmother replied with unusual perception. 'But we must build on this success: Mrs Forrester's ball will be crucial. We must give the utmost care and thought to your new gown. Palest lemon silk with white gauze? Or cream with a floss trim? Or…' Hebe's eyelids began to droop. 'We will talk about it tomorrow. Now, off to bed with you, dear.'

Hebe sank between the cool linen sheets with a sigh of relief and was almost instantly asleep. But behind her closed lids dreams chased each other through the night and a tall girl with her brown hair unbound and wearing only a Grecian tunic whirled and danced in the arms of a tall, dark, beautiful man with fierce blue eyes.

Chapter Six

Both Mrs and Miss Carlton expected the early appearance of Major Beresford on their doorstep, and once again they were disappointed. But on this occasion Mrs Carlton at least declared herself satisfied with the reason.

Sir Richard arrived the afternoon after the party to inform her that he would be absent from her dinner table for the rest of the week and to deliver a note from the Major.

She broke the seal and spread open the crackling sheet of paper. 'How well he expresses his thanks for our soi-rée, and apologises that duty prevents him from calling in person,' she declared after conning the contents. 'The more I know Major Beresford, the more impressed I am by his manners and character.'

Hebe kept her eyes down on her sewing, trying to ignore the constriction of her throat that hearing Alex's name provoked. Her stepmama hesitated, then passed over a small, folded piece of paper, which had been inside the letter. 'This is addressed to you, Hebe. I suppose I should read it, but I know I can trust you to behave prudently.'

The note seemed to curl within Hebe's fingers as

though it had a life of its own. She looked at it. 'Miss Carlton' it said in a strong hand. Slowly she unfolded it, knowing full well that her mama would expect her to repeat its contents: no chaperon would dream of allowing an unmarried girl to receive private notes from a man, and Mama was being most indulgent in not opening it first.

C., it read, *I have gone fishing and will be away for several days. I have remembered to pack those items which you advised me to take. A.*

'He says he is away on duty for several days, Mama,' she said, holding out the note.

'Oh, dear, that is a pity,' Sara Carlton said comfortably, making no effort to take it. She was far too pleased that the Major had written to Hebe to wish to disconcert the girl by insisting on prying. It was not as though Hebe had ever shown the slightest inclination to behave lightly or imprudently with a man—far from it. If she could be encouraged to flirt a little, it might help fix the Major's interest.

With a thankful sigh, Hebe folded up the note and slipped it under her sewing. Sir Richard glanced at the clock and got to his feet hastily. 'My goodness, look at the time! Hebe, my dear, would you care to walk a little with me?'

The Commodore was already treating Hebe very much as the stepdaughter she would eventually become and, liking him very much, she stood on no ceremony with him. Receiving a smiling nod from Sara, she hurried into the hall and found a bonnet and shawl.

She slipped her hand under his proffered elbow and allowed herself to be guided out into the sunlit street.

'Are you happy, child?' he asked her suddenly.

'Happy?' Hebe blinked up at him and he smiled in-

voluntarily at the charming frankness in her wide grey
eyes. 'Why, yes, I am happy. I am very happy.' And it
seemed to her that, without her realising it, a warm tide
of contentment had washed over her these past few days.
But it was not just a placid state: within that warm glow
here was excitement, anticipation, a frisson of something
she did not understand.

'Good.' The Commodore glanced round as they entered a shady square, so small it might almost be a courtyard. An ancient fountain, its pool edged with the battered arms of the ancient Knights, dribbled water over a
moss-covered spout and a stone bench stood under a
dusty plane tree. 'Sit down a moment, Hebe, there is
something I want to tell you.' The little square was quiet,
and, with the exception of two women gossiping outside
a door, deserted.

'You will not repeat this to anyone, Hebe, and I do not
want to disturb your mother yet, but there is a good
chance I will be sailing for England very soon. I do not
know whether she will prefer to be married here, or when
we arrive in London, but I wanted to forewarn you so
you can begin to think about what will need to be done
with the household.'

Hebe sat still, absorbing the news. She had known it
would happen one day and she had looked forward to
returning to the home she hardly knew and the excitements of the long-promised London Season.

'Will you be sad to leave Malta?'

'Yes of course, but London will be wonderful.' There
was a reservation in her voice and he picked it up with
an accuracy that startled her.

'And what about your Major?'

'He is not my Major!' she protested hotly, then caught
his indulgent expression and smiled ruefully.

'But you wish he was? Well, you could do a lot worse. Only a younger son, of course, but an excellent family, and a man of very good character. A brave officer,' he added, watching her face. Not every young woman would want to see a man they were fond of in the thick of danger.

But Hebe's chin came up. 'I know, I can tell.' She glanced around, but they were still alone. 'He is an intelligence officer, is he not?' She took his silence for assent. 'And that is very dangerous?'

'Yes, although probably no more dangerous than storming an enemy fort. It has its particular hazards.' He did not appear to want to add to this.

'Like being shot out of hand as a spy?' Hebe asked point blank. There was no reply.

After a moment's thought the Commodore said, 'I should probably not tell you this, but he will no doubt sail with us when I leave for England.'

'Alex...I mean Major Beresford...is returning to England?' A sea voyage, days together through the Mediterranean, sunlight on the water, the flying fish...

'Certainly as far as Gibraltar. After that, I do not know, and we should discuss it no further. Hebe—' He broke off as though considering carefully what he had to say. 'Hebe, I have no daughters of my own, so I do not know whether I am doing the right thing in encouraging you in this, but you have a good man there...'

'I have not *got* him,' she protested.

'Not yet, perhaps. But I just want you to consider, someone like Alex Beresford will have a long history of, shall we say, entanglements, behind him. More than an inexperienced girl such as yourself might guess. I am sure he would not play fast and loose with you, or I would be speaking to him myself, but I do not want you to build

oo much upon what may only be a flirtation. If it proves
ot to be, well, then, no one will be more delighted than
,'

Impulsively Hebe kissed him on the cheek. 'Thank
ou, sir. And thank you for the warnings about the near
uture. I promise I will say nothing. Goodbye!'

She made her way slowly back up the hill, mulling
ver what Sir Richard had told her, trying to sort out her
motions. Yes she would be sorry to leave Malta, its
unshine, the people, the vivid colours, the ever-present
ea. But she was eager for London…or was she?

Suddenly Hebe's stomach cramped with the sort of
old dread that came sometimes when she woke in the
orning, knowing something was wrong, but not yet
wake enough to recall what it was. There had been long
eeks of that feeling after Papa had been killed, a very
uch milder version of it when she had a bad tooth and
ad to wait a week before the only dentist Mama would
rust returned to Valetta and she could undergo a very
ainful extraction.

London would be fun, of course it would, especially
ow she knew she could cut a passable figure in Society
nd not be regarded as a Plain Jane. But, looking round,
reathing in the smells of hot dust, flowering vines, don-
ey, drains, spicy food, she knew she would miss Malta
ost dreadfully. London would be grey, formal, cold and
he would have none of the freedom she had now.

But it was the thought of Alex that was filling her with
his dreadful apprehension. She wished desperately that
e Commodore had not spoken to her. She was fright-
ned for Alex now in a way that she had not been before.
nd she was also uneasy. The more she thought about
ir Richard's words, the worse the feeling became. Did
e know something? Was he trying to warn her of some-

thing in Alex's past, or even his present? No, surely not, or he would have been more explicit.

What did Alex feel for her? He liked her, he had seemed to enjoy kissing her, but doubtless he enjoyed kissing many young ladies: men did. Mama and Sir Richard appeared to take it more seriously, but they would obviously be hoping for an eligible match for her and could be wildly over-optimistic.

And what did she feel? What would she do if Major Beresford turned up with a ring and a declaration? Hebe gave herself a brisk shake as she reached the front door. *Stop it, you hardly know the man. It won't arise so you can stop thinking about it. Enjoy your first flirtation and wave him goodbye with good grace in Gibraltar.*

This admirable good sense sustained Hebe through the days before Mrs Forrester's ball. Sir Richard started to call in again, so whatever his urgent business had been, it seemed to be done with. A package arrived for Hebe, which on opening contained nothing more than a seashell and a note in a strong black script saying simply, *From Sicily.*

Hebe put it on her dressing table and tried not to keep picking it up and stroking it all the time as she sat making lists in her head of things that must be done in order to leave Malta. It was difficult because she did not dare put anything on paper and Mama appeared to have been given no hint by Sir Richard.

The days were busy, and full of too many secret worries and concerns to allow for much daydreaming. But the nights were different and Hebe dreamt night after night of Alex, of his arms around her, of his lips on hers. Once she dreamt she was running her palms caressingly over his naked chest and woke, quivering with tension, to find she was stroking a silk shawl that she had left lying on the covers when she went to sleep.

Shaken, she sat up against the pillows and watched the dawn slowly lighting the sky until it suddenly burst out over the island in scarlet and gold streaks. Was she very wanton to have these dreams? Did everyone feel like this after just one kiss? She knew the facts of life of course. One only had to be normally observant of life going on around one, without any help from classical male nude statues in the art gallery or one's stepmama's careful explanations, which, Hebe was given to understand, would be expanded upon before her wedding night.

Malta was full of attractive men, and men made even more attractive by dashing uniforms and an air of military glamour. But she had never tried to imagine what it would be like to push their shirts from their shoulders and run her fingers over their backs, or what sensation their lips on her breast would provoke. It must have been that kiss. Yes, that was it. It was being kissed for the first time and nothing to do with the man who had kissed her.

But it was the thought of that man that was foremost in Hebe's mind as she chose her new ballgown. 'That one,' she said unhesitatingly as the ladies flipped through volumes of *La Belle Assemblée and Ackerman's Repository of Arts* in Madame Eglantine's dress shop. Madame Eglantine might have been born Susan Eagles in Basingstoke, but she had skill with scissors and needle, a sharp eye for fashion and an excellent business sense and hers were the undisputed gowns of choice for Malta society.

Mrs Carlton and Madame came to look over her shoulder. 'But charming,' Madame opined. 'Such simplicity, such grace. Naturally, only a young lady with Miss Carlton's height could wear that gown to advantage.'

'Greek?' Mrs Carlton said, not at all so certain. The gown was certainly striking, but not in any obvious way unsuitable for a débutante. It was cut with the perfect simplicity of a Greek tunic, falling in soft folds to the floor and secured at the shoulder and under the bosom with cords and ornate knots. Otherwise it was without trimmings if one eliminated from the picture the diamond parure, the feathers, the toque and the gauze shawl the model was hung about with.

It was the very simplicity that was somehow daring, for it made the observer concentrate on the wearer rather than the gown, and for someone without perfect deportment it would be a disaster.

'Well…Hebe, are you certain?'

'Oh, yes, Mama, please might I have that design?' If Alex saw her in that gown, Circe come to life… The daydream retreated in the face of brisk practicality.

'But your hair, and I do not know what colour…'

'If Miss Carlton's hair was confined in a very tight knot high on her head, with a few ringlets at the neck and a riband, then she would look like that statue in the hall of the Civil Commissioner's house,' Madame suggested.

Fortunately Sara had not noticed the statue on the last occasion she had been a guest of Lieutenant-General Sir Hilderbrand and Lady Oakes. Hebe had, and tried to suppress the memory of one pert naked breast, a flowing tunic cut all the way up the side and the expression on the marble face of a nymph trying not too hard to escape from a satyr. The hairstyle, however, was unexceptional and would allow her to escape yet another threat of having her curls cut off.

As Lady Oakes had graciously loaned her house with its fine ballroom to her friend Mrs Forrester for the ball there was a risk that Sara might notice the statue, but by then it would be to late to do anything about it.

'And the matte silk crepe, in this charming shade of creamy white, will be just the thing.' Madame snapped her fingers and an assistant hurried forward with the bale of cloth. It was indeed lovely. 'I have an assistant who has just the touch with ornamental cords and knots—say in jonquil yellow? And with slippers dyed to match, long white gloves and pearls...' Madame was well away in a trance of creation, sketching rapidly on a piece of paper and holding it up for Sara's approval.

The gown was a total success and the hairstyle just as Madame had predicted. On the night of the ball Hebe allowed Maria to pin a few sprigs of orange blossom into the high knot of curls and sat back. Would Alex look at her and see Circe as he imagined the enchantress? He was back on the island, but not after three more packages had mysteriously appeared and the powder bowl on Hebe's dressing table was full of shells.

Hebe thought she looked very well, but she knew she had no way of judging what it was that Alex found enchanting in her. The knowledge that she was going to see him after almost two weeks brought the colour to her cheeks. Would he kiss her again tonight?

'Are you ready my dear?' Sara Carlton swept into the room, a vision in powder blue and silver, the very handsome diamond earrings that Sir Richard had presented to her as a betrothal gift sparking in her ears. 'Oh, yes! You look...' She paused, obviously lost for words. *Not nice*, Hebe pleaded silently, *please don't say nice.*

'Enchanting,' her stepmother pronounced and was taken aback by the warmth of Hebe's answering smile. 'Come along now, the chair bearers are here.'

* * *

The square outside the Civil Commissioner's mansion
was ablaze with light from torchères, jammed with carriages and chair-bearers and choked with passers-by all
agog to view the guests. Hebe and Sara arrived somewhat
breathless from the jolting as their bearers fought their
way to the steps, but the slow progress up the stairs to
the receiving line gave them plenty of time to collect
themselves. Hebe managed to distract Sara's attention
from the wanton nymph with her hairstyle by pointing
out the quite outrageous décolletage that Lady Gregson
was flaunting and they gained the ballroom without mishap.

The orchestra was playing some light airs while the
main press of guests arrived, giving Hebe time to look
around her. Everywhere there were friends and acquaintances, and a good number of strangers, for Mrs Forrester
had sent out invitations far and wide. But there was no
sign of Alex.

Hebe soon found herself scribbling in her card as gentleman after gentleman asked her for a dance, but she
kept the first waltz, a country dance, and rebelliously, a
cotillion, free. If Alex pressed her she would agree to a
third dance with him, however fast that made her look.
If he asked her…if he was here.

She followed Sara to where a group of matrons were
gesturing for their friend to join them. As she passed
along she heard one lady say, 'Who is that charming gel
in the white Grecian gown? Goodness! Not that dab of a
Carlton gel…' She blushed slightly, but the sensation of
being admired was too pleasant to object to.

She sat with the group of ladies, quietly as befitted a
débutante, and scanned the room as unobtrusively as she
could. The waltz was the first dance: Mrs Forrester had
stuck by her intention of being 'dashing'. The orchestra

had stopped playing their light airs and were adjusting music on their stands. Any moment now, they would begin. Hebe tried to keep the disappointment off her face. Alex Beresford was not here, he would not see her lovely gown, she would not discover what a second kiss might bring.

'Mrs Carlton, ma'am. Miss Carlton, my dance I believe.' Alex was there at her side, apparently appearing from nowhere. His scarlet dress-coat glittered with gold lace, his hair had been newly cut and showed pale skin at his temples and nape against his tan, his blue eyes looked at Hebe as though there was no other lady in the room.

Mrs Carlton opened her mouth to express her doubts about her daughter participating in the first waltz, but it was too late, Hebe was out on the floor, her hand in Alex's, the centre of attention as the onlookers craned to see who was going to be dashing enough to perform the outrageous new dance.

Then other couples joined them and Sara Carlton sat back, fanning herself. Oh dear, if only no one thought dear Hebe fast!

'Dear Hebe' was trying not to quiver as Alex's hand touched her at the waist. He made no attempt to grasp her, but the feel of his hand gave her the sensation of being controlled, mastered. It was surprisingly pleasant. She gathered up her skirts gracefully in her free hand and managed to meet his eyes as the first chord struck. Then they were sweeping through the other dancers, his hand guiding her, her body responsive to the slightest change of direction from his.

Hebe managed a smile after the first few turns. 'Oh, I was so nervous!'

'Nervous?' His eyes were darker than she had ever

seen them against his tanned face. His voice sounded almost harsh and she realised he had hardly said a word.

'I have never waltzed in public before,' she confessed. 'And never with a man.'

He was so silent. She had expected him to ask her how she had learned, so she told him, knowing she was beginning to chatter.

'Lizzie Hawkins got her dancing teacher to show us, and we all danced together. But Mama did not know I could do it; I hope she is not too shocked.'

He was still silent, still guiding her through the other dancers with a skill that left her feeling there was no one else on the dance floor, that they could swoop and swirl here all night. 'Alex?'

'I am sorry. It is just that you look so… Circe, I never imagined… Dammit, I am stammering like a green boy!'

'You think I look nice?' she ventured. 'I thought you might like this gown.' She blushed, for it was not something one should discuss with a man. 'I chose it because of you.'

'Nice? No, you do not look *nice*, you look utterly ravishing.' He seemed almost angry.

Hebe looked up and caught the full power of his hawk-look. She gasped: she had never seen him look like this so close and it was as though all the breath had been sucked out of her.

'I am sorry. It is just that you make me want to—' He broke off abruptly.

Hebe felt a tingling excitement flooding through her. Whatever it was he wanted, she wanted it too. 'What is it you want?' she pressed. They were both keeping their voices low and that seemed to heighten the intensity. She did not know that to those who were watching them it almost seemed as though they were quarrelling, so serious did they look, so locked were their eyes. Across the floor Sara Carlton waved her fan more rapidly and a small moan of anxiety escaped her lips.

Alex swept Hebe into a turn, then again and again until she felt dizzy and clung more tightly to his hand. His fingers seemed to burn through her gown at her waist. She knew she was far too close to him for propriety, which decreed he should hold her almost at arm's length. As they turned she felt her thighs brush his.

Fiercely he said, 'I want to take you out through those doors on to the terrace, down the steps, across the lawn and into the shadows and make love to you for the rest of the night.'

Hebe gasped. 'I told you that what you had was dangerous, did I not?' he went on. 'Enchantment, infinitely more dangerous than even beauty.'

Hebe could hardly keep on her feet, only his hands supported her, only his will kept her eyes locked with his. Then the music came to a crescendo and the dancers swirled to a halt, clapping amid bows and curtsies.

Hebe stood still, her hand still clasped in Alex's. 'I did not know, I had no idea you—'

'No, neither did I. And I should have done.' He was breathing as though he had run a race. 'Come, let me take you back to your seat.'

He escorted a shaking Hebe back in silence, bowed elegantly to Mrs Carlton and disappeared into the crowd. Sara looked at her stepdaughter in wide-eyed surmise. 'What on earth? You looked as though you were quarrelling. Were you, Hebe?'

'I have no idea,' she said slowly, sinking down on to the gilt chair. 'I have no idea at all.'

Chapter Seven

The rest of the evening passed like a strange dream for Hebe. Alex appeared to have vanished, for although she scanned every red coat, every black head rising above shorter men, she could see no trace of him.

Mrs Carlton was deeply concerned, convinced that Hebe had quarrelled irretrievably with the most eligible—the only eligible—man who had ever appeared to take an interest in her. Eventually Hebe's apparent calm and the undoubted success she was having with the other young men present calmed her stepmother and she wrote the whole thing off as a lovers' tiff. Perhaps the Major had been jealous of Hebe's full dance card, in which case that was a very promising sign.

Meanwhile Hebe danced every dance on the card, including the ones she had set aside for Alex, smiling and chatting and giving no sign to either the watchful matrons, her friends or her admiring partners that her mind was working furiously and her body seemed to vibrate like a plucked violin string.

Her first surprise, as she smilingly joined a set for the cotillion, was that she did not feel upset at what had just passed between her and Alex and she set herself to work out why while her feet automatically went through the complex measures of the dance.

There had been nothing to quarrel about, of course, whatever it might have looked like from outside. He was angry, certainly, and some of that anger was directed at her, although she could tell he was chiefly furious with himself.

Yesterday, if someone had told her that Major Beresford was angry with her she would have been distressed and mortified. Tonight, she was not. Why not? That was the mystery. And she should have been shocked at his words: his shocking, thrilling, utterly outrageous words. But she was not.

The cotillion ended and she found her hand claimed by Sir Richard for a country dance. If he had been her stepfather she might have confided in him, asked him why he thought Alex had reacted in that way, but she knew he would not think it proper to discuss such things with her while they could claim no relationship.

She pushed the puzzle to the back of her mind as they whirled energetically through the dance, for he knew her too well not to notice if she was abstracted, but she returned to it over a glass of lemonade with Jack Forrester and his sister and her partner. The others talked and laughed and Hebe joined in, but she was thinking furiously. Some instinct told her that she did not understand because she was innocent, and that very innocence was part of the problem. Some part of her, behind her disappointment that Alex had gone, behind her enjoyment of the ball and of her new gown, was quivering into life.

Then, with a jolt that almost made her gasp out loud, she realised what it was, and what had happened with Alex. He desired her, he wanted her not as a friend, not as an embodiment of a Greek myth, not as a girl to flirt with. He wanted her physically: it was desire, and because she was innocent and unaware, he was angry with himself for feeling like that, and angry with her for arousing those feelings.

Hebe took a long sip of lemonade and smiled at the tale Jack was telling them. Power, that was what she was feeling, growing inside her. Power over a man, power to make him feel so strongly that he had to walk out of a ball.

It was wonderful: exciting, dangerous and…the smile slowly vanished from her lips. Frightening. She did not know what she was doing, she did not know how to control this power and she had no idea how to behave with Alex if he ever came back. Would he come back? Or would he avoid her out of a gentlemanly concern not to alarm her innocence or put her in a compromising position of any sort?

Back home at two in the morning, Sara Carlton was relieved to see that Hebe appeared perfectly composed, if tired. If she was not cast down by Alex Beresford's mysterious desertion, then Sara could not find it in herself to be too worried. She thought of mentioning it, then decided against it. 'Good night, dearest, sleep well.'

Hebe let Maria help her out of her clothes and into a wrapper but she sent the yawning maid away to her bed after that. She was tired, but far too tense to sleep. The night was hot and Hebe wandered restlessly about the room, gazing out of first one window, then another. Her room was on the corner of the house with windows on to the square, but at the side, many years ago, another house had stood. Over time it had fallen into decay and had been demolished, leaving only its ornate façade with empty windows opening on to what had become a some-what neglected side extension of Mrs Carlton's garden.

Hebe's second window with its wide balcony over-looked this nightingale-haunted tangle of shrubs and climbers; now she drew the draperies across the front window, but threw open the side one where she could stand and look out without being seen.

She leaned against the door frame for a long while, twisting the ringlets that lay on her shoulder round and round her finger and trying hard not to think of anything at all. The nightingales were almost silent now, but every now and again a few throaty, bubbling notes came from the deep foliage, heartbreakingly lovely in the moonlight.

With a sigh, Hebe drifted back to her dressing table and reached to pull out the pins that held her hair up in its tight knot. There was a sharp noise at the window and something rattled on the polished boards. Barefoot, Hebe padded across and picked it up. A piece of gravel. There was another impact as another missile hit the glass.

Someone was in the garden below, throwing stones at her window. It was the only explanation, although it was surely something that only happened in novels. Drawing her wrapper tightly around her, Hebe tiptoed out on to the balcony and peered cautiously over. Alex Beresford was standing there, his head tipped to look up, his arm back ready to throw again. As he saw her he lowered his hand.

'''Lo, what light from yonder window shines,''' he quoted.

'Shh!' Hebe leaned out and looked to the side, but none of the windows were open, and Sara's, thankfully, faced the back garden. 'What on earth are you doing?' she hissed.

'Come to see you.' Alex started to unbutton his coat.

'Is that climber well attached?' He made no great effort to lower his voice and Hebe had a sudden suspicion he had been drinking.

'I have no idea!' He threw his coat over a bush and took hold of the thick stem, giving it an experimental shake. 'Go away!' The moonlight was patchy in the garden and odd splashes of stronger light came from the square through the empty windows on the old wall. Alex was hidden now in the darkness at the foot of the wall. Hebe leaned out and touched the tangle of bougainvillea and wisteria stems that were interlaced along the wrought iron of the balcony. Under her hand she felt a tremor. He had begun to climb.

She hung over the edge, trying to see where he was. Goodness knows how strong the climber was, or how tenacious its grasp on the old walls. And if he had been drinking, he was even more likely to fall. There was a sudden explosion of noise, of spitting and yowling, and a violent curse from Alex. A large grey tomcat shot up the climber, on to the balcony, swore at Hebe and vanished up on to the roof.

'Alex!' Her heart was thudding with fright and reaction, but even leaning right out she could see no sprawled shape on the ground beneath.

His head emerged from the darkness, level with the bottom of the balcony. There was a bleeding scratch down his cheek and several twigs in his hair. 'Bloody…sorry, dratted cat.' He gave a convulsive heave, got a leg on to a particularly thick horizontal branch and stood up facing her, his hands gripping the top edge of the wrought iron. Hebe found herself looking at the strong muscles defined under the thin linen shirt and forced her eyes away.

He smiled at her and suddenly Hebe could smell the brandy. 'You're drunk,' she accused.

'I know.' Alex swayed gently where he stood. There was an ominous creaking. 'Give me a hand.'

'No, I will not! What on earth are you doing here?'

'Came to see you.'

'Well, now you have seen me. Go back down at once.' He swayed again, rather more wildly and Hebe reached out instinctively. He grasped her hands, swung a leg over the rail and was on the balcony next to her. Hebe freed her hands and regarded him through narrowed eyes. 'Just how drunk are you, Alex? Or did you sway like that to make me let you on to the balcony?'

'Not drunk, just well to go.' He leaned against the door jamb, as she had a while before, and watched her.

'Oh, look at you,' she exclaimed, half-angry, half-laughing. 'Your face is bleeding with cat scratches, your hair looks like a bird's nest, you have torn your shirt and your cravat's under one ear.'

Alex reached up and tugged the cravat loose, using it to dab at his cheek. He grinned ruefully at her and Hebe's insides seemed to contract. 'I know: half-cut, scruffy as Hades and almost routed by a cat. Hardly the image of the perfect young lover.'

'Is that what you imagine you are?' she retorted tartly, fighting the urge to run her hands through his disordered hair and make him sit down while she bathed his cheek.

'No.' He suddenly sounded sober. With a jerk he stood upright and turned abruptly to step into her room. 'It's all right,' he added as she began to protest. 'I'll be gone in a moment. No, what I am is a damned fool who has come to apologise.'

'Could you not do that in the morning?' Hebe asked, entering the room beside him.

'That would be the sensible thing, would it not?' He sounded bitter. 'It is what I would have done if I had not started drinking in order to forget for a couple of hours.'

'Forget? Forget this evening?'

Alex shook his head sharply. 'No…something else. Never mind that.' He took a step away from her and paused by her dressing table, running his hands through the bowl of shells. 'You kept them, then?'

'Yes, of course. I looked forward to them arriving, and I felt less anxious about you when each one came.'

He turned and looked at her, his eyes bright in the candlelight. 'You worried about me? Why, Hebe?'

'Because I thought you were probably in some danger and I worry about my friends.' She came further into the room, trying to read his face.

'Is that what I am, Circe? A friend?' He tossed down the handful of shells, and the crumpled cravat with its traces of blood fell on the floor.

Hebe kept her voice as steady as she could. 'I do not know what you are to me, Alex. You are a mystery. And sometimes I am afraid of you.'

That brought him round sharply, a look of distress on his face. 'I make you afraid? Hebe, I am sorry, I would never hurt you! You mean this evening, at the ball? I did not intend to frighten you.'

'No,' she said with a shake of her head. 'Not that. When you have that fierce look, when you are like this and I do not know what you want.'

'Only to see you, only to talk to you.' He held up his hands in the fencer's gesture of surrender and relaxed a little as she smiled at him. 'Why did I not frighten you when we were dancing? You knew what was the matter, why I was angry. You know what I wanted, don't you?'

'Yes, you told me,' Hebe said, still managing to keep

her voice steady. She wanted to go to him, hold him, wipe the trickle of blood from his cheek and that dark, tortured look out of his eyes. 'If you hadn't, I might not have guessed. I am not very experienced with men, you know.'

'You do not have to tell me that! Why do you think I was so angry with myself?'

'And with me.'

'I deserve that reminder.' He stood, looking down at the evidence of her undressing that night: the pearl earrings and necklace discarded on the dressing table, a scatter of orange blossom on the boards, one silk stocking that Maria had dropped on her way out. He stooped and picked it up, letting it hang from his fingers. 'If you weren't so sheltered, so innocent.'

'I might be sheltered and inexperienced,' Hebe observed tartly, 'but I am hardly innocent. I understand exactly what the matter is: my inexperience means that I do not know what to do about it.'

That made him laugh, a sudden gasp of amusement. 'I wish I could show you.'

'So do I.' It was out before she realised she was going to say it. Her hands flew to her mouth and her grey eyes stared at him aghast over the shield of her fingers.

'Hebe!' He sounded every bit as shocked as she would expect Sir Richard to be if he had heard her scandalous declaration.

'Oh!' Hebe buried her face in her hands and burst into tears. She was so tired, so confused and now she had shown herself up as wanton and shameless.

The next thing she knew, she was gathered firmly into Alex's arms, her wet cheek pressed against his shirt front. One arm held her tightly, his free hand stroked the nape of her neck with a comforting pressure. 'There, there, poor Circe. Cry all you want.'

But the tears seemed to go as rapidly as they had appeared. Hebe made no move to free herself. The pressure of Alex's arms felt wonderful, strong, reassuring, not at all threatening or confusing. He smelt of the cologne she remembered, and of himself with an overtone of brandy, which prickled her nostrils. Hebe snuggled her cheek against the warm linen and listened to his heart while his hand gentled her nape.

She was vaguely aware of his fingers moving upwards into her hair, then there was the sound of falling pins and her hair tumbled free out of its knot.

'Aah!' He sighed and she felt both hands lift to run through the rippling mass. 'I had imagined what your hair would look like down.'

Hebe looked up at him through wet lashes. 'Mama says I should have it cropped. It is very unfashionable.'

'Never, never do that, Circe. Promise me?'

'I promise,' she said softly and the words seemed to echo in the room. The promise about such a trivial thing was charged with meaning.

Alex stooped and kissed her, gently as he had in the garden, then, as her lips parted under his, with fierce intensity.

It seemed to Hebe that she stopped breathing. The touch of his mouth had excited her before, but now the invasion of his tongue between her parted lips ignited feelings she had only glimpsed in her dreams of him. Instinctively her tongue flickered out to touch his and he groaned deep in his throat, his hands locked in the heavy mass of her hair. Alarmed at his reaction, and shaken by the intense feeling that intimate contact aroused in her, she closed her lips, then hesitantly yielded to the demands of his mouth.

Hebe found her hands were flattened against Alex's chest and began to tug aside his shirt, careless of flying buttons, until she could spread her fingers on the heated skin beneath. The light tangle of hairs against her palms was intriguing, she let her fingers roam further as he showed no sign of freeing her mouth. Then her fingertips found his nipples and froze in surprise as they hardened to her touch.

He freed her mouth and raised his head. For a long moment they stared into each other's eyes, both of them breathing hard. Alex opened his hands and freed her, then tried to step back.

'Let go, Hebe.'

'What, I'm not… Oh!' She found her hands were clenched tight on either side of his shirt front. With an effort of will she opened her fingers, releasing the creased linen.

'Hebe darling, I must go—stop looking at me like that with those great grey eyes.'

'Alex…'

'Hush, I'll call tomorrow. Hebe, I must go—if I don't go now I won't be answerable for what will happen next.'

She backed slowly away as if to make it easier for him. Her knees met the edge of the bed and she fell back on to the covers. Alex closed his eyes and turned away, through the door and out on to the balcony. Hebe hastily got to her feet and ran out, frightened that after all that brandy he was going to fall. But he reached the ground with no more than the sound of ripping fabric and a muffled curse.

She watched him shrug on his coat, the gold lace glittering in the moonlight. He picked his way through the dark shrubs to a point where he could climb out over the wall. Then he was gone.

Something brushed against Hebe's ankle and she jumped. It was only the grey tomcat. He snaked around her bare legs, then jumped up on to the balcony rail, regarding her with eyes that gleamed amber in the candlelight.

Hebe stared at it for a long moment. 'I love him,' she said at last, as much to herself as the cat. 'I love Alex Beresford.'

She turned and walked back into the room, pulling the doors closed behind her. The cat watched her with insolent, ancient eyes, then jumped lightly down on to a branch and began to hunt again.

Chapter Eight

Hebe slept deeply, and, if she dreamt, she had no recollection of it when she woke. She drifted up sleepily through a sort of haze of happiness, which gradually resolved itself into an image of Alex Beresford and a memory of the feel of his lips on hers. There was sunlight on her closed lids and the clock in the church across the square, which was always a minute faster than any of the others, began to chime.

'One, I love him, two, he wants me, three, he's going to ask...' Hebe drowsed on while the chimes stopped at ten, and a ragged chorus of more distant bells straggled to an end.

It was a muttering voice that finally brought Hebe fully awake. Someone was in her room, scurrying about on light feet, talking to herself under her breath. 'Where is it, oh, dear, where did I drop it? Oh, where is it?'

Hebe uncurled herself reluctantly and sat up against the pillows, rubbing the sleep out of her eyes. Maria, a laundry basket under one arm, was straightening up from peering at the floor.

'Maria, what are you doing?'

'Oh, Miss Hebe, *scusì*, I did not mean to wake you. I

was looking for a silk stocking, one of the ones you wear last night. It is not with the other I took out when I undress you, and I must have dropped it. Madame will be angry, it is the new pair, you understand?'

The vivid memory of Alex standing with the stocking in his hand came back to Hebe. 'Oh. I...I have no idea where it is now.' That was true enough. She just hoped he had not dropped it in the garden. The thought of the gardener wandering in with it, having found it caught in a shrub, was too awful to think about. She saw the anxious expression on the maid's face and added soothingly, 'Not to worry, Maria. I will tell Mama I have misplaced it. It will turn up.' It most certainly would, just as soon as she demanded that Alex give it back. Although the thought of the Major carrying her stocking about with him, perhaps next to his heart, was undeniably, wickedly, flattering.

'Thank you, Miss Hebe.' Maria was still looking puzzled. 'But what is this, Miss Hebe?' She held up a long strip of heavily creased white muslin in the folds of which there were flecks of blood.

'That...that is...I mean to say...it is...' Hebe floundered to a halt, then realised her mistake. If she had simply said, 'A rag, put it down' in a confident tone, the maid would have obeyed her. Now Maria was watching her with wide eyes which showed a dawning comprehension.

She smoothed out the long strip and said, 'But, Miss Hebe, it is a gentleman's neck cloth.' Her brown eyes grew wider. 'Oh! It belongs to that beautiful man with the blue eyes? The soldier who looks like a saint?' She giggled. 'Perhaps not a saint after all?'

'Maria, can I trust you to be discreet?'

'Discreet? What does that mean? Oh, I see, Miss Hebe,

you do not want me to tell your mama that you have had this man in your room last night?'

'He was not in my room…well, yes he was, but not in *that* way.'

Maria shrugged amiably. 'I do not think it would be so bad if he was here "in that way". If he makes the love to you, then he must marry you, *sì*? And that would be a fine thing. But even if it was not to marry, I do not think I would say no if he was in *my* bedroom.' Her expression became knowing, and she moved her body with a sensuous little shiver. 'He looks so fierce, so passionate. Very exciting.'

Hebe wondered if Maria had ever… No, she could not ask her about it, it was too shocking. 'He came here to talk for a short while, Maria. It was very wrong of us, and my mother would be most angry with me if she knew, so I hope you will not mention it.'

'Of course not, Miss Hebe,' Maria assured her.

'Thank you. Maria, that sprigged muslin, the one with the blue ribbons.'

'Yes, Miss Hebe?'

'I have grown tired of it, you may have it.'

'Thank you, Miss Hebe, but you do not have to give me presents, I will not tell tales. Do you want the hot water now?'

Hebe got up, washed and dressed with the unpleasant feeling that she had mishandled that encounter. She did not believe Maria was a blackmailer, but a maid with no scruples could expect to receive many tips and presents in such circumstances.

Maria came back in, something folded in her hands. 'The neck cloth, Miss Hebe. Shall I wash it and iron it?'

Thank goodness. If the girl had intended mischief, surely she would have kept the thing. 'No, thank you,

Maria. Just give it to me.' Hebe waited until the maid had gone, then folded the cloth and slipped it into the bottom drawer of her dressing table. After a moment she took it out again, laid it against her cheek and breathed deeply. Citrus, brandy, Alex.

Mrs Carlton and Hebe took a leisurely luncheon, both feeling somewhat heavy eyed and disinclined for much activity after their late night. Chatting in a desultory manner about people they had seen, flirtations observed, and some disastrous gowns, they eventually took themselves off into the garden. Sara had some lace to sew on handkerchiefs, Hebe a new novel.

She curled up in one of the hammocks while her stepmother took a high-backed wicker chair. 'Look, Mama, *Sense and Sensibility*, I had heard it is very good, but I only found it at the bookseller the other day.'

'Well, with a title like that, at least it sounds a respectable book,' Mrs Carlton observed, threading her needle.

Hebe had hardly read more than the first few pages when Maria appeared. 'Major Beresford, Madame.'

'Ah! Show him through, Maria, and bring some lemonade.' Thank goodness, whatever little tiff he and Hebe had had last night, here he was to make it up. 'Major, good afternoon. I do hope you will excuse me, I have just realised I have not yet written to Mrs Forrester, and I must not neglect to do that. Hebe will be glad of your company.'

She fluttered off inside, passing Maria who put down the tray of lemonade, making exaggerated grimaces at Hebe as she did so. Hebe gave her a repressive frown. 'Thank you Maria, that will be all.'

Hebe put down her book and looked up at Alex as he stood by the hammock; her mouth felt dry and a strange sensation seemed to tingle all the way up her body. It was extraordinary—until Alex had touched her she had rarely been conscious of her body at all unless she was ill.

His eyes appeared somewhat heavy and there were three parallel scratches down his right cheek.

'Good afternoon Major. Do you have a headache?'

'A damnable...I mean, yes, I have a headache, Miss Carlton.'

'Would you like a Jameson's powder?' she asked with mock concern. 'Or perhaps a glass of lemonade? Do you have a touch of the sun?'

'No, I have a thundering hangover, Circe, as well you know,' he replied with a grin. 'Did you sleep well?'

'I slept very well.' She glanced up and met his quizzical blue eyes and blushed. 'Surprisingly well.'

'Well, I slept very badly. Can't you guess why?' He poured out some lemonade and sank into the hammock opposite her. 'Ah, that's better.'

Innocently Hebe was considering what he had intended as a rhetorical question. 'Does kissing someone make it difficult to sleep?'

'Damn it, you little witch! Do you really expect me to answer that?'

'You asked me first,' she pointed out reasonably.

'Very well, just don't tell me off for shocking you. Men find it very difficult to simply...er...stop when they have been kissing a woman. Our bodies are not made for flirting, they are made for—' He broke off. 'Stop watching me with those big, innocent grey eyes! This is the sort of thing your mother ought to be explaining to you. The long and the short of it is, when we stop like that, things...ache.'

'Things?'

'Yes things, and I am definitely not going to say another word on the subject.'

'Very well, if I am embarrassing you.' Hebe sipped
her lemonade, the happiness and excitement fizzing inside her. This was the power she had felt last night.
Somehow, something about her made this strong, tough,
confident man unsure of himself, vulnerable. It was very
exciting. But even more exciting was the certainty that
today he was going to make her a declaration, and she
knew exactly what she was going to say when he did.
'Alex? What did you do with my stocking?'

He glanced across at her, and a faint colour touched
his cheekbones. He did not reply, simply touched the
breast of his coat. After a moment he said, 'And my neck
cloth?'

'In the drawer of my dressing table.'

They lay in the two hammocks swinging gently, their
gaze touching, caressing, breaking away and then joining
again. The water in the fountain trickled and splashed, a
Sardinian warbler scolded angrily from a tangle of bamboo and the sounds from the square drifted faintly into
the shady courtyard.

'Circe?'

'Yes, Alex?'

Maria's voice cut through their peace. 'Miss Hebe, the
Commodore is here and I cannot find Madame.'

'Show him through, please, Maria, and go and find Mrs
Carlton. She may have gone upstairs to lie down and rest,
but she will want to know Sir Richard is here.' Hebe
swung her legs out of the hammock and stood up, beside
her Alex did the same, straightening his uniform coat at
the approach of the senior officer. She was disappointed,
but after all, what did it matter, they would be alone again
soon enough.

'Good afternoon, Sir Richard, would you like a glass of lemonade? Mama will be down directly.'

'Thank you, my dear, but I have some news for her—and for you, too, Hebe.' Her eyes flew to his face, and he nodded at her quick comprehension. 'Yes, my dear, I am ordered to England and your mama and I must make plans. Major Beresford, the mails arrived while I was at the port office. A package for you, it looks as though it has been on its travels a long time, so I thought you would like to have it at once.' He opened the leather portfolio under his arm and extracted a stained and battered package with several seals and superscriptions on it. 'I can hear your mama, excuse me, Hebe.'

Alex stood turning the package over in his hands. 'Do open it,' Hebe urged. 'It might be news from your family.' She felt so confident in what he had been about to say to her that a slight delay was of no concern. Happily she curled up again in the hammock and watched him slit the seals and take a letter out of the travelworn wrapper, which must have followed him around the Mediterranean for months. What was his family like? Would they welcome her into the household? Would she grow to love them? She felt sure she would, for, after all, they belonged to Alex.

Alex drew a sharp breath as he looked down at the handwriting. Hebe caught her underlip in her teeth, suddenly afraid that he had received bad news from home. Slowly he ran his thumb under the wafer and unfolded the single sheet. She saw the colour go out of his cheeks as he read, and sat up, suddenly cold inside. Abruptly he walked away from her into the tangle of shrubbery.

Hebe sat and waited. If he wanted her, he would call for her. At last he came back. The colour was in his face again, but his eyes were wide and dark. 'Alex, what is

wrong? Can I help?' She scrambled out of the hammock
and took a quick step towards him.

'No. No, nothing is wrong, Hebe. I have just had very
unexpected news.' He stood, his lower lip caught in his
teeth, then he smiled at her as if he had made up his
mind about something. His eyes were fiercely blue.

'Hebe, before I left England for this posting I proposed
marriage to Lady Clarissa Duncan. I had no real expectation that she would accept me. My birth is good, but I
am only a younger son in a risky profession. And Lady
Clarissa is a great beauty, the toast of Society, and very
much admired and courted. As I expected, she would not
give me an answer there and then.'

He broke off, bending to pick a sprig of rosemary and
twirling it in his fingers. Hebe found she was holding her
breath until it hurt. Slowly she exhaled. 'I gave up hope,
of course,' he said simply. 'I had no real expectation she
would return my love. I doubted that Clarissa even took
it seriously. It is so long ago since I saw her, since I
proposed. She writes to say she accepts my proposal. I
had given up hope,' he repeated incredulously.

Clarissa. The name he had breathed when he saw that
red-headed woman at the party. 'Does she have chestnut
hair?' Hebe asked, amazed, through a sea of pain, that
she had any voice at all.

'How did you know?' He looked at her as if she truly
was the witch he had jokingly called her just now.

'A guess.' Hebe struggled to control her voice and her
face. He must not know how she felt; suddenly that was
the most important thing. Thank goodness she had not
spoken of her love for him. Thank goodness Sir Richard
had come in when he did. It was bad enough as it was,
but at least Alex did not have to extricate himself from

a declaration to a girl he was proposing to on the rebound from his true love.

If he guessed how she truly felt, he would pity her. That was unbearable. 'Congratulations, you must be very happy,' she said warmly. 'How anxious Lady Clarissa must be, not knowing when you would get her letter. She must have realised as soon as you left how she felt, how she valued you.' There, it was perfect, he could never tell that inside her something was breaking, that instead of a heart there was a gaping, aching hole. 'You will be so anxious to return to her.'

'Hebe…I—' Alex broke off, apparently unable to continue in the face of her smile.

'I know what you are going to say,' she said reassuringly. 'We have been flirting, and you feel badly about it. But you must not, you know. I enjoyed it very much and you have made me so much more confident about myself. I was such a little mouse. Now, when I feel intimidated, I shall think, *I am an enchantress*, and unfriendly débutantes and haughty matrons will be as nothing to me!'

He was staring at her as if at a stranger. 'Hebe…'

'No, please, Major, do not be at all embarrassed about it. You forget, I see naval and army officers come and go all the time. I know how they feel, so far from home and loved ones: of course you all flirt. It was just that no one has ever flirted with me before, and that was… special.' She had to stop talking, it was unbearable, any moment she was going to break down into tears.

Mrs Carlton appeared at the doorway. 'Hebe, the most extraordinary news! We are to leave Malta, and in only seven days! And, Hebe, Sir Richard says I must marry him on Saturday. Oh, Hebe!'

Thanks goodness, now she could cry. Hebe ran to Sara

and took her in her arms. 'Mama, I am so happy for you, don't worry, we will manage it all.' The tears were coursing down both their cheeks, only Hebe knew that hers were of the bitterest unhappiness. 'And, Mama, you are not the only one with good news. Major Beresford has heard that a proposal of marriage he made before he left England has been accepted. He can marry the lady he loves—is that not wonderful for him?'

Sara turned in her daughter's embrace with a gasp, but Alex was already picking up his hat and gloves. 'Mrs Carlton, my felicitations and best wishes for the happy day. If you will excuse me, I am sure you have many arrangements to make and will not wish to be encumbered with visitors.' He bowed slightly and was gone before either of the ladies could say anything.

'Hebe! Oh, Hebe darling—' Sara Carlton took her stepdaughter's hands in both hers. 'I am so sorry! How could we have been so mistaken in Major Beresford? Oh, Sir Richard,' she cried as he came into the courtyard, 'Major Beresford is betrothed to a lady in England!'

'The devil he is!' The Commodore stopped dead in his tracks. 'I am going directly to find him: he will soon learn he cannot play fast and loose with a young lady, especially one about to become my stepdaughter.'

'Oh, no, please, Sir Richard, Mama, you are misjudging him, truly you are.' Hebe clung on to his sleeve and looked at him imploringly. 'Please do not say anything, I would be so embarrassed. You see, he proposed to Lady Clarissa, but she would not give him an answer and he had no real hope of her anyway, so he believed he was free. And her letter has been following him around for months. We were only flirting, after all. He made me no promises of any kind.'

'What? Clarissa Duncan, that red-headed daughter of

Bolton's? I knew I had heard some rumour. Well, that at
least explains it: I would have been sorry to find I had
misjudged the man. Still…' he patted Hebe's hand affec-
tionately '…it's a bad business for you, my dear.'

'No, indeed sir, please do not be believing I have a
broken heart or will be wearing the willow for Major
Beresford. And I have London to look forward to—a
season at last!'

She appeared to have succeeded in reassuring her
mother. Sara Carlton peered closely at Hebe's wide, tear-
soaked eyes. 'So you are only crying for my happiness?'

'Yes, of course, Mama. It is so exciting!'

'There is one other thing, Hebe,' Sir Richard said
slowly, 'and I hope you will not be disappointed, but my
orders take me to a posting on Gibraltar. Your mama will
remain there with me.'

'I am not going to London?' Hebe could not keep the
disappointment out of her voice: there were too many
blows this afternoon for her to be able to cope with this,
although compared with the news about Alex it was trivial.

'Indeed you are, dearest.' Sara took her arm. 'Let us
all go inside and I will explain. Your aunt and uncle
Fulgrave will be delighted to have you: your aunt wrote
to me only the other week saying that her eldest girl has
become betrothed and now she is free she would like you
to come and stay and be launched into Society by her.
And she has all the right contacts—just think, Hebe,
Almack's, a court presentation, balls!'

'There is sure to be a suitable couple travelling back
to England who can look after you—probably there will
be a choice,' Sir Richard added. 'With a respectable and
capable maid to attend you, I am sure you will find your-

self quite comfortable on the voyage back from Gibraltar.'

Hebe realised her stepmother was watching her anxiously. The alternative was to exchange Malta for the far more restricted society and less pleasant climate of Gibraltar. The voyage to England would be an adventure, she told herself firmly.

'I am sure it will be perfectly all right, Mama,' she said reassuringly. 'I am sorry you cannot be in England for my first London Season, but it will be delightful to stay with Aunt Fulgrave. How very kind of her.'

Sir Richard hurried off, back to the pressing business that would fill his days until his departure, promising Mrs Carlton that he would send up a reliable and energetic clerk to assist with all her preparations.

The widow sank down in her chair after he had gone and looked despairingly at Hebe. 'My dear, so much to be done! My head is in a whirl, what shall we do first?'

'Obtain your bride clothes, of course,' Hebe said firmly. 'And send out the invitations, order the wedding breakfast—or will Sir Richard look after that? Perhaps the Admiral would lend his banqueting hall?' She jumped to her feet. 'I am going to fetch some paper and we will make lists. Cheer up Mama, it will all be done in time.'

Chapter Nine

Hebe was right: everything was done in time and only seven days later the new Lady Latham was standing on the harbour side in Dockyard Creek, dabbing her eyes with a scrap of lace and bidding a tearful farewell to the friends who had gathered to see her on her way.

Her stepdaughter was trying very hard to maintain the bright smile that everyone appeared to expect from her. It seemed to occur to no one that she might be sad to leave Malta, and of course, none knew that she felt as though she was leaving her heart behind her.

'You lucky thing,' Miss Smithson lamented for the fourth time. 'A London Season, all the shops, the balls… You are so fortunate, Hebe!'

'Yes, I am,' Hebe replied firmly. If she said it often enough she might believe it, and one part of her was looking forward to the new adventure. But she did not view the prospect of weeks at sea with nothing much to think about than Alex Beresford with anything other than the deepest misgiving.

The last week had not been too unendurable during the day at least. There was so much to do, and all the excitement of the wedding, that it was impossible to mope.

But Hebe cried herself to sleep night after night, smothering her sobs in her pillow and trying to dry her tears on a crumpled neckcloth. Maria, almost beside herself with excitement once she discovered she was going too as ladies' maid, kept trying to remove it to wash it, but Hebe would not let her take the sorry-looking rag, not while it retained the faintest scent of Alex.

There had been no sign of him, which was what she expected. She knew he was staying away, not to neglect her, but because, as a betrothed man, it would be wrong of him to give the slightest appearance of courtship, or even flirtation with her. Hebe could only hope he had believed her when she told him her affections were not deeply engaged.

Their luggage was being swung aboard the frigate HMS *Audacious* in nets, most of it bound for the depths of the hold where it would remain until Gibraltar. Only a few valises could be accommodated in their tiny cabins and Maria was having the time of her life bossing around the sailors deputed to seeing them stowed safely, while giving them the full benefit of her big dark eyes and curvaceous figure.

Sir Richard was sailing as a supercargo, with no command position at all on the sleek warship, but he was already deep in discussion with Captain Wilson. The captain, far from showing either resentment or nervousness at having a distinguished senior officer on board to watch his every move, was eagerly exchanging views on the current state of the campaign against the French fleet.

The first lieutenant came briskly down the gangplank and saluted Sara. 'Lady Latham, ma'am, we will be sailing within the hour, may I show you to your cabins?'

'Yes, thank you. Hebe, Maria, come along. Oh, good-

ye, Georgiana...' She turned to kiss her friends and
topped with a gasp. 'Hebe, look, it is Major Beresford.'

Approaching them along the dockside, a porter trun-
ling a laden barrow at his back, was Alex Beresford.

Of course, how had she forgotten that he had expected
o be posted back? But on this ship? *Oh, please, no*, Hebe
prayed silently. Alex stopped where a pair of midshipmen
were supervising the loading and spoke to them briefly.
Hebe held her breath, only too aware that she could not
ake her eyes off the tall figure. They touched their hats
and showed the porter where to leave the Major's trunk,
hen called up a sailor to manhandle his cabin luggage
aboard.

'If you ask for the Captain of Marines, sir, I believe
you are billeted with him,' one of the lads added.

The Major thanked him and made for the foot of the
gangplank, stopping as he came face to face with the
Commodore's ladies. Hebe suspected he had known they
were there all along, but he made a creditable show of
pleased surprise. 'Lady Latham, Miss Carlton! May I
help you on board, ma'am?'

His face showed no more than the pleasure to be expected upon coming across a party of acquaintances, but
Hebe recognised the bleak, hawk-look in his eyes and
shivered. Had he known she would be on this ship? And
how did he feel? Possibly he was concerned that she
might make things awkward for him by wanting to flirt,
Hebe thought grimly. Well, if that was what he feared he
would find that Miss Hebe Carlton could be just as cool
and polite as he, whatever the circumstances.

With a flustered look at Hebe, Sara took his proffered
arm and walked up the gangplank, Hebe and Maria at
her heels. They were welcomed by the Captain and Alex
melted away after making himself known. She saw him

talking to a tall, harsh-featured man in Marine uniform
and the two vanished below decks.

One of the midshipmen escorted the ladies down, taking great care that they came down the companionways
backwards and holding on to the ropes. Maria tried to
run down facing forward, and was hastily put right. 'No,
no, miss! Not like stairs in a house, you'll soon fall if
you do that when we are at sea. Along here, Lady
Latham, ma'am, mind your head at the entrance, here we
are, ma'am.' He threw open a door on to a tiny cabin
with two bunks, a folding washstand, a few coat pegs
and not much else. 'The First Lieutenant's cabin, ma'am.
He presents his compliments, and says if there is anything
he can do to make you and Sir Richard more comfortable,
please do not hesitate to ask.'

The lad seemed anxious that her ladyship might be
shocked at the tiny space, but Sara had been on a warship
before, with Hebe's father, and accepted the accommodation without a blink.

'And Miss Latham...sorry, Miss Carlton, you are
along here, ma'am, with your maid. The Second
Lieutenant's cabin.' Hebe and Maria found themselves in
an even smaller space with curving walls that followed
the lines of the ship.

'And what happens to the displaced lieutenants?' Hebe
asked, earning a smile for her concern.

'Well, ma'am, First has Third's cabin, Second has
Fourth's. They have the senior midshipmen's mess—
that's me and Wilkins, ma'am, and we have the junior
midshipmen's quarters.'

'And they have...?'

'Hammocks with the men, ma'am.'

'Oh dear, I hope they will not be too uncomfortable.'

'No fear of that, ma'am, do them good, toughen them

up,' the boy said stoutly with all the confidence of a sixteen-year-old confronted with a charming and sympathetic young lady.

Hebe looked round her new home with interest, while Maria, who had had visions of a cabin much like that to expected from a Spanish galleon of romance, was aghast. 'Miss Hebe, we cannot sleep here! It is like a cupboard. And what do we do if we want…I mean, all those men…'

Hebe who was exploring, opened what was no more than a wardrobe and disclosed a close-stool with a chamber pot. 'There you are, Maria, every comfort.'

'Comfort! Miss Hebe, a lady like you cannot live like this! *I* do not wish to live like this! How do we wash?'

'Look.' Hebe hinged down the pewter washbasin, which was set into a plank. 'I expect you will be able to get hot water from the galley.'

'Galley? What is this galley?'

Hebe left the maid lamenting and went to see how Sara was faring. Her stepmother already had her valises open and was shaking out some gowns and trying to decide what to put in the one drawer under the lower bunk and what to leave in the cases.

'Shall I send Maria to you, Mama? I warn you, she is having the vapours. I think she imagined gilded carving, brocade sofas and great sterncastle windows.'

'No, thank you, dear, keep her with you. I am used to life on board, and I would rather you had her with you at all times. Not that I have any worries about this ship, it appears a well-disciplined command, with respectful men.'

There was one on board whose behaviour had not been respectful in the past, but Hebe bit her lip and made no comment. Alex Beresford would be taking no liberties with her now.

Her bitter musings were ended by the midshipman again. 'The Commodore's compliments, my lady, and we are about to cast off if you wish to come on deck.'

'Thank you,' said Hebe. 'What is your name?'

'Murray, ma'am.'

'Then would you tell my maid, please, Murray? She is in my cabin.'

They made their way up, successfully negotiating the companionways, and found the dockside a bustle of activity as the lines were cast off and sailors laboured to coil the dripping ropes on deck.

Captain Wilson walked over and asked them if they would like to come up on to the quarterdeck as the frigate sailed out and they readily agreed. 'Never go on to the quarterdeck without an officer inviting you, Hebe,' Sara warned her, low-voiced, as they took their places at the rail, well out of the way of the officers who were shouting orders to the men. The longboats were out, towing the frigate out of Dockyard Creek into the Grand Harbour, and familiar as they were with the scene, both women gasped at this view of it.

'Dramatic, is it not?' The First Lieutenant paused beside them, then leaned over to shout at a sailor who had dropped a line. 'Beg pardon, ma'am. Yes, you can just imagine the Knights' great fleet at anchor here, or the Turkish ships attacking, when you look at those massive walls.' He touched his hat and walked on.

Hebe's gaze followed him and she saw Alex standing alone, hands on the rail, staring down the length of the deck. All at once he straightened and turned to look at her before she could glance away. His eyes were dark and his expression severe, then, as their eyes locked, he smiled at her before turning back to contemplate the view.

Hebe breathed out as though she had been holding her breath, then realised that was just what she had been doing.

Hebe was particularly dreading meal times, for she was sure the Captain would invite his passengers to dine with him each evening, and that was exactly what he did. But to her relief he also invited a selection of his officers every time and Hebe found herself seated between them, and not in a position where she had to make conversation with Alex.

The first three days soon settled down into a comfortable routine. The Captain had a sail rigged in one quiet part of the deck to provide shade for the ladies and the ship's carpenter produced chairs that were a mixture of armchair and hammock and swung comfortably to and fro with the motion of the ship.

The weather was good and there was enough to watch to prevent the ladies being forced back on the books or sewing they had prudently included in their cabin luggage. Hebe managed to complete the first two chapters of *Sense and Sensibility*, but more often than not it stayed closed while she watched the sailors climbing high in the rigging, or eavesdropped on the midshipmen's navigation lessons.

Alex had stopped to exchange a few words with Lady Latham as he passed, but he seemed to spend most of his time with the marines and Hebe overheard snatches of what sounded like a particularly technical discussion of artillery.

The only problem appeared to be that the winds were unseasonably light and they were not making the progress the Captain had been hoping for. He and Sir Richard disappeared below for a while and emerged to talk to the first mate. All three men appeared anxious, and, following their gaze, Hebe saw banks of cloud massing from the south.

'Is there a problem, Sir Richard?' she asked as he paused beside them on his way along the deck.

'Nothing to worry about, my dear,' he reassured her. 'But we might be in for a bit of a blow from an unexpected quarter.'

'Will that not take us too close to the French shore?' Hebe queried. She knew they had safely rounded the southern tip of Sardinia but there was a way to go before they had the archipelago of Balearic islands between them and the French coast.

'Nothing to worry about,' Sir Richard repeated, but Hebe could not help feeling a little uneasy. At least they did not appear to be in any danger from the French fleet. Sir Richard said they were believed to be close in to Toulon and, given the weather, he did not expect them to be beating south into the teeth of the coming wind. There was the odd brigantine about, causing the masthead lookout to alert the quarterdeck, but everything they sighted was far too small to risk the *Audacious*'s bristling guns.

But during the night the weather became rougher and Hebe woke to find Maria wailing in terror and the luggage skidding about the floor of the cabin. The whole vessel seemed to be corkscrewing in the most extraordinary fashion.

Hebe struggled out of her bunk, tying her wrapper tight around herself. Maria did not appear to be seasick, merely frightened. Hebe recalled that Sara had some laudanum in her luggage and was wondering if a small dose of that would calm the girl's nerves when there was a knock at the door. When she opened it Sir Richard was outside, fully dressed.

'Hebe, dear, can you spare your maid to look after your mama? Poor Sara seems to be feeling very sick, and I cannot stay with her.' He looked over Hebe's shoulder at the wailing Maltese girl and back to Hebe.

'I will come,' Hebe assured him, 'Maria is all right really. I will give her something to calm her nerves.'

She hurried along the passageway to Sara's room to find her stepmother retching miserably into a bowl, her face white and strained in the flickering lantern light. 'Ohh!' was all she could manage before being miserably sick again.

Hebe searched through the medicine bag and found the laudanum. With a promise to return directly she took it along to Maria, mixed her a very weak dose in a glass of water, and assured her that she would instantly fall asleep. To her amazement it worked, and within a few minutes Maria was calmly dozing.

Things were not so simple in the other cabin. Sara was desperately sick, unable to keep down any of the soothing medicines Hebe tried, or even small sips of water. Hebe battled her way to find the cook, only to discover that all galley fires had been extinguished on Captain's orders and there was no warm water to be had.

Hebe struggled back, bouncing off the walls as she went and did her best to make Sara comfortable. She wrapped her up warmly, bathed her brow, found lavender water for her temples and tried to get a little water down her every time she was sick.

The hours crept by in a noisy, violent turmoil. The smell of the bilges filled the cabin, mingling horribly with the smell of sickness, and Hebe realised that Sara was so exhausted that she was beginning to be delirious. Hebe looked at the pocket watch which Sir Richard had left beside the bunk: six o'clock.

With a reassuring murmur to Sara, Hebe battled back to her cabin where, by a miracle, Maria was still dozing, and clambered into her clothes. Then, clutching the walls at every step, she found her way up on deck.

It might be dawn, but there was hardly any light in the sky which seemed to be a mass of swirling black clouds. The wind was fierce, battering the elegant warship from constantly changing directions, howling in the rigging like damned souls in torment. And it was pouring with rain.

Hebe was drenched as soon as she emerged, her hair plastered down and into her stinging eyes. Somehow she managed to struggle towards the ladders up to the quarterdeck and collided with an officer.

'Look out, damn it! Oh, my God, what are you doing up here, Miss Carlton?'

'My mother is very ill, I must find the ship's doctor.'

'I'll send for him, ma'am—for goodness' sake, let me get you below.' He took her arm and began to guide her back.

'What is wrong?' Hebe gasped against the buffeting wind. Somehow, even this dreadful weather did not seem enough to explain the crazy wallowing of the ship.

'Top mast gone, snapped in the first blast. We've got men up, trying to cut it away, but it's wedged fast and we can't get control of the sails.' He seemed to remember who he was talking to and added hastily, 'Not that it will be quite all right soon, ma'am, these things blow themselves out.'

At that moment there was a shriek, half-carried away

by the wind and a spar crashed to the deck. Falling with it, tangled in rigging, Hebe saw the young midshipman Murray.

The lieutenant pushed her unceremoniously into the mouth of the companionway and ran for the mainmast. No one seemed to be doing anything about the boy and Hebe ran out on to the slippery, tilting deck, her first rush carrying her to the point where she could clutch the fallen rigging.

'Murray! Murray, are you all right?' The she saw his skull was crushed and turned away, gasping with shock. There was nothing she, or anyone, could do for him.

Shakily she pulled herself to her feet, almost blinded by spray and tears. The deck was dipping wildly, the entire ship was bucking like a horse. Something else must have been damaged as the spar fell.

'Hebe!' Alex's voice cut through the storm and she turned to see him with a party of marines, frantically cutting at another mass of fallen rigging. 'Hebe, hold on!' He began to fight his way across the deck to her and she realised his feet were bare on the treacherous wet surface. He reached her side and seized her in a grip that hurt.

'Damn it, woman! What are you doing here?'

'I…came for…doctor,' Hebe gasped. 'Mama…'

'Get down below.' He began to drag her back across the deck. She saw he was still wearing his scarlet coat, but it was black with water. His hair was plastered to his skull and his teeth showed white against his unshaven chin in the fitful light of the wildly swinging lanterns.

There was a sudden lull, the ship seemed to hang in the water, then with a roar a great blast of air hit them, followed by a swamping wave of water. Hebe found herself swept off her feet. Something hit her hard in the ribs, then she was falling, still with a ruthlessly painful grip on her right arm. Her mouth was full of salt water, she was blinded by it, unable to breathe, then with a force that knocked the remaining air from her lungs she hit something solid, struggled, and found it was not the deck, but the surface of the sea.

I am going to die, she thought with surprising calmness. So this was what it was like. *Oh, Alex...*

The agonising vicelike grip on her arm let go, then she was grabbed ruthlessly under the chin and found herself being dragged up to the surface. 'Kick, damn it!' ordered a voice in her ear, and she did. 'Breathe!' the voice demanded, so she took a deep, agonising breath and found she was inhaling air, not water. 'Good girl,' said Alex Beresford. 'Now hold on to me as though the devil were after you—and pray.'

Hebe had no idea whether she managed to pray or not. She had a confused impression of being held, of kicking, and of Alex's voice praising her, then everything finally, mercifully, went black.

Chapter Ten

This was the most incredibly uncomfortable bed. And it was wet, the roof must be leaking. And cold. She was certainly going to complain to the landlord of this inn when she…

Hebe stirred, found her mouth was full of wet sand and spat it out. Everything hurt, her ribs creaked when she breathed, her throat was raw, her eyes would hardly open. Shakily she managed to raise her head and found she was sprawled face down on a beach of shelving sand, the waves just tugging at her frozen feet as the slight Mediterranean tide slowly ebbed away.

What? With an effort of will she levered herself up on her arms, then pushed herself over until she was sitting up. Gradually she found her memory coming back. The great wave, going overboard, Alex's voice in her ear, shouting at her, willing her to survive.

'Alex!' It was a cry of pain that tore her raw throat, but there was no answer. Somehow she got to her feet and looked around. The beach seemed to stretch for miles in every direction, deserted. The rain had stopped, the wind had dropped, but the sky was lowering and overcast and the air was bitterly cold for May.

Frantically Hebe scrubbed at her sore and swollen eyes with numb fingers and searched the beach again. Nothing, only a pile of storm wrack tossed up on the water's edge. Or was it? She stumbled towards it and realised it was a man, face down, totally unmoving. 'Alex!'

With the strength of desperation Hebe heaved him over and pressed her ear to his chest. Nothing. Then she saw the slightest movement of his white lips. 'Alex! Alex, wake up!' Still nothing. Desperately she slapped his cold face, then again. 'Wake up, damn it!' she yelled in his ear. 'Don't you dare die on me!'

With an effort that was visible one blue, bloodshot eye opened. 'Don't swear, Circe,' he croaked. 'It isn't lady-like…oh, hell!' and rolled over and was violently sick. Hebe held on to him, until he stopped retching. 'Sorry.'

'Sorry?' she stormed at him, utterly, ludicrously furious. 'You save my life, I thought you were dead, and you say ''sorry''?' And promptly burst into tears.

'Oh, Circe.' She could tell he was laughing painfully. 'Come on, we must get off this beach and get dry or you'll catch your death of cold.' Holding each other up— Hebe was not sure which of them was in the worse case—they managed to get to their feet. Alex took her hand and they began to trudge slowly through the sand and up the shelving dunes that fringed the beach. At their feet a lagoon stretched parallel with the coast. To their left Hebe could see the land beginning to rise sharply into cliffs.

'Damn.' He looked down at her. 'I am going to apologise comprehensively for my language when we get out of this, in the meantime I'm afraid you will just have to put up with it.'

Hebe had not even been aware he was swearing. 'Do you know where we are?' she croaked.

'Yes. In France, although it could be worse. That lagoon is fresh water for a start, so I suggest we have a drink and wash our faces. And if we had come ashore any closer to Spain we would probably have been dashed on the base of the cliffs.'

Hebe felt undeniably better once the drink and the wash had been achieved, although she was shivering with cold and famished with hunger.

'Now, can you walk?' Alex pulled her to her feet. 'I daren't leave you here, you'd be dead of cold before I could get back.'

'Where are we going?' Hebe forced one foot in front of the other. Both her shoes had gone, and in her haste to dress she had not troubled with stockings. At least they were walking on hard mud, not through the shifting sand.

'South, into Spain.'

'But southern Spain is occupied!'

'I have friends amongst the *guerillas*. If we can get across the border we will be safe. We are close now, thirty miles perhaps.'

'Close!'

'If we steal mules, it is not too bad. If we can just get into the foothills behind Argelès, I know a shepherd's cabin we can rest in.' They trudged on in silence for a while, Hebe biting her lip as she thought about her step-mother and Sir Richard and what they would be feeling now, believing her dead.

'Alex? Will the frigate be all right?'

He looked down at her. 'I think so, there was enough sea room for it to run before the wind if they got that wreckage down.'

Hebe was grateful for the qualified reassurance. She would not have believed a hearty declaration that all would be well, but she had faith in the crew: if there was a chance, they would save the ship.

'Hebe...' Alex hesitated, obviously choosing his words. 'If we are seen, I want you to run, immediately. Get under cover and keep heading south. Steal what you have to, but don't be seen. Once you are in Spain, find a village, go to the headman. Tell him who you are, what has happened. You will be very unlucky to find yourself in the hands of collaborators: if you do, emphasise how wealthy Sir Richard is. They would rather sell you to him than to the French.'

'But what about you?' Hebe realised with a sudden jolt that Alex's uniform coat had gone and that he was in his shirtsleeves. He did not answer. 'If they catch you, they'll shoot you, won't they? *Won't they?*' At last, reluctantly, he nodded. 'But they won't shoot me, surely? They won't think I'm a spy?'

'No, Hebe,' he said harshly. 'They'll rape you first, then shoot you.'

'Oh.' Hebe's voice was very small, then she rallied. 'Well, we will just have to make sure they do not find us. You do this sort of thing all the time, don't you, and you keep coming back.'

'I don't do it without a disguise, without backup, when I'm soaked to the skin, exhausted and with a young lady to look after,' he said grimly, then added with a smile, 'Otherwise, of course, it is just the same.'

'I don't need looking after,' she declared, prompting yet another smile. 'And as soon as we can steal some clothes and a mule and some food, we won't be cold and wet and tired, either. Look, there's a hut, where the lagoon ends. Perhaps we can steal something from that.'

'Really, Hebe,' Alex said mildly as they staggered on, 'I find it hard to believe that your mother could have brought you up with such a cavalier attitude to other people's property.'

She was almost too exhausted to laugh, but she managed a hoarse croak as they reached the hut. Alex yanked at the door, found it locked and without hesitation picked up a stone and battered the catch until it opened.

The hut was primitive, dirty and smelled strongly of fish. Hebe thought she had never seen a more beautiful sight. In one corner was a pile of nets; without a word they walked towards it and fell down on the rough tarred heap. Alex dragged some free, wrapped Hebe in it, dragged more over himself and before he had finished she was asleep.

Hebe woke to find she was alone. She felt the hollow next to her where Alex had slept, but it was cold, although the netting seemed to hold little warmth in any case, so it was no indication of how long he had been gone. A faint dawn light showed around the edge of the ill-fitting door. She lay still for a few minutes, trying not to cry and reflecting that she had just passed the night with the man she loved and had no recollection of a moment of it: no memory of the warmth of his body next to hers, no touch of his hand to treasure.

How long had he been gone? She rubbed the sleep out of her sore eyes and found a rough earthenware pot beside her, full of water. She took a grateful drink and walked cautiously across the heavily shadowed floor to the door. It creaked open easily to her touch and she stood for a moment, looking out across a turbulent sea. But the wind had dropped, the clouds had largely gone and the sun was coming up on what promised to be a lovely May day. Hebe sent up a silent prayer that all was well on the *Audacious*, then looked up and down the beach.

A mule was plodding towards her, led by a tall figure in a slouch hat and rough clothing. There was a blanket thrown across his shoulders and he was wearing *culottes* cut off just below the knee, flapping over bare calves and feet.

Hebe shot back inside, her heart banging wildly. A Frenchman! She looked around in the gloom for a weapon, remembered the water pot, and with it raised over her head ran to stand behind the door. There was a muttered curse outside as the man remonstrated with the mule in what sounded like some form of *argot*. Then the door creaked open.

She drew a deep breath, stepped forward and brought the pot down, only to find herself thrown on to her back on the nets, the pot shattering against the boards of the wall and the man's weight full on her. Hebe brought up her knee with vicious intent and was stopped just in time by a shout of 'Hebe!'

'Oh, Alex, I thought you were a Frenchman,' she gasped, struggling in his grip. After a moment he seemed to recall the position they were in and stood up.

'I feel sorry for any Frenchman who decides to attack you,' he said with a grin.

'Did I hurt you?' she asked, getting to her feet and attempting to smooth down her disastrous skirts.

Alex gave a smothered snort of amusement. 'I think my manhood is safe on this occasion.'

Hebe decided that if she was going to be thrown into maidenly confusion by everything he said in these circumstances she would have a very uncomfortable journey. 'You reacted incredibly fast.'

He glanced at her sideways. 'I am normally reckoned

o be reasonably alert, Circe, but even so, I seem to have
a second sense for where you are. Come along, let us
have some breakfast outside where I can keep an eye on
things.'

Wrapped in the blanket, Hebe hunkered down in the
shelter of the hut and devoured the odd breakfast Alex
had managed to steal. Some incredibly high cheese, half
a loaf, some form of preserved fish that had seen better
days, a handful of olives and a piece of sausage that
appeared to consist largely of garlic and fat.

'Delicious,' she said warmly, her mouth full, accepting
the small pitcher in a woven straw casing that he handed
her. She took an incautious swig and subsided, gasping.
'What on earth is that?' she managed to say after she got
her breath back.

Alex sniffed cautiously and then took a healthy gulp.
'Goodness knows, distilled goat by the taste of it.' He
munched on the bread for a while. 'I'm afraid I couldn't
find you any clothes, but you should be warmer wrapped
in the blanket.'

'Where did you find these things?' Hebe gestured at
his clothes, the food and the mule. Then she saw there
was a long-barrelled musket hanging from its saddle and
a wicked-looking knife in Alex's belt.

'A poor sort of farm up along there a couple of miles.
I don't think there's a woman in the household.' Alex
tossed down the heel of the loaf and got to his feet.
Although his face was half-turned to her, Hebe caught
the slight grimace of pain that twisted his mouth for a
moment.

'Alex, are you hurt?' Now she looked closely, there
was a trace of blood on his shirt. He had left in a perfectly
decent, if salt-stained shirt, now he was wearing one of
rough weave.

'No.' He tightened the girth, his back to her. Hebe got silently to her feet and reached out to touch his side under the stain. There was a hissing indrawn breath and he swung round to look at her, blue eyes dark. 'A scratch.'

'Let me look.'

'No.'

'Let me look!'

With a resigned shrug he unbuttoned the shirt and revealed a long, angry-looking cut across the bottom of his ribs on the left hand side. 'That is not a scratch.' Hebe regarded him, hands on hips. 'Honestly, men are so… And I'm not wearing any petticoats.'

Alex's frown vanished and his lips quirked into what Hebe could tell was about to be a suggestive smile. She gave him a repressive look and added, 'Bandages.'

'Doesn't need anything.'

'Yes, it does, it will chafe on that rough shirt. What did you do with your own shirt?'

With the sigh of a nagged man, Alex fished it out of the saddle bag. Not only was it slashed, but it was covered in blood.

'Alex! That cannot all be from that cut—where else are you hurt?'

'I'm not. It was the other man.'

Hebe opened her mouth, then shut it rapidly. The man had been a Frenchman, an enemy. If Alex had let him go, then he would have raised a hue and cry after them and they would both be dead.

She took the shirt gingerly and shook it out. 'Give me the knife.' With care she managed to cut a long, clean strip off from the back. 'Take that shirt off.' Alex shrugged it off with a resigned expression, which turned into one of comical apprehension as Hebe cut off another piece of cloth, soaked it liberally in the strong spirit and applied it to the cut.

'Damn it, woman, that hurts!'

'Please do not use that language sir,' Hebe said calmly, bandaging up the cut with a firm hand, giving herself no opportunity to think about the feel of his skin under her fingers, or of how closely they touched as she reached around him to catch the end of the bandage. 'There, you can put your shirt on again.'

'Thank you.' He eyed her balefully. 'You are a very managing young lady. I had no idea.'

'No such thing,' she retorted cheerfully. 'Your welfare is essential to my survival; naturally I must take care of you.'

Major Beresford did not rise to the provocation, merely checking inside the hut to make sure they had left nothing, then tossing Hebe up into the saddle. 'If you wrap the blanket around you like this, and pull it over your head like so, you will not look out of place from a distance. I must steal you some clothes as soon as possible.'

'And another mule?' she asked as they set off along the beach.

'Not unless I find one away from a settlement. A valuable animal gone missing is likely to result in a search party, whereas a petticoat here and a shawl there might go unnoticed for a while.'

The long day passed without more than half a dozen alarms as they gave the town of Argelès a wide berth. From time to time they saw riders on the horizon, or passed men working in the fields who raised curious heads to stare at the strangers. Alex called greetings in the local *patois*, or waved a hand, and no one seemed unduly curious.

He left her with the mule hidden in a grove on the outskirts of the village of Sorède, and returned after an hour with a loaf of bread, some cheese, a pair of poorly made small leather shoes and a petticoat, all wrapped up in a worn woollen shawl.

Hebe, who had been trying to keep herself from worrying while he was gone by staring at the tumbled mass of mountains ahead of them, emerged from behind the bush where she had scrambled into the petticoat and asked, 'Where are we spending the night?'

Alex nodded towards the apparently impenetrable wall in front of them. 'Up there.'

Hebe gasped. 'But we can't get over there! Surely we will go around the coast road?'

'Ideal if you want to get caught,' he responded briefly. 'Another five miles by a mule track will take us into the foothills: I have a hut there I use. Tomorrow we can start to climb.'

Now they were clear of habitation he unslung the gun, checked it and began to walk with it held in one hand, the mule's halter rope in the other. The apparently casual walk he had been using all day changed and he began to walk briskly with long, swinging strides. After a while he began to jog, then dropped back into the walk again. The mule trotted obediently after him on its neat hooves.

They crested a rise and he stopped to check the area, glancing up at Hebe. 'Are you all right? That isn't much of a saddle.'

His voice sounded a little strained. Hebe wondered if he was breathless and, more to make him stay standing there than for any other reason, said, 'I have never seen soldiers march like that.'

'Learned it from the Rifles,' he said. 'Looks sloppy, covers the ground like nothing else.'

No, he wasn't breathless, but his voice was rough and, as Hebe leaned forward from the saddle, she thought his face looked pale in the evening light. 'Alex, are you feeling all right? Is it that knife wound?'

He began to walk again. 'I'm perfectly all right.'

They continued in silence for another half-hour, the narrow track becoming steadily steeper, the light ebbing. Alex paused again at a sharp bend, listening, and Hebe suddenly leaned forward and laid her palm on his forehead. 'You are burning up! Alex, you have a fever.'

'It is nothing.' Now she could hear the rasp in his breathing plainly. Surely it could not be that wound already?

Hebe began to swing her leg over the saddle. 'Let me walk, you ride.'

'No.' He jerked the bridle, forcing her to sit back. 'It is a marsh fever. It comes back occasionally if I become very cold or wet. If I march I'll stay focused on what I'm doing, the rhythm keeps me going. Once I get on that damn mule I'll start getting sleepy, and you don't know the way.'

Hebe forced herself to keep quiet. She had to trust him to do what was best. Surely Alex didn't have the sort of stiff-necked pride that would force him to walk on if that was not the best thing in the circumstances? But Hebe's resolution to keep quiet was soon stretched to the limit.

Chapter Eleven

The climb seemed endless. The slope was too steep now to jog any more, but Alex did not stop. He was not keeping to the Riflemen's easy-going slouch, but increasingly marching like a disciplined trooper. Hebe could only suppose it was his way of keeping going, banishing all thought in the hypnotic task of putting one foot in front of the other.

Suddenly they rounded a bend and found themselves on a small flat terrace, roughly paved with flat stones. A trickle of water ran down the rock face into a rough trough and then spilled out across the terrace in a muddy puddle, eventually falling over the edge. At the back of the space was a large hut, huddled into the craggy rock of the slope.

Hebe slipped off the mule and stalked round to confront Alex, anxiety sharpening her voice. 'Is this where we are going? Because whether it is or not, this is where we stop.'

He looked down at her, an amused smile tugging at the corner of his mouth. 'Shh, not so loud. Yes, this is the hut I use: stay here until I check it out, and do not walk in the mud.'

He cocked the musket and walked cautiously to the doorway. Hebe led the weary mule over to the water trough and let it drink. It showed no sign of wanting to wander off so she dropped a stone on to the end of the lead rope and followed Alex into the hut, jumping over the muddy patch.

It was surprisingly roomy inside, although of a very odd shape, for the back wall was made out of the bare rock. There was a large, open, earthen-floored space with a stone fireplace and chimney, a rough wooden bench and table and a pile of old straw on the ground. Furthest away from the door the space narrowed abruptly, ending in a planked wall that was hung with old mule harness and empty sacks.

Alex was standing with one hand on the wall, quite still, apparently lost in thought. Hebe walked up quietly and, before he realised what she was about, put her hand on his forehead.

'You are burning up! Alex, will you lie down and rest *now*!'

He pushed himself away from the wall, catching her hand in his and bringing it down close to his chest. Hebe twisted in his grasp and fastened her fingers over his wrist. 'And your pulse is racing.' He was pale under his tan, his eyes were dark and Hebe could feel that he was shivering.

'Managing woman,' he said, apparently with an effort. 'There are things to do before we can rest, let me get on with it.'

'No, I will not.' Hebe kept hold of his wrist, realising with a frisson of fear just how ill he must be, and amazed that his strength and sheer will-power had kept him going for so long. 'Tell me what to do, I have been sitting on that dratted mule all day, I need the exercise.'

That provoked another smile. 'Language, Hebe!'

'What, "dratted"? I am sure by the time we get home I will be using far worse, given the example you have been setting me.' She pulled him towards the bench. 'Now, sit down and tell me what to do.'

To her surprise he yielded. 'Very well. Unsaddle the mule and bring the saddle in here. Lead it up the path and when you have passed the roof of the hut you will see another track to your left. Go up there and it opens into a tiny patch of meadow where the stream runs. You can tether it up there where it can drink and graze out of sight.'

Hebe ran to do as she was told, casting him a suspicious glance when she lugged in the heavy wooden saddle and dumped it against the plank wall under the old harness, but he made no move to get up, so she felt reassured enough to leave him.

The mule followed willingly enough and stood quietly while she tethered it to a wind-bent sapling near the runnel of water. When she got back to the hut, though, Alex was no longer sitting on the bench but was pulling planks from the wall at the narrow end of the hut. Behind them Hebe could see a dark space which, when she ran to help him, she saw was like a large cupboard containing a bed.

Alex removed four of the vertical planks, then stopped. 'You see, they slot in like this. They can be held in place from the inside if necessary. If anyone comes, get in here with anything which could give away our presence and pull them back.' He stacked the planks in order against the wall and reached inside, bringing out a small lantern. 'Do not light this unless the door is closed, and, if someone comes, blow it out or the light will show through the cracks in this false wall.' Every word seemed to be an effort.

Hebe peered round the edge. 'Did you build this?'

'When I found the hut this was just a typical cupboard bed, built into the alcove to keep the draughts down. I made the wall and fitted shelves inside.'

Hebe eyed him: he was becoming sicker by the minute, now having to grip the edge of the planks so tightly that his knuckles showed white. 'What is in here?' she asked, scrambling into the space. 'Let me see, then come and lie down. Please, Alex—if you collapse, I will never be able to lift you.'

There were shelves with clothing stacked on them: rough shirts and culotte trousers, a pair of buckled shoes, woollen socks, a heavy cloak. There was a small wheel of cheese with a knife sticking in it and a thick rind that would deter most mice, an evil-looking sausage and a water container. The bed itself was a vast hay-filled sack lying over boards and covered with country-weave blankets.

Hebe lifted out the food and wriggled back into the room. 'Go on, lie down, Alex.'

To her intense relief he did as she asked, falling back on to the mattress with a sigh, but he still would not relax and let go. 'Hebe, listen to me…'

'No, stop talking, Alex. I understand what I need to do. I must be careful not to do anything that will give away the fact we are here, and leave no footprints in the mud. I must keep a look out and if anyone comes I must put up the planks and hide in here. Now lie still and I will get you something to eat.'

But when she returned a few moments later with a little cheese, bread and the water flask, he was heavily asleep, perhaps unconscious. Hebe forced herself to leave him while she checked outside. Darkness was falling and a faint powdering of lights showed from the villages in the foothills. She lit the lantern, left it on the table, then went outside and shut the door. Even in the darkness out there she could see no chink of light escaping, so she hurried back inside and, after an anxious glance at Alex, ate and drank.

Now there was nothing else to distract her she found it difficult to keep her mind calm. To see such a strong man collapse so utterly filled her with dread. Was he dying? No, she told herself firmly, he says he has had this before. No, he will be all right if you only look after him.

Hebe picked up the light and went and looked down at the long figure stretched out on the bed, fully clothed. She had never done any sick nursing and she had certainly never had to look after a helpless man.

'Do not be feeble, Hebe,' she said out loud. The sound of her own voice was strangely comforting. 'Just imagine he is Mama in the same circumstances. Now, what do I do?' It seemed an unlikely comparison, but it did at least help her think.

To get him comfortable and warm seemed the first thing, and he certainly seemed to be neither, dressed like that. Hebe clambered up on to the bed and set about undressing him. At first it seemed daunting to touch a man like this, let alone one she loved. Then the practical difficulties turned the whole enterprise from embarrassing to infuriating and she stopped worrying about the impropriety of it.

Alex was a dead weight to move. She started with the easiest things and took his shoes off. She unbuckled the heavy leather belt and pulled it from under him, then unbuttoned his shirt and peeled it open. His chest was hot and dry and under her hand his heartbeat was rapid. The bandage around the knife cut was badly stained but the skin around it felt no worse than the rest of him so she decided to leave it until the morning and better light.

The shirt felt rough to the touch and was soaked in sweat. Hebe looked at the others on the shelf and found some which were softer linen: one would do as a night-shirt if she could only get this off. She tried rolling him and slipping off one side and then the other. That did not work. She tried pulling it up, but it would not shift. Finally Hebe simply hitched up her skirts, straddled his prone form and, linking her hands behind his neck, heaved. It worked and she found herself with her arms full of unconscious man.

Hastily she pushed off the old shirt and began to pull his arms through the sleeves of the fresh one. Finally, after what seemed like hours, she managed it. For a long minute she sat there, Alex's body in her arms, his head resting on her shoulder. 'Oh, Alex darling,' she mur-mured, stroking his damp, disordered hair. 'I do love you.'

As gently as she could she lowered him back to the bed and fastened the shirt, smoothing it down. Then she eyed the canvas trousers. They certainly looked ex-tremely uncomfortable to sleep in and the waistband cut across the bandage on one side. If that got trapped in one position during the night it could chafe very badly and open the wound up.

She bit her lip and reached uncertainly for the crude bone buttons on the waistband. 'Come along, Hebe,' she chided herself. 'You are a rational young woman dealing with a sick patient. And, after all, you have seen plenty of classical nude sculptures: there is nothing to be sur-prised or alarmed about.'

Naked male flesh was, perhaps, rather more of a rev-elation than she had bargained for, but Alex was soon

wrapped snugly in the softest of the blankets and even to
Hebe's anxious eyes seemed to be resting more comfortably. She tried to coax him to drink a little but only
managed to moisten his lips, so she put a pannier of water
and a cloth carefully on the shelf close at hand, tidied
away all traces of her presence from the hut and began
to fit the planks back around the bed-cupboard.

It was a little like doing one of the popular dissected
puzzles, but after a brief struggle she worked out how
everything fitted and dropped the cross-piece down that
effectively held everything tightly in place. She wriggled
down into the space beside Alex's unconscious form,
blew out the light and, despite her anxiety and the
strangeness of the place, fell instantly into an exhausted
sleep.

But her rest did not last long. Hebe was wakened
abruptly by a sharp blow and realised that Alex was tossing restlessly in his fever, his arms free of the blankets.
She lit the lantern and managed to open the boards up,
sliding out of the cupboard-bed and into the chilly darkness of the room. She found her shoes and dragged down
the heavy cloak that at least kept her warm while she
tried to make him more comfortable.

It seemed hopeless. Whenever she had him covered he
would throw off the blankets, his head tossing restlessly
on the pillow, which became hot and crumpled. Hebe
managed to trickle a little water into his mouth, but she
could not rouse him enough to make him drink properly.
She became increasingly frightened for him, but odd
snatches of conversations came back to her and kept her
going. There had been a friend of her stepmother whose
son had been very ill with a fever and Hebe recalled her
saying how terrifying the nights had been because the
fever was always worse then. Sir Robert had told a tale

of how one sailor had become completely delirious, throwing off the combined weights of the ship's surgeon and two of his messmates, yet had made a complete recovery.

Once or twice she managed to nod off, her head resting on the bed, but always woke with a start to find Alex no better. Then he began to talk, muttering at first, then more and more clearly, although none of it made any sense. Doggedly she struggled on, replacing the blankets, smoothing the pillow, putting wet cloths on his forehead and trying to get a little water into his mouth.

Finally morning came. Hebe heard the sound of birdsong, intermittent at first, then swelling into the full chorus. She got up stiffly, took the water pannier to the door and went out. It was going to be a beautiful day she saw thankfully, for she did not think she could cope if it turned wet and cold. A splash of cold water on her face, a drink and a piece of cheese seemed to give her renewed strength and somehow in the daylight she felt more optimistic.

She left the door wide and went back to sit by Alex, holding his hand, her fingers lightly on his wrist where the pulse raced, and willed the fever to break. He was silent for a while, then said clearly, 'Of course I love you.'

Hebe gasped and sat up straight. 'Alex?' But his eyes were shut and he was moving restlessly, still obviously unconscious.

'Give me a straight answer,' he added, then, 'Clarissa, must you always tease? You know I am serious.'

Hebe dropped her face into her hands and felt the tears wetting her palm. It was one thing to have him tell her that he had made a proposal, quite another to, in effect,

hear him make it. It hurt horribly, and it made her feel
like an eavesdropper. What more might he say?

'Shh, Alex, shh,' she whispered. 'Do not talk, just rest.
I am here, Alex.'

'Hebe?' Had he heard her? 'Hebe, no!' Then he was
quiet again.

She sat down abruptly. What did that mean? It was
hopeless to speculate, she thought drearily, but one thing
was plain—her name seemed to provoke rejection,
Clarissa's, love.

By mid-afternoon Hebe had managed to work out a
routine. She would spend ten minutes or so by Alex's
side, talking to him, trying to get him to drink, bathing
his forehead, then she would walk around the terrace,
checking that there was no sign of anyone on the hillside,
soaking in as much sunshine and warmth as she could.
She checked on the mule, moving it to a better patch of
grazing, then came down again to resume the pattern she
had set herself.

Gradually she felt herself becoming calmer, more
hopeful. Alex, although no better, was no worse. She
could manage what was necessary and there was enough
food for her for several more days yet. She was strong
and fit for a young lady, thanks to her frequent walks:
when Alex was a little stronger and able to guide her,
she would dress in men's clothes, help him on to the mule
and they would climb up to the pass, high above.

She came to this conclusion standing on the edge of
the terrace, stretching, her hands in the small of her back
which was aching after spending so much time bending
over the high bed. Feeling better in her mind made her
realise just how awful she felt physically. Her hair was
a tangled mass of salt-sticky rats' tails, her feet were grey

with dust, her clothes had not been off her back since she had dressed in haste two—or was it three?—nights ago on board ship.

Hebe ran back into the hut. She paused to lay a gentle hand on Alex's dry, burning forehead. He seemed quieter. She trickled a little more water between his cracked lips, then began to search the shelves around the bed, finally emerging triumphant with a piece of rough olive oil soap and a length of torn sheet.

A long, cautious scrutiny of the slopes below convinced Hebe that she was quite alone. Standing by the trough she stripped off her stained clothing until she was quite naked in the hot sun, then plunged her arms right into the water. The cold made her gasp and shudder, but she worked the soap into a lather and began to wash all over, finally dunking her whole head in until her hair was soaked. Getting the salt out with the coarse soap took forever, but finally the strands squeaked and she could rake the tangles out with her fingers.

With the makeshift towel wrapped around her she went to sit in the sun on the edge of the terrace to let the sun dry her hair. After perhaps fifteen minutes it was still damp, but she was worried about leaving Alex any longer. Hebe stood up, automatically checking the hillside as she had been doing all day, and froze.

Far beneath her was the unmistakable sight of a column of men beginning the climb she and Alex had made only the day before. She could see the glint of sunlight on musket barrels, the flash of red uniform coats and the dust kicked up by the boots of men and the hooves of mules and donkeys. How many? She craned to see, trying to count as they vanished and emerged between stunted trees, bends in the path and fallen boulders. Twelve, perhaps fifteen.

She spun round and scanned the terrace with fierce concentration: the soap was on the edge of the trough. She snatched it up, rubbing a few suds away. The water flowed clear and clean, all sign of the lather gone. She had remembered to jump over the muddy patch every time so there were no betraying footprints.

Hebe hurried into the hut, replacing the stool by the fireplace, bundling the plate and remains of her lunch on to a shelf in the cupboard. She threw her shoes and clothes on to a shelf, then ran outside to fill the water pannier, taking care not to spill any on the dusty ground.

There was nothing she could do about the mule—with any luck they would pass by the tiny path that led off to its clearing. She left the door ajar, thinking it looked less suspicious, dropped a sack over the mule saddle and climbed into the cupboard.

Her fingers fumbled with the planks, sending splinters into her palms. 'Steady,' she told herself. 'Steady, like doing a puzzle.' And suddenly all the planks had slotted into place, the locking bar was down and all she had to do now was to slide carefully down the bed until she was lying alongside Alex.

How long would they be, reaching this point? she wondered, wriggling into a comfortable position and pulling a corner of the blanket over her slightly damp legs. She curled into Alex's back and put an arm across him; he murmured something, then lay still and quiet in her embrace. Hebe let her forehead rest on his back, feeling the strength of his muscles through the thin shirt, the heat of his fever. 'Lie still, darling,' she whispered. 'Just lie still for a little while.'

Time seemed hardly to pass, then there was the alarm call of a jay outside and she began to make out the sounds of the approaching troop. Men calling to each other, the sound of metal striking rock and finally, as they reached the terrace, the jingle of harness.

They will stop a while, she told herself, *they will want to check the hut, water their horses, have a rest. Then they will be on their way.*

The door swung open with a crash: Hebe stifled a little gasp of fear and froze. Boots came across the earth floor towards their hiding place, someone kicked the sack over the mule saddle, she caught of few words of French, none of which made sense. There was laughter, and outside, someone shouted an order.

Outside there was activity. Suddenly a horse whinnied, almost at her feet, and after a moment's panicky thought she realised that they were tying their animals up on the rail on the other side of the wall from where she lay. *Tying them up?*

Boots tramped into the hut again and there was the sound of things being thrown down on the floor and of logs being tossed on to the hearth. *They were staying! Oh, no, oh, please, no*, she prayed silently. *Don't let them stay.*

Chapter Twelve

There was no divine intervention: the troop of French soldiers continued with their preparations with the casual efficiency of men who were used to making themselves comfortable wherever they found themselves. The only mercy was that they created a considerable amount of noise.

Hebe strained her ears and finally began to pick up the odd word. *Espagne…fille jolie…demain…*someone being chaffed about a Spanish girlfriend he would be seeing tomorrow. Thank goodness, at least they were not settling in to use this hut as an observation post.

She knelt up and, leaning carefully over Alex's still form, put her eye to a knothole in the planks. They had lit the fire and several lanterns that stood around the room. Packs were set out around the hearth and a few men squatted on them, one slicing something into a pot at his feet. Another was fixing a bar across the fire, apparently to take the great kettle and iron cauldron that stood beside him.

Suddenly more men came in and turned towards Hebe's hiding place. She jerked back from the wall as though they could see through it, but they were piling saddles and panniers up in the smaller space in front, obviously considering that part of the room too small for the men.

Hebe eased herself down in the bed again, taking advantage of the bustle outside to make herself and Alex as comfortable as possible. She felt along the shelf with infinite care until she found the water, then soaked the cloth in it, before trickling it into Alex's mouth. She dipped her fingers in and sucked them, too nervous to risk picking up the water container in case she spilled it.

Then she lifted the blanket and slid under it, curving her body around Alex's again. Only this time her bare legs touched his and she remembered with a frisson that she was naked. She realised she was blushing and almost laughed. Alex was in no state to know whether he had one or a dozen naked women in bed with him. It was an indulgence to relax, to feel the sensation of his skin against hers, the rough hairs on his legs tickling the smoothness of her calves. Hebe wrapped her arms around him and let herself drift into a state that was as near sleep as it was possible to achieve under the circumstances.

She was sleepily aware of a rise in the level of talk and activity in the room and woke, realising the French soldiers were coming in to eat their evening meal. The smell of boiling beans, bacon and onions insinuated itself through the gaps in the planks and tortured her empty stomach.

Then Alex began to move, restless again, murmuring. Hebe tried to keep him still, but he turned within the circle of her arms until he was lying on his side facing her. 'Wine,' he said clearly but softly. 'Red wine.'

'Oh, hush, darling,' she whispered back, her lips almost against his mouth.

'Wine!' This time it was louder. Hebe laid her palm over his mouth, but he twisted his head away. 'Landlord!'

In desperation she placed her mouth on his and silenced him with a kiss. It worked wonderfully. He kissed her back gently and Hebe relaxed again. In a moment his fever-driven fantasy of an inn would have passed. She tried not to think about the kiss as a kiss, or to let herself be aware of the feel of his nape where her hand rested, holding him to her.

Cautiously she drew back, but he moved sharply in reaction and some part of his body, perhaps his heel, hit the plank wall with a force which sounded to Hebe like a hammer blow. She froze, but the noise in the room was too loud for it to have been noted, or perhaps it had sounded like the horses tethered outside.

But while a knock might be ignored, an English voice could not fail to attract attention: she had to stop him speaking. His mouth found hers again and Hebe let the unconscious man kiss her, too frightened and distracted to realise at first what else was happening as his hands began to caress her.

Alex's fingers slid over her shoulder and found the curve of her breast. Hebe gasped against his lips and tried to wriggle away, but his hands were strong and she was held, not painfully, but with a firmness that told her that she would have to use some force to free herself. And then what? There was hardly room in the cupboard-bed for the two of them as it was. Hebe wriggled again, then realised that her naked body moving against Alex's was only making things worse.

She was on her back now, his weight over her, his hands still caressing, apparently by blind instinct. And there was the growing realisation that classical statues did not tell the whole story: there were mysteries about the male body she was just beginning to learn. What had Alex said wryly in the garden when she had innocently asked him why he had had trouble sleeping? That the male body was not designed to stop once it had begun, that kissing led on…

Oh, Alex! This was not how it should be, not how she had hazily dreamt of being in his arms. Here, in this remote French mountain cabin with enemy troopers the other side of the wall, and a lover who was making love to some phantom woman who inhabited his fevered dreams.

She knew she could not fight and part of her did not want to. But her untutored, unprepared body was not going to yield easily, whatever her mind told it, and the pain shocked a cry from her that was muffled against Alex's lips. Tears began to run down her face in the darkness, but even as they flowed, her hands were caressing his shoulders and her legs were twining with his.

'I love you,' she whispered against his mouth. 'Alex, darling….' And something miraculous was happening: through the discomfort and the shock and the fear, despite the sound of French voices singing marching songs only feet away, something was happening to her body. Hebe felt it begin to follow Alex's movements, felt a deep, building sensation that made her want to cling even tighter to him. His hands made her body flame everywhere he touched her. Something was happening, something that in a moment she would understand. Hebe felt her whole body tense as she reached for it, then Alex went rigid above her, his cry lost against her shoulder, and finally collapsed against her, still and quiet.

The rest of the night passed for Hebe as though she and not Alex was in the fever. The noise outside, the fact that death was the thickness of a plank away and that a cough, a sneeze, an inquisitive soldier, would end everything—none of that seemed important any more.

She fell into an uneasy doze, her aching body trapped under Alex's, far too hot where he touched her, her feet cold to the point of numbness. She tried to think about what had just happened, tried to find out just what she was feeling, but could not.

There was almost quiet in the room beyond now. Men snored, the fire crackled and she could hear the sentries outside exchanging desultory conversation as they passed each other. Finally dawn came and the troop, grumbling and muttering, roused itself for the new day.

Someone was brewing coffee: Hebe felt her mouth watering and swallowed, hurting her dry throat. Would they never be gone? At last they began to pack up and finally went on their way and she even remembered to hold her breath with anxiety as she heard their climbing footsteps pass the roof line of the hut, pass the path leading to the mule's little pasture—pass it and be gone.

Hebe heaved against the weight pinning her down and managed to slide out from under Alex's body. With hands that shook she unfastened the planks and climbed down into the room, pulling the cloak with her. Wrapped in it, she tiptoed out, stepping over discarded rubbish, and surveyed the scene outside. It was all clear.

Somehow, as though she had shut off her mind entirely, she managed to wash and dress. A pair of the culotte trousers came to her ankles, but could be belted in tightly and were easier to move in than a skirt. She tucked in a shirt and threw the shawl over her shoulders, crossing it in front and then knotting it at the back. A length of thread unravelled from a blanket tied back her hair, and the crude leather shoes at last seemed to be moulding to the shape of her feet.

Now she could not distract herself with dressing any longer, Hebe took a deep breath and went back to Alex. He lay still, a lock of hair falling across his forehead making him look absurdly young. 'Oh, darling,' she whispered, reaching for the water and beginning to wash his face.

She managed to eat a little and drank thirstily, then sat by the bed, holding Alex's hand and trying to make sense of what had happened to her. She had lost her virginity, so she supposed that even if she found someone else she wanted to marry, she could not do so. She could hardly imagine the man who would accept or tolerate a tale of unconscious seduction in a French mountain hut.

And Alex was already betrothed. In fact, she realised with a cold shiver, she had to make very, very certain he never suspected, or he would be in an impossible position and would probably have to end up marrying her, simply because it was the lesser of the two evils. Hebe let herself imagine being married to Alex, then firmly put it out of her mind. What would it be like to be married to a man who had been forced into it, when all the time he loved another woman? No, it did not bear thinking about.

Despite her efforts to be brave, a large tear welled up in the corner of her eye and spilled over to trickle down her cheek. She put up her free hand to wipe it away and a hoarse voice whispered, 'Don't cry, Circe.'

'Alex! Oh, Alex!' She burst into tears, throwing herself on his chest and holding him with all her strength. Then she realised that his skin was damp and that the fever had broken. 'I'm sorry,' she said shakily at last, pushing away and standing up to reach for the water. 'It must be the relief. Here, please try and drink.'

He managed to push himself up on one elbow and
Hebe thrust a rolled-up blanket behind him so he could
sit up and drink deeply. She found she was avoiding
meeting his eyes, frightened by what he would read in
hers. She forced herself to do it and managed a tremulous
smile, despite her shock at the sight of his deep hollowed
eyes.

'Poor little love,' he said huskily. 'What a nightmare
for you. Have you managed to get any sleep at all? How
long have we been here?'

'Two nights, and yes, I managed to doze.' She added
with more confidence, 'You have been a dreadful patient,
calling for wine, refusing to drink water, throwing off
your blankets.'

He smiled at her and as he did so she saw his face
change. His eyes darkened as he stared and the colour
began to stain his cheekbones as a look of appalled recollection came over his face.

'Hebe…I…we…Hebe, no, I could not have done such
a—' He broke off and leaned back on the makeshift pillow, his eyes still fixed with painful intensity on her face.

Hebe made an instant decision. 'What is the matter,
Alex? Are you remembering one of those nightmares you
had?' She made herself laugh. 'I am not sure I should be
telling you this, but at one point I think you imagined
you were…er…kissing a woman. I could not possibly
repeat what you said! Why, I had to put my hands over
my ears and run outside.'

'A dream?' He swallowed painfully.

'A delirium, I should have said,' Hebe corrected. 'It is
all right, I am only teasing, I was not so very shocked,
you know.'

Alex looked deeply relieved, and she could only be
thankful that he was still so weak and was not seeing her

with the same sharp intelligence he normally brought to anything he observed. But he seemed uncomfortable meeting her eyes still, and his gaze strayed over her shoulder and into the room beyond.

'My God, Hebe, I know you have had things to think about other than housework, but what have you been *doing*?'

Hebe followed his eyes. 'Oh, that. That was the French soldiers.' After the shattering thing that had happened to her last night, the soldiers were fading into something akin to a bad dream; easily forgotten once daylight comes.

'French soldiers!' Alex struggled up against the pillow, all thoughts of embarrassing dreams and fantasies banished utterly. 'Hebe, if you are teasing me about this, I'll put you over my knee the moment I've the strength to do it.'

'No, truly,' she assured him, getting up and beginning to look through the rubbish the troop had left. 'They came late afternoon yesterday, about fifteen of them, and spent the night.'

'And you cooked a nice dinner, I suppose,' he said, with the air of a man who has reached the limit of what will surprise him.

'Certainly not, I did exactly what you told me to do. I made sure everything had been put away and that we had some water, then climbed into the cupboard and closed the planks. They were very noisy, so I didn't get much sleep.' She poked in the still-warm ashes and emerged triumphant with a battered coffee pot. 'Look, they've left some coffee.' She began to rake together the embers and pushed the pot deep into them. 'Now, what else have they left, I wonder.'

'Hebe, stop that and come here.' Reluctantly she came

over and stood by the bed. 'Are you telling me that you had to sit in here all night with me delirious and who knows how many French soldiers feet away?'

'Yes.' He looked so appalled that her frayed nerves broke and she snapped, 'Well, what else could I do? I wasn't feeling very enchanting. I doubt if emerging and seeing if I could turn them into swine would have worked.'

'How did you keep me quiet?'

'You were only muttering by then, and they were very noisy,' she said, with perfect truth. 'Would you like some coffee?'

'Damn the coffee. Look at me, Hebe.' She met his eyes and almost cried at the deep, warm, admiration in them. 'I can't think of any man I know who would have gone through what you have had to endure these past few days and managed as well, or have stayed as calm. Or have had the humour to tease me at the end of it,' he added ruefully.

It was suddenly very difficult to breathe, let alone speak. Hebe stammered, 'I owe you my life, I was not going to throw it away by doing something stupid.' She went and picked up the coffee pot. 'If you do not want this, I am most certainly going to drink it.'

She turned back to find Alex had swung his legs out of the bed and was sitting on the edge, regarding his bare limbs as they emerged from under the blanket. 'And I suppose you asked a Frenchman politely to help me out of my clothes and into a nightshirt?'

Hebe reached past him for a battered tin mug and poured the coffee. 'No, I did it, of course. It was hard enough trying to keep you comfortable like that, let alone if I had left you dressed in those awful clothes.' He took the mug, but his eyebrows were raised incredulously.

'Oh, for goodness sake! I have seen nude statues, do not flatter yourself that you are any different.'

'No fig leaf,' he commented wickedly, taking a deep swallow of coffee. 'That is quite the worst coffee I have ever had, but I can't think when I have been more grateful for it.'

Hebe ignored the jibe about the fig leaf and held out her hand for the mug. 'Have you left any? Thank you. Yes, it is awful, but something hot is wonderful. I am going to put some water on the embers; it will at least get it warm. Then I am going to dress that knife cut and you can have a wash.'

'Only if I can have my trousers back and you leave the room.'

'I cannot dress that cut if you have your trousers on.' She balanced the water bucket in the embers and stood regarding him, hands on hips. 'Oh, wrap yourself in the blanket and take off your shirt, Alex—or are you afraid I will hurt you?'

He glared back. 'You sound—and look—like my old nurse. Very well, turn your back.'

Patiently waiting while muttered oaths marked Alex's unsteady progress towards a decent covering, Hebe wondered if his fever-clouded memory of what had happened last night was colouring the way he was reacting to her now. She supposed it must be, even if he did believe it was a dream. Whatever he had felt for her before Clarissa's letter arrived he had suppressed, and in their mutual struggle to survive he had treated her simply as a companion. Now all his consciousness of her as a woman had returned. Her problem was how she was going to hide her own new knowledge of him as a man.

She carried the bucket over and found another piece of old sheet to tear up, then gently freed the old bandage.

It was impossible to do it without touching him, encir
cling him with her arms, resting her cheek against the
flat planes of his chest as she unwrapped the bandage.
She felt him sitting unnaturally still, and thought he was
holding his breath.

The slash was, by some miracle, starting to heal with
out any sign of infection. Hebe rebandaged it, found Alex
his trousers, a clean shirt and the soap and went outside,
expecting him to call when he had finished.

To her horror she heard his voice just behind her at
the door of the hut. 'Is this all the bread that's left?'

'Get back to bed!'

He was holding on to the door jamb with a visible
effort, the lines of strain visible even through the stubble
which was now heavy on his face.

'No, we leave just as soon as we've eaten. I'll make
breakfast, if you can fetch the mule.'

'I'll not go a step until you promise me you'll ride and
I'll walk,' she said.

He grinned at her belligerent tone. 'I can promise you
that, Hebe, but I'm sorry to do this to you—it is a steep
climb now.'

The mule was patiently standing where she had teth
ered it, and seemed more than willing to follow her down
and be saddled up. Hebe brought out extra blankets, a
canteen of water and all the remaining food, and went
back to board up the secret cupboard again. When she
came out Alex was in the saddle, white about the mouth
and with his eyes closed. Hebe took the rope and began
to lead the mule up the path again. After a few hundred
yards she came to a point where the track split. One path
went up, the other, wider and heavily marked by the

oots of yesterday's French troops, turned along the flank
f the mountain.

'Up?' she asked, turning to look at Alex.

He opened his eyes and smiled at her. 'Up,' he agreed
uefully.

Chapter Thirteen

Hebe found she enjoyed the climb up the steep track a
it zigzagged through the scrubby, rock-strewn pasture
The wide trousers were a revelation to someone who ha
always had her desire to stride out and enjoy a wal
hampered by clinging skirts. After two days of being tie
to the confines of the hut the freedom and fresh air wer
wonderful and the physical exercise and the need to con
centrate on her footing stopped her brooding.

The mule followed sturdily behind, nimble on its nea
hooves. At first Hebe stopped herself from looking bac
every few yards as she was tempted to do. She had n
wish for Alex to feel she was clucking over him like
mother hen. Considering how frustrating it must be fo
him to feel so weak when his instincts and his pride wer
all driving him to protect her, he was being extraordi
narily good tempered. In Hebe's experience, wounde
male pride normally showed itself in thorough-going ir
ritation.

Finally they reached a sharp hairpin in the path wher
Hebe thought she could legitimately stop to rest. Sh
turned, taking in the breathtaking panorama spread befor
them with a gasp of pleasure. 'How wonderful! I hav

ever been so high up before—look, Alex, you can see
he sea.' Round their feet the short turf was studded with
pring flowers, flowering later in the cooler mountain air
han those down on the plains.

After a few minutes Hebe felt that she had demon-
trated an admirable disinclination to fuss and looked at
Alex. He was sitting, the musket lying across the saddle
n front of him, the reins looped casually in one hand and
is head tipped back to watch the vultures circling lazily
verhead in the cloudless sky. He appeared to feel her
yes on him and looked at her, smiling. 'Are you out of
reath yet?'

'A bit,' she confessed. 'But I love this: it is so good
o be able to walk freely, scramble about. Do you think
could start a fashion for divided skirts when I get back
o England? I had no idea trousers would be so...
iberating.'

He considered her strange costume seriously. 'I think
ou would set all the old Society tabbies by the ears. But
f you marry a man with a large country estate, why, then
ou can wear what you choose and stride about to your
eart's content.'

Hastily Hebe turned away and started to climb again.
After last night she was never going to be able to accept
proposal of marriage, whoever it came from. 'Or I shall
ecome an eccentric spinster and have a country cottage,'
he tossed back over her shoulder in an attempt at light-
ess.

They went on in silence for another hour, interrupted
nly by Alex calling to her to stop and drink from the
anteen at the saddlebow. She insisted he drink first, not-
g with relief the colour that was coming back into his

face and the sharp, alert look in his eyes as he scanned
the slopes around them.

'Are we likely to see any French?' she asked, made
uneasy by his constant watchfulness.

He shrugged, shifting his grip on the musket. 'I doubt
it. They hold territory on the other side of the border
almost to Gibraltar, so they have no need to patrol unless
they have intelligence that a *guerrilla* band is on the
move. You were unlucky with that group last night; I
suspect they were moving along the flank of the mountain
to provide high-level lookouts over the coast.'

'So we are no safer when we cross the border?' Hebe
twisted in the cork and handed the canteen back to him.

'Much safer. The French are on enemy territory there
and I know the partisans.' He pointed up the mountain-
side. 'You see that break of slope there? We will stop at
that point and have something to eat. After that it gets
much steeper.'

Hebe squared her shoulders and climbed on, beginning
to realise that, despite taking far more exercise than most
of her friends, long rambles on Malta were not at all the
same as scrambling over the foothills of a mountain
range. She could feel her face glowing and damp and her
hair, despite being tied back, kept blowing irritatingly
into her eyes.

She flopped down when they finally reached the natural rock step that Alex had pointed out and tried not to
look up. Above them the surface seemed to be entirely
composed of frost-shattered rocks through which the narrow mule track was a hardly visible thread, looping its
way to the top.

Alex threw his leg over the pommel and slid to the
ground, stretching with a deep sigh of relief. He looked
so much better Hebe could hardly credit it. She supposed

that underlying strength and fitness told, even after his sharp bout of illness. He pulled the remains of their food from the saddlebag and came to sit beside her, pulling the knife from his belt to cut the bread and cheese.

They ate in companionable silence, so quiet that a blue rock thrush flew down in a flash of iridescent wings and perched on a rock for a few moments, and the mewing of the buzzard circling overhead reached them clearly.

Hebe looked up at it, then pushed her hair out of her eyes irritably.

'Let me.' She could feel Alex untying the knot in the strand of wool that held her hair back at her nape, and then his fingers began to comb through the long, tangled mass, carefully teasing it out. 'What have you been doing to it?' he asked, puzzled. 'It is remarkably clean, but it feels as though it has never been combed.'

The rhythmic movement was strangely soothing, despite the occasional tug when his gentle teasing failed to untangle a knot. 'I had just washed it when the French came. I was sitting on the edge of the terrace in the sun, drying it when I saw them. I suppose it never got combed out properly.'

'Hmm. Well, I have done the best I can, but it is hardly…I know.' She could feel his fingers working again, more purposefully now, and realised he was braiding her hair into a long tail. The closeness of him and the touch of his fingertips against her nape made her want to lean back into his embrace, twist in his arms until she could kiss him…

'Where did you learn to plait?' Hebe said, trampling firmly on the clamorous demands her body was making.

'It is no different than plaiting a horse's tail,' Alex said prosaically, knotting the thread at the end of the long braid. 'There, that will keep it out of your eyes.'

Hebe stood up. The sooner they got going again the better. The closeness of him, the warmth of his body so near to hers, the touch of his fingers were all potent reminders of last night.

'You ride now, Hebe.' He stood by the mule, obviously waiting to toss her up into the saddle.

'No! I am perfectly all right, and it is far too early for you to be exerting yourself.'

His eyes narrowed. 'Hebe, come here and get on this mule. *Now!*'

'No. And do not shout at me, I am not one of your troopers.'

'More's the pity, they do as they are told.' There was a long pause, then he turned away sharply and said, in quite a different tone, 'Hebe, please do as I ask. If you fall and break your ankle on that slope I will never be able to lift you on to the mule. Can't you tell I am half-crazy with worry about you? Don't make me have to beg you to help me.'

Hebe choked down a shocked sob. 'Alex, I am so sorry, yes, of course I'll ride the mule if you think that is best. I don't mean to be a burden to you.' She felt quite sick at the reproof and at the thought that she had forced him to admit his weakness. His face was unreadable as he lifted her into the saddle, but as he picked up the long rein and turned to start walking Hebe caught a glimpse of an expression of wicked amusement on his face, transforming the lean, strained, heavily stubbled countenance.

'Major Beresford!' she stormed, kicking the mule to try to bring it alongside him. 'That was the most unprincipled, dishonest, ungentlemanly trick to play on me!'

'I agree, Miss Carlton,' he replied calmly, but with a hint of a laugh in his voice. 'But it worked.'

Hebe subsided into fulminating silence. She knew she was sulking and that it was a completely unworthy thing to be doing, but she was suddenly tired of coping and being cheerful and pretending that last night had not happened. She just wanted to be taken in Alex's arms and to have a good cry. As that was obviously impossible, being furious with him was the next best thing.

For the next hour she sat on the mule, hanging on to the pommel as it lurched and clambered up the slope, glaring at Alex's back and keeping herself from worrying by rehearsing all his numerous faults. Unfortunately she could not find any, other than being as stubborn as the animal she was riding, and having the poor judgement to fall in love with a red-headed beauty called Clarissa.

They reached the pass so suddenly that it was a shock to find the mule standing on level ground. 'Downhill all the way now,' Alex said with satisfaction, leaning against the animal's shoulder. He twisted round to look at Hebe. 'Are you talking to me again?'

'No,' she said tightly. 'You almost made me cry.'

'I can't believe that, Hebe, you are much too brave to cry. Come on, we'll be with friends by evening.'

He set off down the track into Spain and Hebe kicked her heels and followed him, biting her lip. She knew he was not intending to be unkind, and was trying to bolster her spirits by complimenting her on her courage, but his words were having quite the opposite effect to that he had intended.

She blinked hard and swallowed. Hebe, capable, sensible Hebe wouldn't cry, of course. And as for Circe, well, whenever she was upset she probably just went out and turned a few more hapless sailors into animals, so she didn't *need* to cry. But she was not either any longer.

She was a new Hebe: a ruined woman, a woman in love
with a man who did not love her, an Englishwoman cast
adrift in a foreign, enemy-occupied country—and this
new Hebe wanted a good weep.

'Wait!' she called. Alex stopped and turned round. 'I
want to get down.'

'Why?' He came and lifted her from the saddle.

Hebe glared at him. 'Because that shrub over there is
the first bush I have seen in over three hours and I intend
to take advantage of it.' She stalked off and took refuge
behind the spiny foliage, not emerging until she had
rubbed all the tears out of her eyes and blown her nose.

The track snaked down into the valley, becoming
wider and less rocky as they descended. It was much
easier going and they seemed to be covering miles after
the steep climb of the morning. Hebe noticed that the
slopes were greener on this side and that great stands of
sweet chestnut cast welcome shade from the sun, which
was now low in the sky.

'Are we nearly there?' she asked, and was answered
by Alex's gesture to further down the slope where thin
columns of smoke could just be seen. The track suddenly
met a wider cart track at right angles and Alex turned on
to it, then stopped. Around the bend, approaching them
came the sound of voices and the rumble of wheels.

'Leave the talking to me,' he said urgently as a group
of people accompanying two laden carts came into view.

Hebe held her breath. They were all civilians, four men
and two younger women, and by the look of them they
were returning to their village after a day gathering wood
or looking after animals on the pastures. Alex stood quietly by the side of the road, one hand on hers as it rested
on the mule's neck, his eyes on the approaching group

who were regarding the pair of them with undisguised
curiosity as they came.

Then there was a cry of 'Major Alex!' and they were
in the centre of a laughing group, slapping Alex on the
back, grinning at her, firing rapid Spanish at him despite
his efforts to slow them down. Hebe sat, weak with relief,
and studied them, liking what she saw. They were all
dark, the men rather stocky and dressed very much alike
in knee breeches over rough woollen hose with heavy
buckled shoes. Their shirts were generously cut and on
top some wore leather waistcoats, others jackets. One
woman was about Hebe's age, shy and long haired in a
plain gown kirtled up to show her sturdy shoes and dusty
petticoats; the other was a little older, with a thin, ex-
pressive face. She sat up on the box of the first wagon,
the oxen's reins held loosely in her hand, her eyes vivid
as she smiled at Alex.

The excited group suddenly fell silent and turned as
one to look down the cart track towards the village. They
had heard what it took Hebe a moment longer to recog-
nise, the beat of many hooves on the hard-packed surface.

'Los francès!' one of the men said and before she knew
what was happening Hebe was sitting in the back of one
of the wagons, a sack thrown over her trousers and the
musket tucked down beside her. One of the men had
clapped his hat on Alex's head, the mule was hitched on
behind and suddenly the little group had acquired two
more weary workers returning home for the evening.

They stood aside, sullen, but showing no obvious hos-
tility, as the small troop of cavalry swept past them, the
officer giving them a sharp, dismissive glance as he
passed. Then they were walking again, keeping to the
pace of the oxen. Hebe let her head fall back against the
side of the cart and fell into a doze of sheer weariness.

* * *

She was woken by Alex shaking her gently by the shoulder to find they had stopped in the tiny square of the village. Whitewashed houses interspersed with others built from the local granite formed three sides, with the church on the fourth. Lanes ran off from it, busy with small children playing and chasing chickens and dogs, old women sitting outside their front doors preparing vegetables and their menfolk wearily making their way home.

'We are safe here,' he said, smiling at her as she knuckled her tired eyes. 'You go with Anna, she will look after you.'

'But, Alex!' Hebe started to scramble down, conscious that several old ladies were regarding her attire with surprise. One crossed herself. 'Alex, I do not speak any Spanish!'

'But I speak English,' said the woman who had been driving the oxen. She jumped down from the cart in a swirl of skirts and Hebe saw she was perhaps thirty years old, and tall. 'I am Anna Wilkins. *Mrs* Anna Wilkins. And you are welcome to my brother's house as is any friend of Major Alex.'

Her accent was heavily Spanish, but Hebe could make out an underlying edge of cockney. She was urging Hebe towards the front door of one of the larger houses, talking as she went. 'Do not worry about the Major, he is talking to the headman of the village. 'Ere we are.' The tranquil shade hit Hebe like a breath of cool air. The shutters were closed and the evening light sent bars across the terracotta-tiled floor, falling here and there on the few pieces of massive oak furniture that flanked the wide fireplace.

'Is this your house?' Hebe asked. 'It is beautiful.'

'My brother Ernesto owns it. I keep house for him

now I am a widow.' She steered Hebe towards a door that opened to reveal stairs. 'You like a bath?'

'Oh, yes, please. I am sorry, was your husband an Englishman?' It seemed quite unreal to be making polite conversation with this woman in a remote mountain village.

'Yes, 'arry Wilkins, one of the Major's sergeants. I follow him all over, until he died of the fever.' She glanced at Hebe. 'The Major had it too, it comes back I think, sometimes. He does not look well now.'

'Yes, he was very ill for two days: we were washed overboard from a frigate on the way to Gibraltar. Al— the Major saved me.'

Anna nodded sharply as though she would expect nothing else, and shouted down the stairs, 'Donna! *Venga aqui!*'

A woman appeared, was deluged with a rapid fire of instructions and retreated again, muttering. Anna rolled her eyes and showed Hebe through to a bedroom with a wide bed with a headboard of chestnut planks and a billowing mattress covered in white sheets.

'Now, you have a bath...' Anna tugged a hipbath out from behind a screen '...and then you go to bed and I fetch you some food and some drink and you sleep or eat as you want. *Sì?*'

The maid must have had hot water on the fire awaiting her mistress's return, for it seemed only a few minutes before she was puffing up the stairs, followed by a youth, both of them carrying buckets that steamed gently. When the bath was full Anna shooed them out of the room and lifted towels, fine but worn, and a long white nightgown out of the chest at the foot of the bed. 'I help you undress?'

She took Hebe's tired fumblings with buttons and ties

as assent and began to help her out of her clothes. Hebe
was too weary to either feel any embarrassment, or wonder what state her adventures had left her in. It was not
until the older woman gasped and took Hebe by the
shoulders, turning her so she could look at her properly,
that she realised that perhaps she was rather bruised and
battered.

'I must have got very knocked about in the sea,' she
said, looking down at her shins and the state of her forearms.

'This was all not the sea,' Anna said harshly, twisting
her round until she faced a long mirror. Even in the
gloom Hebe could see the finger marks on her upper arms
and shoulders, the bruises on the white skin of her thighs.
'The man that raped you, the Major has killed him, *no*?'

'No!'

'I find that hard to believe,' Anna said sternly. 'And
what is he about, not telling me so that I can look after
you properly. I shall have words with him!'

'No!' Hebe said again with such an edge of desperation that Anna stopped fulminating on the idiocy of men
and looked at her closely.

'He does not know?' Hebe shook her head. 'But how
is this? These are not old bruises, they are newer than
the ones on your...' She lost the English word and gestured at Hebe's calves.

Hebe gave a little sob and found herself wrapped in a
warm embrace. 'Come along, tell Anna. Who was it,
ducky?'

The foolish English endearment overturned what was
left of Hebe's resolution. 'Alex,' she whispered. 'Last
night,' and burst into tears.

Chapter Fourteen

'The Major? The Major ravished you?' Anna sounded incredulous as she gathered Hebe into her arms, wrapping the bedcover round her shoulders, before hugging her tightly.

'Yes…no. I mean, it was him, but he didn't know…'

Anna was muttering in Spanish, then she broke into angry English. 'How can I be so mistaken in a man?' She produced a choice expression that she had obviously acquired from her sergeant. 'And he shows no shame, no sorryness. There, there, ducky, you cry and then you have your bath and go to bed and I will talk to him. And if he does not do the right thing, why, then my brother will talk to him also and then he will be sorry!'

'No!' Hebe wriggled until she could look Anna in the face. 'Anna, please, say nothing. He did not know it was happening, he was in a fever, delirious.' At the look of puzzlement on Anna's face she stumbled on, recounting the story of the French soldiers, that dreadful night trapped in the secret cupboard bed. 'He remembered something in the morning, but I made him think he had been dreaming,' she finished, wiping her eyes on the towel.

'But why do you not want him to know? He will marry you then.'

'He cannot, he is betrothed to a lady in England.' Hebe squared her shoulders. 'You promise you will not say anything, *please*, Anna.' The Spanish woman gave a reluctant nod. 'Thank you. May I have my bath now?'

Anna helped her off the bed. 'You want that I stay?'

'Yes, please.' Hebe sniffed. 'I am sorry I am being so feeble, it is just such a relief to feel safe and to have a woman to talk to. Alex has been wonderful, but it is not the same.'

'Indeed, no,' Anna agreed grimly, picking up the soap and starting to work a sponge into a lather.

Hebe feel asleep as soon as her head touched the pillow, only to wake, crying out in alarm, 'Alex!' to find the room in darkness except for a candle burning on a side table, and Anna hurrying to her side from the big chair by the window where she had been resting. She took Hebe's hand and talked quietly in Spanish until her eyelids drooped and she drifted off again.

She woke to find herself alone and the room flooded with light from half-opened shutters. The comforting noises of the village going about its everyday life drifted up from the square outside. Hebe sat up, wondering where her clothes were, then heard feet stumping up the staircase and the door opened to reveal the elderly maid, still muttering, and with a tray in her hands.

Hebe summoned up her few words of Spanish and ventured, *'Buenos dias, señora.'*

This earned her a glare and a returned greeting, pronounced with such emphasis that she was made quite aware that her own pronunciation had been sadly lacking.

Hebe took the tray, considered trying a 'thank you', thought better of it and simply smiled and nodded before the old woman stumped out again.

She must have reported that the Englishwoman was awake because a few minutes later Anna appeared, her arms full of clothes and a frown between her strong, dark brows.

'Good morning, Anna. Is anything wrong?' Suddenly anxious, she pushed aside the tray and started to get up. 'You haven't said anything to Alex about…you know?'

'I promised not, so I don't,' Anna said, heaping the clothes on the end of the bed. 'But I talk to him about your journey, and you are right, he does not remember. I say, it is very difficult for you, a young lady to be alone with a man in all that danger, and he agree. So I say, what a good thing you are there, Major, or she would have been ravished by those dogs of Frenchmen. And he agrees, but he is worried that he was sick and you had a bad fright and he could not protect you that night, and says you were very brave and sensible.'

She began to shake out a selection of skirts. 'And so I say, and it is wonderful, there is this nice English girl, so respectable, and she is rescued by a man who treats her just like a brother would.' She raised an eyebrow at Hebe, 'And you know, he goes red, what is it you call it?'

'Blushes?'

'Yes, blushes. But he does not look guilty like a man who has done something bad, just awkward, like a man who has thought things he should not. So I am not angry with him any more, just worried.'

'Worried?' Hebe queried. 'What about? The more time passes, the more he will be certain it was all a dream in his fever. Oh, what pretty skirts, is one of them for me to borrow?'

'Yes, whichever you like.' Anna unrolled some white cotton stockings and laid them out. She added, half to herself, 'It is not his memory I worry about. Still, time will pass, we will see what we will see.'

She left Hebe to get washed and dressed. Anna's words puzzled her, then she shrugged her shoulders and began to climb out of bed, shocked to discover just how stiff and sore she felt when she stood up. All her bruises seemed to ache at once, and her leg muscles were protesting violently about their steep climb the day before.

Still, it was a pleasure to wash in warm water and to dress in clean clothes. She pulled on the stockings, tying the red garters, then tried a petticoat. It was much fuller than the English fashion and flounced, although it was plain and untrimmed. There was a chemise with pin tucks and a white cotton blouse with full sleeves. Hebe pulled a skirt in a deep blue home-weave with a narrow red stripe running down it over her head, admiring the way it flared over the petticoat and showed a pretty glimpse of ankle. There was a jacket with short sleeves to go over the blouse and a shawl, which she would probably be expected to wear over her head.

Hebe unplaited her hair, remembering Alex's fingers gently untangling it, and re-made the plait so it hung smooth and heavy down her back with just of few curls around her face. The face that looked back at her from the glass was subtly different: lightly tanned, thinner, her cheekbones more pronounced and the severe hairstyle showing off her wide brow and grey eyes. Hebe wondered what her stepmother would think when she saw her, and had to fight down the surge of worry about just what Sara would be going through.

When she walked slowly downstairs, the shawl in her hand, the living room was deserted, so she opened the front door and looked out. Someone had set a table and benches in the shade outside their house under a tangle of vines stretched across wires and Alex was sitting on the table, talking to several men. Anna stood on the edge of the group watching him with an unreadable expression.

She turned as Hebe approached, drawing the men's attention to her and they all got up and greeted her, mostly in Spanish, but with the odd English word thrown in. Hebe smiled, and tried her Spanish again, this time to better effect and they moved away, leaving her with Alex, and the watchful presence of Anna.

He looked at her for a long moment as though he hardly recognised her. 'Hebe, you look—'

'If you say "nice",' Hebe remarked, 'I will scream.'

'I was going to say, you look enchanting, but different.' He put his head on one side, studying her. Hebe shifted a little under the scrutiny.

'What? I know I have a tan. Mama is going to be livid.'

'No, it isn't that. You are Circe still, but a...grown-up Circe all of a sudden.'

'Circe?' Anna interrupted. 'Who is this Circe? The child has lost weight, no doubt.'

'Yes...' Alex sounded dubious. He stood up and before she could stop him he had cupped Hebe's face in both hands as he had done on the boat in the harbour. And as they had then, his thumbs gently traced the line of her cheekbones. 'Yes, that must be it. Your eyes look enormous.'

Anna coughed sharply and the moment was over. Alex crossed his arms and became expressionless, Hebe threw the shawl over her head and pretended to concentrate on tying it. 'When do we start, Major?' Anna said briskly. 'Everything is ready.'

'Start?' Hebe asked, clashing with Alex who said, 'We? Who is we?'

'Me, and you and Hebe,' Anna said simply. 'I go with you and we are careful about what we tell Hebe's *madre* and she thinks I have been with you all the time. And then you don't have to marry her, because it is all respectable. *No?*'

Alex glanced sharply at Hebe. 'Indeed? Hebe and I have not yet discussed this. I suppose you think we can convince Lady Latham that you were conveniently standing on the beach in France, Anna?'

She gave him a withering look. 'Of course not, *stupido*, but even the fiercest mother would not believe you are able to…what is the word? Disgrace? Ah, compromise, a young lady in the sea, or on the beach when you are just washed up. I see it, exactly as it happened. You are on a *Spanish* beach—unconscious, that is most proper I think—and a peasant, known to me, of course—rides by and he rescues you both and he recognises the Major and tells the *guerillas* and I come and all is quite as respectable as if the nuns from the convent of Santa Maria had found you.'

Alex looked from her to Hebe and back from under hooded lids. 'It might do, I suppose, if we work on it a little. Anna, do you not mind coming? It might still be dangerous.'

She made a contemptuous gesture. 'No, I enjoy the change, and I look after Hebe. And when we get to Gibraltar, perhaps I find a handsome English sergeant. Poor 'arry has been gone a long time and I miss him, but I think I would like to be married again.'

'Hebe, what do you think? Will Lady Sara believe that story? Do you really want to tell something that is less than the truth?'

'What is the alternative?' Hebe asked, trying not to sound waspish.

'We tell the truth.'

'And then Sir Richard demands that you marry me, but you are betrothed to Clarissa, and it all becomes very awkward and embarrassing.' He opened his mouth to speak and Hebe added tartly, 'When—if—I marry, I want a love match.'

'Well, that is very clear,' Alex snapped back. 'Just so long as we all know what tale we are telling.' He clapped a slouch hat on his head and turned to walk off across the square. 'I will be ready in half an hour.'

'Tch!' Anna watched him go. 'Men! Now you have hurt his...' She waved a hand in the air. 'Do not tell me, I must practise my English. His proud, no, pride. You hurt his pride, now he will be cross with us all the way to Gibraltar and that is very good because then he does not think about how lovely you are and how much he wants you.'

'He is in love with Lady Clarissa Duncan, not with me.'

Anna snorted. 'You are here, she is not and he is a man. Come, Hebe, we will pack some things and you will tell me who this Circe is.'

Anna was still puzzling over the Greek enchantress when they returned to the square with two battered valises, which she threw into the back of an old donkey cart. 'But why does he think you are like a witch? That is not very flattering, I think.'

'Not a witch, an enchantress. Someone who makes spells to make men fall in...I mean, admire her.'

'That is a good word, enchantress.' Anna rolled it round her tongue. 'You tell me how you become an enchantress, Hebe, and I will try it on a handsome sergeant.'

'You do not need any lessons,' Hebe laughed, looking at Anna's flashing black eyes and sensual, swaying walk.

'What are you laughing about?' Alex asked, joining them and loading some wicker baskets of food into the cart.

'Men,' the women said in unison.

'Are you ready, Major?' Anna added, managing to make it sound as though he had been keeping them waiting for an hour.

Alex narrowed his eyes at her, but did not rise to the bait. 'Quite ready, thank you, Anna, let's go.'

Afterwards the days the three of them spent walking towards Gibraltar seemed to Hebe to be part of a story from a book that she had been told but which she had not really experienced. It had all the hazy quality of a dream as they walked steadily through green farmland and dusty plains, climbed ridges that seemed like hills after the foothills of the Pyrenees, and made their way across old bridges arching over rivers still swollen from the spring snowmelt.

Sometimes they saw French troops, but they seemed to be convincing in their role as three farmers moving from field to field or travelling to the next village and they were not challenged. Each night Alex found friends, or friends of friends, to stay with and Hebe began to develop a Spanish vocabulary she was quite proud of.

But somehow she and Alex were never alone and never spoke about more than the most commonplace hings. Hebe missed their closeness, even as she recognised its dangers. And, she told herself as she trudged along beside their patient donkey, she would be parting from him soon, so the earlier she got used to it, the better.

That evening she wandered away from the house where they were staying with a large and exuberant family who proved to be distant cousins of Anna's. Anna was admiring the new baby and Alex was deep in conversation with the village mayor and several leading citzens who were describing in detail what they had observed locally of French troop movements so close to the front line with the English. Hebe felt restless and lonely. She knew that if she stayed where she was she would spend the evening gazing at Alex, wishing they were alone, wishing she was in his arms again.

She found a spot where a large tree trunk had been washed up on a bend in the river and sat on it to watch the swallows hunting gnats over the water. It was quiet and she fell into a sort of doze, thinking about Alex, aching for him and trying to find the strength of mind to stop. He would be gone from her life soon, back to England and the woman he truly loved and would marry and raise a family with. It was wrong of her to feel like this, and dangerous too, for she knew she must not let her guard down and let him glimpse her feelings or guess at what had happened that night.

A footstep behind her jerked her awake with a start and she half-fell, half-stumbled off the tree trunk, ending up with one foot in the stream. Alex jumped down beside her and lifted her on to the dry shingle, his face alight with amusement at her predicament.

Hebe, thoroughly startled at finding herself in his arms, jerked away abruptly and made a pretence of holding on to a willow branch while she shook the water from her shoe. Alone with him in the evening light she was acutely aware of his masculinity, of his looks, which she had become so accustomed to and which now struck her with renewed force. The casual way he wore the loose linen shirt, the way the tight trousers followed the lines of his long legs and the dark stubble that he was shaving only every other day, all of these served to emphasise the strength and elegance of his body and the severe perfection of his face.

She felt a wave of desire that startled her with its intensity and made her avoid his eyes lest he read her feelings in them.

'Hebe? What is the matter?'

'Nothing! I mean, you made me jump, I was sitting there daydreaming and I suddenly heard you and I was startled.' She bent to put back her shoe, making too much of a business of lacing it.

'I am sorry, I did not mean to scare you.' Alex took a step towards her as she straightened up and, without thinking, she stepped round the fallen tree until it was between them. He was regarding her with a slight frown between his dark brows. 'Hebe, have I done something to upset you? You seem to have been avoiding me these past few days.'

'No, no, not at all.' *Stop twittering*, she told herself fiercely. 'It is probably better if we keep more of a distance, do you not think? I mean, we are almost back to Gibraltar now, and it will not do to give any impression that we have been intim…close.'

Alex leaned his hip against the tree trunk and folded his arms, still watching her closely. 'We can revert to society manners and distance the moment the gates of Gibraltar come into sight. I hardly think we need any practice.'

'Umm...' Hebe felt cornered. 'Well, I still think it is better if we get used to it now. After all, you are engaged to be married and we have fallen into the habit of...'

'Intimacy?' he supplied drily.

'Friendship,' Hebe retorted, recovering her wits somewhat.

'Very well, we will behave as though we have just been introduced at a dull evening reception, although if I was your mama I would find that considerably more suspicious than the natural degree of familiarity one might expect to develop between two people cast adrift on a foreign shore. However, you know her best.'

Hebe opened her mouth to retort that she did not mean they should act as total strangers when he added, 'And speaking of foreign shores, Anna is throwing herself into the role of duenna with some enthusiasm, is she not? What is the matter with her? Do the pair of you think I am about to leap upon you and ravish you?

'I am sorry!' He broke off at the sight of her rosy cheeks and wide-eyed shock. 'I did not mean to put you to the blush. Really, Hebe, you know I find you damnably attractive, but I can promise you, I would never do anything to alarm or compromise you.'

The first part of this was so near the knuckle that Hebe gasped, then his last sentence penetrated. 'Did you say you find me ''damnably attractive''?' she demanded.

'Oh, lord! I do recall saying I was going to give you one comprehensive apology for my language at the end of this adventure.' He raked his hand through his hair and regarded her ruefully. 'Yes, for my sins, I did say just that—but you knew it already.'

'You said I was enchanting, not attractive,' Hebe pointed out, throwing caution to the winds. This was dangerous ground, but she could not resist.

'Same thing.'

'No, it is not. People say kittens are enchanting, or babies.'

Alex pushed himself away from the tree trunk and regarded her with a look that made her heart beat hard in her chest. 'I do not think of you as a kitten, Hebe. A small wildcat sometimes, but never a kitten. I will go back to England, and I will become a respectable married man, but I will never quite forget you, because you are an enchantress.'

Hebe thought she had stopped breathing. She knew she should turn his words, make some light remark, start to stroll back to the house, but all she could do was stand there, her eyes locked with his, grey with blue. He took one step towards her and she found that her own feet, without any conscious decision on her part, were also moving. One more step and she would be in his arms.

Chapter Fifteen

'Hebe!' Anna's voice broke the spell and Hebe turned aside, her face flaming. 'Hebe! Where are you?'

'Here, Anna,' Hebe ran up the slight slope of the bank and waved. 'Just talking to Alex.'

Anna looked sharply from one to the other, then linked her arm through Hebe's and began to walk back to her cousin's house. 'It is time you were in bed, tomorrow we cross the lines into English territory. We need all our wits about us.' As they reached the door she ushered Hebe through and towards the stairs. 'Goodnight, Major.'

'Goodnight, Anna. Goodnight, Miss Carlton.'

Anna raised interrogative eyebrows at Hebe as they turned up the wicks of the lanterns in the bedroom they were sharing. 'Miss Carlton? Have you had an argument, you two?'

Hebe unlaced her jacket wearily. 'He thought I was being distant.' Anna looked puzzled. 'Formal, cold. He thought he had done something to alarm me and that was why you were such a strict duenna. I told him that it was only that I thought we had better seem to be less good friends before we got back to Gibraltar.'

'*Sì?*'

'And then he said something…that he thought I wa
attractive, and—oh, Anna, I do not know what happened
but suddenly we were looking at each other and…'

'You find you are in love with him?' the other woma
said drily, as she folded her wide skirts and laid them o
a chair.

'I knew that already,' Hebe said, equally drily. 'I knew
that on Malta, but thank goodness, the letter from Lad
Clarissa came before I could do or say anything tha
might make him suspect I was doing more than flirting.

'And the Major?'

'He loves Lady Clarissa. But, as you said the othe
day, I am here and she is not and he is a man. And on
who appears to find me attractive, although no one els
ever has.'

'*Qué?*' Anna said, looking amazed. 'No one? Wh
not?'

Hebe shrugged as she rolled off her stockings. 'I wa
ordinary—I *am* ordinary, only Alex makes me feel spe
cial. I was the sort of girl who is a good friend, a *nic*
girl. Nothing special, no charm, everyone tells me thei
problems but never thinks I might have an interestin
secret of my own. Mama is always saying what a pity
have no looks.'

Anna made a complicated, very Spanish, sound. 'Wha
nonsense. Me, I would like to box your mama's ears, silly
woman! I suppose she is one of those little white—no
blonde, is that the word?—blonde English women wh
get fat when they are forty. All giggles and no bones
Now you,' she glared at Hebe, who was trying not t
smile at this pungent description '—you listen to me
You have the bones and the charm and yes, you are
nice girl, but with a man who loves you, you will be

beautiful woman. Especially,' she added with a wicked winkle, 'especially if he *makes* love to you.'

'Yes, but he must not make love to me!' Hebe said, scrambling into bed and pulling the covers up. 'He is going to get married to someone else whom he loves. Just because a man wants to make love to you, it does not mean he is in love, does it?'

'No, more is the pity.' Anna sighed, climbing into bed beside her and blowing out the light. 'The trouble with men is that they are all ruled by their—' She suddenly seemed to realise to whom she was speaking and broke off. 'Good night, Hebe, *querida*. You will be home with your mama tomorrow, if the good Lord allows.'

The next day seemed so much like the ones before it that Hebe could not truly believe the end of their journey was almost over. But as the morning wore on, Anna's tenseness and Alex's hawk-like watchfulness began to make her nervous, and when they rounded a corner to find themselves walking straight into a troop of British horsemen Hebe almost cried out with the shock of it.

She stood by the cart, her hand tight in Anna's, as Alex spoke to the young Lieutenant in command of the troop. The discussion was too quiet for Hebe to hear, but the officer glanced once or twice in her direction and she could see him nodding repeatedly as he listened to Alex.

Then Alex came back to the cart, the first smile Hebe had seen on his face all day lightening his expression. *Audacious* made harbour safely with no more loss of life. Your mother and Sir Richard are quite safe—but in deep mourning for you.' He broke off as Hebe turned her face into Anna's shoulder and burst into tears, waiting patiently until she managed to get her emotions under control and turned a watery smile on him. 'Lieutenant

Farthing is offering to send a messenger on ahead wit
the news. You know best how your mother would react–
is it better for a stranger to give her the good new
quickly, or do you want to wait and see her yourself?'

'Send ahead, please.' Hebe had no doubt what sh
would prefer if the position was reversed. She turned t
the officer, who had ridden a little closer to hear he
decision. 'Please, Lieutenant Farthing, I would be s
grateful.'

He touched his hat to her and called over a troope
'Find Sir Richard Latham and tell him that his stepdaugh
ter Miss Carlton is quite safe and in good company an
will be with him within two hours. Only approach Lad
Latham if you cannot locate Sir Richard and make sur
she has her woman with her before you break the news–
good tidings can be as shocking as bad if they are un
expected.' He made the man repeat his instructions an
they watched as he spurred his horse away down th
road.

'I can send another trooper back with you, Major, bu
I regret I cannot spare the horses to mount all of you
The road ahead is quite safe. Peters! Escort the Majo
and his party back into the town. Ma'am, my congratu
lations on your safe return!'

The short distance to safety seemed endless to Heb
now her anxieties about her mother were at rest. Ho
soon would the trooper reach Sir Richard? How lon
would it take to find Mama? What state of health wa
she in after that nightmare sea voyage and the shock c
her stepdaughter's apparent death?

She wanted to talk to Alex, to ask all these question
none of which he would be able to answer, simply fc
the comfort of talking to him, but he seemed to be grow
ing colder and more distant with every step. The mon

she had at first compared him to was back in control and the Alex she had come to know over the past days seemed a distant figure.

The trooper had done his work well, for they were expected at the gate and escorted efficiently to a carriage. Hebe understood vaguely that they were being taken to the Governor's house where her parents were lodging, but she hardly took it in, nor was she at all conscious of the streets through which they were passing.

She was vaguely aware of Alex starting to say something and Anna hushing him sharply. 'Not now, she needs her *madre*.' Then they arrived at the foot of some stone steps, the carriage door was opened and she was hardly out of the coach before Sara, sobbing, had run down and gathered her into a smothering embrace.

How much later it was that she found herself sitting beside her stepmother in an elegant sitting room she had no idea. Sara, still clad in deep black, was alternately dabbing her eyes with her handkerchief, kissing Hebe and clutching the hand of Sir Richard who stood beside her, beaming at the reunited pair.

Hebe took a long sip of the glass of wine someone had pressed into her hand and looked around her. Of Alex and Anna there was no sign. 'Where are A…the Major and Mrs Wilkins?'

'Major Beresford is outside, he thought you would want to be alone with us. So considerate. But who is Mrs Wilkins?'

'Mrs Anna Wilkins, the Spanish lady who helped us.' Sara was looking puzzled, so Hebe continued, hoping she would say something that fitted with whatever story Alex and Anna would tell. 'She is the widow of a sergeant who served with Major Beresford and she has connections with the Spanish partisans. After we were washed ashore she took us in: I stayed at her brother's house until we could make our way back here.'

Sara was watching her with painful intensity. 'So she was with you, chaperoning you all the time?'

'Why, yes, from the first day in Spain,' Hebe replied, crossing her fingers. 'It was such a mercy that we found ourselves in Spain where the Major has so many connections with the *guerillas*.' Provided no one realised that they had not arrived in Spain from the outset, they might brush through this.

'Thank heavens!' Sara closed her eyes in relief. 'It must have been a terrifying ordeal for you, Hebe darling. This Mrs Wilkins: she is a respectable woman? Not a…I mean, not a camp follower?'

'Goodness, no!' Hebe was, and sounded, outraged. 'A most respectable lady. I suppose, in English terms, her brother would be a yeoman farmer: the family would never have agreed to anything at all irregular. Now she keeps house for her brother, but such is her regard for Major Beresford she offered to come with us. He was obviously extremely anxious that I was properly chaperoned,' she added.

She saw Sara exchange a rapid glance with her new husband and Sir Richard nodded and strolled towards the door. 'Just leaving for a moment, dear.' The faint sound of male voices reached them through the heavy panels then faded as the men walked away. No doubt Sir Richard was having a frank man-to-man talk with Alex who, thank goodness, would be able to answer him with a perfectly clear conscience in all matters except their exact point of landing.

'And you are quite all right, Mama, other than your worry about me?' Hebe asked anxiously. 'You were so sick on the *Audacious*, and I was in terror of it having foundered in that storm.'

'Quite all right, dearest,' Sara reassured her. 'Mercifully Sir Richard kept the news of your accident from me until the worst of the weather was over and I could at least think coherently. We tried to cling to the hope that you had been washed ashore—and, of course, the knowledge that Major Beresford had gone over with you gave us some hope.'

'He was wonderful,' Hebe said warmly. She did not care if she raised suspicions that she felt deeply for him, she just wanted everyone to know that he had saved her life. 'I would have drowned at once if he had not been there.'

Sara dabbed her eyes. 'I know, dear, he is a truly admirable man and one can only be sorry that—' She broke off. 'Still, it is no good repining, I am sure Lady Clarissa is a highly suitable match for him.'

'And Maria?' Hebe asked, not wanting to discuss the excellent Lady Clarissa.

'Wretched girl!' Lady Latham said with exasperation. 'She could not help being sick, of course, but now she is declaring herself homesick and demanding to be sent back, but the minute she sees a ship she bursts into tears. Sir Richard says that she is going on the next one back to Malta if he has to tie her to the mainmast.'

Sir Richard came back into the room, looking relaxed and smiling. Hebe noted the reassuring look he sent his wife and knew that his interview with Alex had set his mind at rest.

'Where is the Major?' Sara asked. 'I am sure I did not begin to thank him properly—not that one ever can give satisfactory thanks for such courage and care.'

'Gone to report to the General, my dear. They'll keep

him busy and no mistake, with all the intelligence he will
have gleaned, walking though Spain with the *guerilla*
for days.'

'And Anna?' Hebe asked, fighting a ridiculous urge to
burst into tears. She wanted to talk to Alex, be alone with
him and now he was gone and they had never made up
that stupid quarrel. 'I would not want to neglect her, she
has been the most wonderful friend to me.'

'Indeed, yes,' Sara said, getting to her feet. 'Let us go
and find her, Hebe. Do you know if she wishes to return
home at once? Sir Richard—would we be able to help
with that?—or could she stay a little? I would so like to
show my appreciation.'

Remembering Anna's frank interest in finding herself
a handsome sergeant, Hebe was quite sure she would
enjoy staying in Gibraltar for a while and said so. 'I think
she would like to stay, Mama. She wishes to improve her
English, she tells me, although it is very good, and I do
enjoy her company.'

'Here she is!' Sara let go of Hebe's hand and held out
her own to the Spanish woman who was standing by the
window in the adjoining salon. 'Mrs Wilkins, I cannot
begin to tell you how much I appreciate what you have
done for my daughter. The relief at knowing she was in
the care of a respectable lady such as yourself was im-
mense, and our feelings of obligation at the inconve-
nience, and perhaps danger, you put yourself to in order
to escort her, are great.'

Anna took the proffered hand and dropped a very neat
curtsy. 'Thank you my lady. I am very fond of Hebe and
I have a great regard for the Major: I could do nothing
else but help.'

'We all hope you will stay with us for a few weeks,
Mrs Wilkins,' Sara continued, sweeping her towards the

door. 'Perhaps you will join us in my chamber: I was going to discuss clothes with Hebe, and put off my own blacks. We can discuss how long you can stay.'

But by the time they had reached the chamber Hebe was already swaying on her feet. Anna caught her arm and pushed her gently into a chair. 'She is exhausted, my lady. The sea, the fear, the long journey and her worries about you. Now she no longer has to be brave I think she will sleep for many hours.'

'Oh, dear, I should have thought.' Sara fluttered round. 'I will call for a maid, dearest, and we must put you to bed.'

'I will do it, my lady,' Anna said firmly. 'You too need to rest and Hebe is used to me: she does not need a strange maid at the moment. Show me her room, *por favor*, and I will look after her.'

Hebe found herself in the merciful quiet and cool of a lofty room with shutters closed against the afternoon sun and the comfort of a soft bed to fall back on. 'Not yet, *querida*.' Anna stopped her sinking down. 'You must take off those clothes and get into your nightgown. We do not want anyone else seeing those bruises, *no*?'

Thank goodness for Anna's quick wits, Hebe thought as she struggled out of her clothes and looked down at her body. The bruises, fading into green and mauve stains, were graphic on her thighs and upper arms. She touched the finger marks with tentative fingers, wincing.

'He would not have hurt you, of purpose, ever,' Anna said gently. 'It is just that he is a very strong man.'

'I know,' Hebe said, sleepily struggling into the nightgown. 'You will stay, Anna?'

'Oh, yes,' Anna agreed, pulling the covers up around

Hebe's shoulders. 'I will stay: I think you may need me,' she added, almost to herself as she watched Hebe's eyes close.

The next morning Sara bustled in, her complexion restored, her clothing once more in pretty light colours, ribbons streaming. 'How are you, my darling?' She noticed Anna and smiled. 'Mrs Wilkins, I cannot tell you what a relief it is to have you here! Are you sure you will be able to stay a while? Will your brother manage without you?'

Anna smiled back. 'Why, yes, my lady. I think my brother will do very well without me for a while. There is a certain widow in our village who would make him a very good wife, but while I am there making him comfortable he is too lazy to—oh, what is the word?—to bestir himself to make court to her.'

'Good, now you must promise me that you will say if there is anything you need.' She hesitated. 'I have no wish to offend you, but I am sure you set out without much money on you, given the nature of your journey. Would you consider acting as my daughter's companion while you are with us and accepting the salary I would pay a gentlewoman in such a position in England?'

'Why, yes, my lady, if Hebe is happy.' Anna received a glowing look of agreement and said, 'In that case, I accept for as long as Hebe needs me.'

'Excellent. Then if I were to pay you a month in advance, would that suit?' Terms agreed, Sara got up. 'Now, Hebe, you are to stay in bed. I am going out to talk to the excellent *modiste* that has been recommended to me—she made my blacks in next to no time. I will arrange for her to call here tomorrow and we will order clothes for you, and for Mrs Wilkins. And a hairdresser for you, Hebe dear. Then the day after that we will see if you are strong enough to go out shopping yourself. Now rest, dearest.'

As soon as the door closed behind her Hebe was out of bed and hugging Anna. 'Oh, thank you! Now, I am not going to stay in bed: I do not want to lie there with nothing to think about but…I mean, I do not want to brood…'

'No,' Anna agreed sympathetically. 'I am sure your mama will not mind if you sit quietly in the salon, at least you can look out of the window.'

They found a shady balcony overlooking the garden, screened from prying eyes with vine-clad trellis and with comfortable wicker chairs and footstools. Anna settled Hebe in one of the chairs and went out to fetch lemonade. No sooner had she gone than a footman came in.

'Beg pardon, Miss Carlton, but there is a gentleman below asking to see you. I said I did not think you were at home.'

'Who is it?'

'Major Beresford, miss.'

Hebe hesitated, not knowing what she wanted to do. The man added, 'But as your companion isn't here, miss…'

Contrarily Hebe made up her mind. 'Mrs Wilkins will be back in a moment. Please show the Major up.'

She lay back in the chair, schooling her features into calm. The door opened, Major Beresford was announced and then there was silence as it closed behind the footman.

'Hebe?'

'Out here, on the balcony,' she called.

Alex came out, unfamiliar in immaculate uniform. 'Good morning,' she said with a smile. 'I see you have found your baggage from the ship. Please sit down.'

There, she told herself, *that was in your best social manner. No one would guess your heart was thudding and you were having to hold on to the arms of the chair so as not to reach out for him.*

Alex dropped into the chair opposite, long legs stretched out in front of him. 'How are you, Circe?'

'I am very well thank you, but you should not call me that.'

'No, I suppose I should not,' he agreed. 'But I think I will not have another opportunity.'

'Why?' Hebe sat up sharply. 'Surely you will visit us? It would present a very odd appearance if you did not.'

'I sail for England tomorrow. I have come to say goodbye.'

How could he say it like that, as if he was saying he would be away for a day or two?

'Tomorrow?' Hebe said lightly. *I am not going to cry, I will not cry.* 'My goodness, that is fast! Surely there is much you have to report?'

'I have been keeping a log in cipher and I have been up half the night reporting.' He looked at her, unsmiling. 'There were orders awaiting me, and a ship bound for Portsmouth is in the harbour. We sail with the morning tide.'

'You must be pleased. How long is it since you were in England?' She pressed on without waiting for an answer. 'How happy your father and brother will be—and Lady Clarissa, of course.'

'Yes, it is a long time since I saw any of them,' he agreed. She could feel his eyes on her face, but she did not look at him. He was retreating behind the taciturn front he had used when she first met him. Hebe was determined she was not going to betray her feelings.

'I expect there will be an early announcement of your

wedding in the newspapers,' she said brightly, making herself look at him. A stranger would have seen nothing there, but she knew him too well. 'You seem surprised?'

'No, of course not, only there will be all the planning to do.'

'Lady Clarissa will have been planning ever since she made her decision,' Hebe said with a light laugh. 'What woman would not? Why, she and her mama will have every detail all fixed. What flowers for the church, what menu for the wedding breakfast, exactly how many of the more remote or difficult relatives to invite. You are just the husband-to-be, you will have nothing to say in the matter.'

Across the salon, the door opened and shut quietly. Anna tiptoed to a chair in the furthest corner. If she stood up and peered round the screen she could see the balcony: that was chaperonage enough, she decided.

Hebe, feeling she had established a suitably light tone to the conversation, allowed herself to look directly at Alex. It was as though she was seeing him for the first time. She had grown accustomed very rapidly to Alex's extraordinary good looks: for her that was a minor detail in how she felt about him.

Now, knowing she was losing him, knowing she was perhaps seeing him for the last time, her eyes hungrily recorded every detail. The way his hair grew at his temples, the depth of colour of his eyes, the exact curve of his ear. She remembered the incredible softness of the skin behind his ears, the tautness of the tendons of his neck under her spread fingers.

Her body recalled the strength of his as it lay against her own, the heat of him, the scent of him and she longed for his touch. He ran his hand though his hair and im-

mediately she knew how the spring of it would feel
against her own palm.

Her whole body ached for him. She closed her eyes
and could see the rangy, naked form, the patches of light
and dark where tan met protected skin, the long, strong
muscles that had kept him going despite a raging fever
past the point of exhaustion, to protect her. She could
trace in her mind the dark hair on his chest, the narrowing
trail of it going lower, lower…

Hebe's eyes snapped open and she realised that only
a few moments had passed since she had last spoken.

'You are doubtless right,' he said drily, getting to his
feet.

Right? What about? Hebe had no recollection of what
she had said and now he was going out of her life. She
had to say something, she had to touch him, kiss him one
last time.

A chair moved in the salon behind them, its legs grat-
ing on the tiled floor as its occupant shifted slightly.
was enough warning. Hebe got to her feet, holding out
her hand. 'Goodbye then, Alex. You know how I feel
about what you did for me, I can never repay that. I wish
you very happy.'

He took her hand and reached for the other, carrying
them both to his lips in an unconventional salutation.
'Goodbye, my Circe. Be careful who you enchant next
I do not think you have any idea of your own power.'

And then Alex Beresford was gone out of her life for
ever.

Chapter Sixteen

Hebe expected to find herself on a ship bound for England within a week or two, but in the end it was six weeks before she left Gibraltar.

Lady Latham had expected it would be an easy matter to find a respectable lady to entrust her stepdaughter to, but by ill chance no one she considered suitable was embarking for home. And Hebe's health and spirits were giving her cause for concern as well. Hebe, despite doing her best to look lively and interested in the diversions offered her, spent most of her time inside, growing paler and thinner.

Try as she might, she could not feel quite well: her back ached, she felt slightly light-headed and her appetite had vanished. She rebuked herself for moping, but in fact she managed quite successfully not to brood about Alex every moment of the day. It was difficult at night not to lie awake, staring open-eyed into the darkness and wondering where he was and what he was doing, but Hebe had a strong vein of common sense and even more courage, and she knew she could not fall into a decline over this. He was gone, and somehow she had the rest of her life to get on with.

Then the news came that Sir Richard had been pr[o]moted to Rear Admiral and was being posted back [to] Malta and Sara was faced with the decision of takin[g] Hebe back with her or sending her on the voyage [to] England and her aunt.

'I do not know what to do for the best, dearest,' s[he] said, looking anxiously at her stepdaughter. 'I wor[ry] about you spending another summer in all that heat whe[n] you are so pale and tired, but I cannot send you back [to] England by yourself.'

'If you will excuse me, my lady,' Anna interjecte[d]. 'Would you consider me accompanying Hebe? I wou[ld] like to go to England, if you permit it.'

'Hebe?' Sara regarded her pale face. 'Would you li[ke] that?'

'Oh, yes.' Hebe smiled gratefully. 'I would like th[at] very much.'

Somehow she had grown to dislike Gibraltar intensel[y.] She could not settle, she felt completely rootless ther[e.] And the thought of going back to Malta, where she ha[d] been so happy, felt like returning to a hollow drea[m.] England was different, England held no memories, s[he] had left there when she was very young. And somewhe[re] there, although she would never see him, was Alex.

'I do not want to leave you, Mama, only…'

'I know, dearest. You deserve your come-out and yo[ur] holiday. And I will feel happier about your health wit[h] all those good London doctors at hand.'

The voyage, once the tearful farewells had been mad[e,] was calm and uneventful, marred only by Hebe sudden[ly] becoming seasick. 'I do not understand it,' she puzzle[d] to Anna. 'I had no trouble at all before, even in th[e] dreadful storm when Maria and Mama were so poorl[y] and here I am, in the gentlest of swells, unable to stomach my breakfast.'

Anna said little, concentrating on keeping Hebe warm, making sure she got some exercise and persuading tempting morsels out of the ship's cook to coax Hebe into eating.

Despite the light winds, they made good time and within two weeks had reached Portsmouth. Sir Richard had sent a message ahead to reserve them rooms at a respectable widow's lodging house, for Hebe's aunt would not know when to expect her and they would have to spend several days in the port before arrangements could be made.

Anna inspected the accommodation with a critical eye, but expressed herself satisfied with the two bedchambers and little private parlour. Hebe, swaying somewhat and unable to get her land-legs again, was sent firmly off to bed with the promise that she should write to her aunt the next morning.

But the next day when she ventured into the parlour she found Anna sitting at the table, an almanac open before her and a serious expression on her face.

'Anna? Is something wrong?'

'I hope not, ducky.' Anna had shed almost all her Spanish phrases after several weeks of talking nothing but English and even her cockney accent was beginning to disappear. 'Come and sit down.' She bit her lip and seemed, uncharacteristically, lost for words. Eventually she said, 'How long is it since you crossed the border into Spain?'

Hebe blinked in surprise, but obediently began to work it out. 'A week, just over, before we reached Gibraltar,

then six weeks there, and two weeks at sea, and a few
days here and there. Nine weeks I suppose.'

'And your monthly courses, have they come?'

Too surprised to feel embarrassed at the question Hebe
said, 'Well, no, they have not. I suppose it is because I
had such a shock and I am not feeling well. It happened
once before when I had a bad fall from a horse, and one
month missed.'

'But two? And you feel queasy and dizzy.'

A horrible cold feeling was creeping over Hebe.
'Anna, what are you saying?'

'I think you are with child, my dear.'

'Pregnant! No, I cannot be!'

'No?' Anna said gently. 'Why should you not be?'

'No! I won't believe it!' Hebe was on her feet, pacing
the room, her hands pressed to her cheeks. 'I will not
believe it!'

'You must see a doctor, Hebe,' Anna persisted. 'And
see one soon. Better here where no one knows you than
in London.'

But all Hebe would do was shake her head and pace
repeating, 'No, I am not! I cannot be.'

Anna slipped from the room and returned after a few
minutes. She took Hebe by the shoulders and forced her
to sit down. 'Now, listen to me. If you are not with child
then you are very unwell in some way and must have
medical attention. And if you are, then we must know as
soon as possible so we can plan what to do.'

Hebe just stared at her blankly, so Anna kept talking.
'I have spoken to Mrs Green, our admirable landlady. I
tell her I have a woman's problem and I need to see a
doctor and can she recommend a nice one, because I am
shy of seeing a doctor in a strange country. And she tells
me of this Dr Adams, who looks after her sister and her

daughters who have all got children and have had problems and she says he is a very good doctor and nice and fatherly and will not make me shy.

'So, we will go and see him and you will wear my wedding ring and we will tell him your husband is a soldier on Malta and you have come home to be with your mama because the hot weather does not agree with you. But now you think you are expecting a baby and you are not feeling well and are very upset because neither your husband nor your mama are with you.'

And so Hebe allowed herself to be walked to Dr Adams's surgery that afternoon. He was, just as Mrs Green had said, a kind and fatherly man and quite understood how ill and frightened young Mrs Smith was feeling. Yes, she was indeed two months pregnant, and she must not cry any more because soon she would feel much better and would be with her own mama. And in the meantime she must rest and eat—even if she did not feel like it—for the sake of the baby.

When they returned to their little parlour Hebe said virtually the first thing she had uttered since they had left the consulting rooms. 'Anna, what should I be eating?'

'You are hungry?' Anna said with relief. 'You do not feel so sick?'

'No, I do feel sick and I am not hungry. But the doctor said I must eat for the baby, so I will.' She stared out of the window as if seeing something beyond the roof tops and the circling gulls and the grey clouds.

Anna bit her lip and went down to order their dinner, much to the relief of Mrs Green, who had been getting anxious that the poor young lady was so pale and had so little appetite.

Hebe doggedly ate her way through a chicken wing, some vegetables, a slice of bread and butter and a glass of milk with the air of someone who had to finish a hard, but essential task. She put down her knife and fork on her empty plate and smiled at her companion. 'Thank you very much, Anna. I am sorry I have been so…foolish. You have been so kind, I do not know what I would do without you. You have been fearing this from the start, have you not?'

Anna, who was feeling quite sick herself with mingled anxiety and relief that at least Hebe was at last talking rationally and eating, managed to smile back. 'It is a common consequence of lying with a man, my dear. I could not help but worry.'

'And that is why you came with me? Oh, Anna, I am so sorry. I have dragged you hundreds of miles from home.'

'But not at all! I wanted to come to England. I told you, I want to find another handsome English husband like my 'arry.'

Hebe smiled weakly at her. 'Harry, not 'arry! All your other "aitches" are perfect now.'

'He called himself 'arry, so I do too,' Anna said. She suddenly wiped a tear from the corner of her eye. 'Now you go to bed, Hebe. You must sleep for this baby as well as eat.'

Hebe took herself off to bed as she was told, but instead of sleeping she sat up against the pillows and forced herself to think. It was as though she had been frozen in a block of ice since Alex had gone and the shock of this discovery had shattered the icy cage open. Now every bit of her was melting into awareness again: slowly, painfully.

'I am carrying Alex's child,' she whispered into the

gathering gloom. 'And he is probably married by now. Even if he is not, he does not love me, and soon will be married. So I am going to have to have this baby by myself.'

She thought for a while, trying to come to terms with it. She did not *feel* pregnant—however that was supposed to feel. The idea of a child as an individual did not yet seem real, although the idea of Alex's child as something she was responsible for, something she must cherish for his sake, did.

What to do? Tell her aunt? Impossible. Hebe lay there, wondering why she did not feel more frightened. Shock, perhaps: well, she must take advantage of it and plan while she could.

Anna found her at the table early the next morning, fully dressed and with a sheet of writing paper before her. 'Hebe? Did you sleep?'

'Not much,' Hebe answered honestly. 'I have been thinking—planning what to do. I have written to Mama.'

'To tell her?' Anna hesitated. 'Wait one minute before you tell me, I will ask Mrs Green to send up breakfast.'

As she came back Hebe was signing her name. 'No, I have said nothing to her, but I have to write or she will be worrying that I have not arrived safely.'

She pushed the letter across the table to Anna, who pushed it back. 'I cannot read English as well as I speak it.'

'Dearest Mama,' Hebe read, *'We both arrived safe at Portsmouth the day before yesterday after an uneventful voyage and found Mrs Green's lodgings to be both comfortable and entirely suitable for ladies travelling alone. I was somewhat tired, so I hope you will forgive my not writing immediately we landed, but I am glad to tell you*

that I find I am now eating much better than I have for some time. I am about to write to my Aunt Fulgrave, and I believe the best course will be for us to hire a chaise and make the journey to London ourselves, rather than wait until my uncle is able to come and collect us. I will write at length as soon as I reach London. Mrs Wilkins begs to be remembered to you, and please convey my respectful affection to Sir Richard. I remain, trusting you are both in the best of health, your dutiful and loving daughter, Hebe.'

Dutiful. She wished she was certain exactly where her duty lay. But one thing was clear, her first, her only, concern now was for the baby. She was becoming reconciled to the idea that she was carrying a child, but she simply could not *feel* pregnant. Sick, tired and frightened, yes. But not a mother to be. Doubtless that would come.

'A chaise?' Anna queried. 'Will that not be expensive?'

'Sir Richard gave me money against that contingency. He was not sure whether, when we arrived, we would want to wait for my uncle, or travel on. He said we should not pay more than two shillings and six pence per mile for a chaise and pair. I think it is about seventy miles—if we were to go direct.'

'*If?* Hebe, what are you planning—?' Anna broke off as Mrs Green tapped on the parlour door and entered with a laden tray.

'Here you are, Mrs Wilkins. A nice big breakfast to tempt Miss Carlton.' She whipped the cover off a platter of bacon and kidneys. Anna, with one glance at Hebe's face, took the cover and replaced it firmly.

'Thank you, Mrs Green. How delicious, we must not let it get cold.'

The landlady was turning to leave when Hebe said, 'Do you have a *Peerage* in the house, Mrs Green?'

'Why, no, miss, but there's a very good circulating library down along Bath Street.'

'And do they have the London newspapers?'

'Oh, yes, miss, all of those, and they keep them for months, miss, because of the naval gentlemen wanting to catch up on all the news when they come into port.'

'Excellent. Thank you, Mrs Green.' Hebe waited until the door was closed, then said, 'I need to find where Alex's family seat is: there is a fair chance he will be there, having been away so long and with the wedding to prepare for. And I must discover whether or not the wedding has taken place.' She eyed the covered platters uneasily. 'I think I will just have some toast and a cup of tea.'

Anna lifted the teapot and began to pour. 'Hebe, what are you planning?'

'I know what I must do, I think, although there are some details I cannot yet see clearly. But how I must do it will depend on where Alex is and whether or not he is married yet.' She picked up the butter knife, thought better of it, and began to cut dry toast into pieces. 'Do not look so worried, Anna. I am not going to do anything foolish, and I know I must be very discreet.'

The ladies found Hodgkin's Circulating Library without any trouble, and the proprietor was only too happy, on receipt of a day's subscription, to settle them in a comfortable corner with a table, the *Peerage* and the past two months' issues of *The Times*.

The Beresfords' family seat was quickly found. 'Oh, thank goodness,' Hebe exclaimed. 'It is in Hertfordshire: see Anna, Tasborough Hall near Tring. I will ask to see an atlas in a moment, but I should imagine that will not be too great a detour on our way to London. Now, let us work backwards through *The Times*, looking at the announcements for a wedding notice. I should imagine the betrothal notice was placed before Alex returned to England.'

They worked their way steadily backwards, their fingers becoming grimy with newsprint. 'Surely the wedding cannot have taken place so soon after Alex's return to England,' Hebe puzzled, after they had scanned a full month. 'Oh, well, it is better if it has not, for I would want to avoid Lady Clarissa if at all possible. Look, we are back to a date before Alex could possibly have landed.'

Anna, who had taken the week earlier than the pile Hebe was scanning, broke off with a gasp. 'Hebe, look here in the Deaths! It is the Major's father, is it not?'

Hebe snatched the paper and spread it out on the table between them. '*George Beresford, third Earl of Tasborough, as a result of a carriage accident, at his seat, Tasborough Hall, Hertfordshire…succeeded by his son, William, Viscount Broadwood*. Oh, my goodness! No wonder the marriage notices have not appeared: the family will be in deep mourning. Why, it must have happened just before Alex arrived in Portsmouth. How dreadful, to return home to such a tragedy!'

They sat, staring at each other, too stunned by the news to speak. Then Hebe said, 'Much as I hate to intrude on him at such a time, I cannot afford to wait. It is, after all, four weeks since the accident: the family will be receiving calls again. Mr Hodgkin!' The proprietor hastened over, hoping that these well-dressed ladies who were making such good use of his facilities might be tempted to take out a longer subscription. 'Do you have an atlas

I could consult? I need to plan a journey to London, by way of an estate in Hertfordshire.'

A gazetteer was speedily placed before her, Mr Hodgkin helpfully opening it at the correct page. 'Thank you,' Hebe said. 'Could you recommend a reliable livery stable? I wish to hire a chaise and pair and, as you may imagine, with two ladies travelling alone, the assurance of a reliable postilion is most important.'

Mr Hodgkin, while disappointed that these ladies seemed bent on leaving Portsmouth, was hopeful that they would recommend him to their friends and did his utmost to be helpful. 'Certainly ma'am. I would suggest Porter's Livery Stables, which is not too far. When you are ready to leave I will send the lad with you to show you the way, if you wish. A long-established and most reliable outfit: I assure you I would have no qualms about entrusting my mother or my wife to their care.'

The livery stable proved as respectable as Mr Hodgkin had promised. Hebe and Anna emerged from the office with a carriage bespoken for the next day, with a pair and one postilion. After careful consideration of Hebe's need to visit old friends near Tring and then continue to London, while not tiring herself, as Anna interjected firmly at this point, the owner suggested easy stages to Guildford. There they might stay at any one of a number of highly respectable inns that Mr Porter himself could recommend, then travel on to Berkhamsted. 'The King's Arms, ma'am, is the place to stay, although I would not despise the Crown if the King's Arms cannot accommodate you. The next morning you would be able to make a morning call and still be in London that evening by a good road.'

Calculations were made and Hebe handed over what

seemed to Anna a large amount of money. 'And for that we get one man?' she protested as they walked back slowly to Mrs Green's lodgings. 'No armed outriders?'

'Anna, this is England, not the wilds of Spain with French troops around every corner,' Hebe teased her gently. 'Now, I think I will write to my aunt and warn her that I will be arriving in three days' time.'

Three days, she thought as they climbed the stairs to their rooms. *Three days, and by then I must have planned everything.* There were so many gaps in the scheme she had worked out through the long night. And if Alex was not at Tasborough Hall, what would she do?

Chapter Seventeen

Three days later the chaise turned out of the King's Arms in Berkhamsted and drove briskly west. The postilion had proved excellent and at every stage had secured strong, steady horses so that the journey, although tiring, was not exhausting. Now, obedient to Hebe's instructions, and after consulting the grooms at the inn, he was setting out for Tasborough Hall to arrive at eleven o'clock.

'But what are you going to say to him—if he is there?' Anna queried. She had asked over and over again, but all Hebe would do was shake her head and reply, 'I am still working it out.'

That was nothing less than the truth. There were still the gaping holes in her plan that she could not quite solve, but with every turn of the carriage wheel she was getting closer to the problem of how to break the news to a man that he was going to be a father, and in such circumstances.

In many ways Hebe felt better in herself. She was eating, although it was an effort, and she no longer felt so dizzy and weak. But her back ached and the cold, nagging fear at the enormity of what was happening lurked like a beast in the recesses of her mind, ready to spring out whenever she let her guard drop. And she would soon see Alex: she could not let herself dwell on that, on how she would feel, on how she must control the urge to throw herself into his arms and pour out the story.

Instead she must keep calm, rehearse what she had to say so that it was rational, sensible and he would see the inevitable good sense of what she proposed.

The chaise turned off the pike road and began to follow a winding road across gently rising fields. Then, abruptly, after a sharp turn, it became steeper, shadowed by huge beech trees on either side. Anna peered out of the window. 'Mountains?'

'No, just the Chiltern Hills. I think we must be there.' The carriage swung between a pair of lodge houses built of grey stone with split-flint panels and into a driveway that led, at last, into an open space before a rambling mansion. Hebe peered through the window at the building, which appeared to have grown over centuries, added to in the style of the day as each succeeding generation saw fit. A heavily panelled front door, heavily draped in black crepe, was set in the centre of what appeared to be the Jacobean heart of the building.

As she waited for the postilion to dismount, the door opened and a footman hurried over, let down the carriage steps and opened the door. When he saw the occupants, he stared in surprise before recollecting himself. 'I beg your pardon, ma'am, I was expecting Lawyer Stone.'

'Is Major Beresford at home?' Hebe asked. 'I realise this is a very difficult time...'

'The Major.' The man stared at her blankly and for a moment Hebe wondered if they had come to the wrong house. 'Er...yes, ma'am. Well, that is, he is here, ma'am, but I do not know if he is receiving visitors now.'

'I do appreciate that. However, I have a very urgent essage from Spain—I hope I do not have to say more? uld you tell the Major that I come from Rear Admiral r Richard Latham.'

'Oh, yes, ma'am. Of course. Would you care to come side?' The footman helped them down and directed the stilion round to the stables. 'This way, ladies.'

A very superior butler was crossing the hall as they tered, a harassed frown on his face. His expression be- me professionally blank the moment he saw the visi- s. 'Good morning, ladies. May I be of assistance?'

The footman went and whispered in his ear and the tler's face became, if anything, blanker. 'If you would re to step into the Panelled Salon, ladies, I will inform Major. That is—' he broke off suddenly and threw en a door. 'I think you will be comfortable here, ladies. hat name shall I say?'

'Miss…Circe, and companion,' Hebe said.

'Miss Sersay, very well, ma'am.'

The wait, although it was probably no more than ten nutes, seemed endless. Hebe thought she had never en in a more silent house. Only the ticking of the clock the mantle broke the smothering quiet.

He was here, and in a moment she would see him. As e thought it, the door opened and Alex walked in. He s dressed from head to toe in black, relieved only by e white of his shirt. Even his neckcloth was black. His ce was paler than Hebe had ever seen it, for not only d the tan begun to fade, but he appeared to have no lour left under his skin at all.

'Hebe!' His eyes blazed blue at the sight of her. 'What earth? What is wrong? You look so—'

'I will wait outside,' Anna said, although neither of the

others appeared to notice she had spoken. She slip
out and went to sit in the hall.

'Hebe?' Alex took one long stride towards her
halted as Hebe put up both hands as though to ward
off. 'Please, sit down here.' He pulled forward one of
brocade chairs that flanked the empty fire. 'Wha
wrong? Starling said you had a message from
Richard.'

'No, I told him I had *come from* Sir Richard, whic
true. Alex, I am so very sorry to hear about your fathe
what a tragic homecoming for you.'

'Thank you. It has been a…difficult few weeks.
why are you here, and looking so thin and tired? Did
have a very bad voyage from Gibraltar?'

'No.' Hebe bit her lip, twisting her hands tightly in
lap. Now she was here, with him, all her carefully
hearsed phrases vanished from her head. 'Alex, ple
will you not sit down? I cannot order my thoughts v
you standing over me.'

'Of course.' He dropped into the chair opposite
leaned forward, his forearms on his thighs, hands loo:
clasped in front of him. 'What am I thinking of? Wo
you like some refreshment?'

'No!' Hebe took a deep breath and said more caln
'No, thank you. Alex, I do not think there is any e
way to tell you what I have come to say. I hope you
forgive me for intruding now, of all times, but I da
not write in case the letter fell into other hands, ai
dared not leave it for any longer to see you, or app
ances might cause talk. I checked the newspapers
saw there had been no mention of your marriage, s
thought I had every chance of avoiding seeing L
Clarissa as well.'

He broke in, 'Clarissa and I…'

'No, please let me finish what I have to say. This is hard enough as it is.' She raised her gaze and looked deep into his troubled, shadowed blue eyes. 'Alex, you remember the shepherd's hut on the border?'

'Yes, of course. How could I forget it?' There was a small vertical frown line between his brows. Obviously, whatever else he had been expecting her to talk about, it was not this.

'You were very ill, delirious.'

'Yes.'

'Do you recall when you woke? When the fever had broken, the morning when the French troops left?'

'Very clearly! I hope I never again have to live through another moment like the one when you told me you had been trapped like that.'

Hebe knew she was about to plunge him into even greater anxiety, but doggedly she talked on. It felt as though the words were being strangled in her throat.

'When you woke, you were suddenly embarrassed because you had been dreaming, and you could remember your dream very clearly.'

That did bring the colour back into his face, and she could tell it was an effort for him to keep his eyes steady on her. All he said was, 'Yes, I recall.'

'That was not a dream,' Hebe said quietly. 'That was the recollection of what had happened while you were delirious.'

'What?' The word came out as a whisper. Hebe dropped her gaze from his appalled expression.

'You remembered having…making love to me, did you not?'

'Yes. But Hebe…surely not? Surely it was as you said, a dream? You joked about it.'

'Do you think I wanted to discuss it?'

He reached out for her hands and Hebe, knowing if h[
touched her she would fall into his arms, recoiled sharpl[
back into the chair. He was Clarissa's, he must neve[
suspect how she felt about him, never be allowed [
throw away the true direction of his life for this.

'My God!' Alex flung himself out of the chair and too[
two jerky strides away from her to stand, one hand res[
ing on the wing of his chair, his back turned to her. '[
happened that night? While the French were there?'

'Yes. That was why I could do nothing. I could n[
struggle, I could not cry out and try to rouse you, or the[
would have found us.'

There was a long silence, then he said, 'So you had [
lie there, while I… Hebe, how could you bear it?'

'Better you than fifteen Frenchmen,' Hebe said, wit[
out realising the effect her words would have.

Alex spun round, his face white and sick. 'Yes, as y[
say, better to be raped by one man than fifteen.'

'It was not rape,' she tried to say. 'You did [
know…' But he was not listening to her.

'I must have hurt you.' She stared into her lap. 'Heb[
Reluctantly she nodded.

'And the next morning you get up and you wash a[
you dress, and you look after the weak, useless, sick m[
who has just ravished you, and you walk over that da[
mountain to nothing but strangers and more danger [
you never let me suspect a thing. I said I thought y[
had courage Hebe, I never knew until now how muc[

'You were not useless,' she said hotly. 'I would [
dead if it were not for you. And how could I tell yo[

'I would have married you the moment we reac[
Gibraltar, Hebe, you know that.'

'Yes, and jilted Lady Clarissa? Caused a scan[
Forced me into a loveless marriage?'

She looked up and saw him staring at her, his handsome face frozen into an expressionless mask. What was going on behind those blue eyes?

'And when you did find a man who proposed a love match to you—always supposing, after what I had done, you could bring yourself to contemplate marriage—what would you do then?' He sounded as though he was interrogating a prisoner. If Hebe had not known him so well, loved him so deeply, she would have been frightened of him. As it was, she could hear the pain behind the harsh words.

'I realised I could never marry,' she said calmly. 'I will not marry without love. I could not deceive a man whom I did love, and I cannot expect any man to accept with complaisance such a history.'

He took another few steps across the room, then turned and looked at her. Through the unshed tears that clouded her eyes he was an indistinct figure silhouetted against the window. 'Anna is with you. She knows, I presume? When did you tell her?'

'I did not need to,' Hebe said simply. 'She saw...'

'She saw the bruises I had left on your body, I suppose.' Hebe could not bear the self-loathing in his voice. The tears gathered and began to roll slowly down her cheeks. 'Of course, that explains her strict chaperonage—and the way you withdrew from me as soon as you had reached safety with her. Very wise: you never know when a man who acts as I did might not turn on you again.'

'Alex, stop it! I never feared that.'

'You forgive me, then? Is that what you are saying?'

'No! There is nothing to forgive. You were not responsible for your actions that night.'

'I am not weak-minded. I am, and should be, responsible for my actions, all of them. If I had not thought about you in that way—yes, I admit it, I desired you— if I had not allowed myself to think like that, then this would not have happened when my guard was down. As you have so accurately pointed out, I was an engaged man, I had no business being attracted to you.' Alex stalked back to the chair and threw himself into it, then saw the tears pouring helplessly down her cheeks. 'Oh, Hebe, Hebe dearest, don't…'

He was on his knees in front of her, holding out a handkerchief, reaching for her. Hebe took the linen square, but pushed him away with her other hand. 'No, Alex…'

He recoiled as though she had slapped him. 'Of course I am sorry. How insensitive of me. I promise I will not touch you again.'

Hebe buried her face in the soft cloth, trying not to let the lovingly remembered scent of citrus and sandalwood overturn her completely. She managed to dry the tears and looked up. Alex was watching her, his lips tight, his hands clasped in front of him. 'Hebe, why have you told me now?'

'Because…because…' The words just would not come. Hebe raised her head, took a deep breath and said steadily, 'Because I am pregnant.'

She saw him absorb the shock. The only outward sign of the blow her words must have delivered was the way in which he leaned back in the chair, let his head rest against the deep crimson fabric, and closed his eyes.

After a moment he opened them again. 'You are certain?' She nodded. 'It must be what…two months?'

'Yes.' Now the worst was said, Hebe found she was recovering a little strength. If only that nagging ache in her back would stop, it was exhausting. 'You see why had to come and see you? If I wrote and the letter fell into other hands, it would be disastrous. And I could hardly call when the pregnancy had begun to show—what a stir that would cause.'

'Yes. Thank goodness you have come, and that I was here.' Alex sat up straight, some of the colour back in his face again. 'Now, what we must...'

'Alex, please let me finish. I cannot say what I came to, if you keep interrupting me.'

'But there is little choice in the matter.'

'There is a choice. I have been thinking, and this is what I intend to do.' Hebe straightened her aching back and said with determination, 'I will go into the country, somewhere I am not known. A small town, perhaps. I will wear black and a wedding ring and take a modest house and let it be put about that I am newly widowed. I will say that my husband was killed at sea, in the navy. I can speak of that with enough knowledge to convince anyone. When the baby is born, I will bring it up there.

'But,' she persisted as he opened his mouth to speak, 'I need your help. I would never ask this for myself, but I find I am quite unscrupulous when it comes to this baby. It is extraordinary how that changes everything. I am not thinking twice about asking you for money, or about deceiving my family. I have little money of my own: enough, I suppose, to just manage on. But that will not do now. This child is going to grow up in modest, respectable comfort. If it is a boy, then he will need an education, and a start in a career. If it is a girl, then she will need a marriage portion.'

'Hebe...'

'I need you to find me that house and to make the child an allowance. That is all I ask.'

Alex looked at her over his clasped hands. 'And your aunt and uncle? Your mother and Sir Richard?'

'That is the problem,' Hebe admitted, relieved that he appeared to have accepted her proposal. 'I will have to slip away from London very soon. Perhaps I will leave a note saying I cannot face Society and have decided to go and live in the country.'

'They will have the Bow Street Runners after you.'

'If I hide well enough, they will not find me. And as for Mama and Sir Richard...I do not know, but they are a long way away, so I have time to think.'

'They are as far away as the mails to Malta,' Alex said drily, then broke off at the sound of a discreet tap on the door. He shot Hebe a piercing glance, saw that the tears had dried on her cheeks and her chair was turned from the entrance, and called, 'Yes?'

Hebe heard the door open and there was a slight cough. 'Mrs Wilkins thought perhaps Miss Sersay would like some refreshments, my lord. I have taken the library of bringing tea and some biscuits, which I understand would be acceptable.'

'Thank you, Starling. Please put them on that table.'

The butler left, but Hebe was staring at Alex. 'My lord?'

He turned from pouring her a cup of tea. 'Both my brother and my father were in the curricle when it overturned. My father, we believe, had a heart attack when handling the reins. He was killed instantly. William, my brother, was thrown clear, but hit his head. At first it did not seem too bad, and he has been up and about, although shaky. Then last week he began to have severe headaches and fell into a coma. The doctors say it must have been an effusion of blood on the brain. There was nothing the could do: he died yesterday without regaining consciousness.'

'And I walk in here with this news.' Hebe pressed her fingertips to her lips, which were trembling. 'Oh Alex, I am so sorry! To have lost your father was tragedy enough, but your brother as well, and in such a way, when you must have had every hope of his recovery. I am so very, very sorry. I must go, I cannot stay here talking to you, you must have so much to do, so much to reflect upon…'

'There is nothing I can do for my brother now,' Alex said harshly. 'At least I was with him at the end. We were never close—he was five years my senior—but we had time to talk, these past weeks after the accident. I am glad we had that. But my man of business is here, the lawyer is expected. There is nothing else I can do at the moment. And, as you have discovered, this baby changes priorities.'

'You will do as I suggest, then? Perhaps there is a London agent you can recommend to me who will find me a house? I thought Suffolk perhaps, or Norfolk. I know no one there and we have no relatives at all in that part of the world. I do not know how much money I will need: I have not had the chance to think about it yet, and I am so out of touch with what things cost here.'

'No, Hebe.'

'No? You would prefer to deal with the agent yourself? Oh, yes, and I must find the direction of the bank where my trust fund is situated and make arrangements for that to be paid. There is so much to think about.'

'I mean, no, Hebe, I will not agree to this insane plan.'

Hebe put down the cup of tea he had just handed her. The fragile bone china chattered in the saucer. 'You will not help me, then?' She had never dreamed he would reject her like this. How would she manage?

'Very well.' She got to her feet, amazed to find her voice was steady. She turned and took a step towards the door, then swung round to face him. 'I was not asking you to love this child, my lord, just to provide a little for it. If you will not help me, then I will manage as best I can.'

The inimitable, handsome face stared into her own white one and the room began to spin.

Chapter Eighteen

'Hebe!' She blinked and found herself being lowered gently into the chair again. Alex picked up the cup and pressed it to her lips. 'Try and drink a little. Hebe, listen to me, I am not going to abandon you and the baby, it will be all right. Just rest a little, I will call Anna.'

Hebe took a sip, then shook her head. 'No, no, I do not need her. What do you mean? You said you would not agree to my plan.'

'It is madness, Hebe. Did you really think I would abandon you like that, baby or no?'

'But Lady Clarissa…'

'Lady Clarissa Duncan is now Lady Westport.'

'What?' Hebe stared at his face, but there was absolutely nothing there to read other than the pain in his eyes. 'But she wrote to you—I was there when you read the letter.'

'Yes. I now find, from talking to my brother, that she never had any intention of taking my proposal seriously. I would never have heard another word after we parted, only she burned her fingers very badly when she thought she could ensnare the heir to a dukedom—never mind which one—and she appears to have written to accept me on the rebound.

'A younger son of an earl, with no fortune and only his army career to support him was not, it appears, a very appealing prospect when she had time to think about it. As far as I can tell, she told no one that she had accepted me in whatever fit of pique it was, and a little while later, at about the time I was reading her letter in your garden, she snared herself her lord. Her letter informing me of this arrived here a few days after my return. Presumably she heard I was back and decided it might be kind to let me know I was no longer betrothed to her.' He smiled wryly, with absolutely no humour. 'It is amusing, is it not? If she had only waited, she would have found herself a countess.'

'Alex, I do not know what to say.' Hebe tried to contemplate the blows that were falling on Alex's broad back and quailed at the thought. His brother and father dead; a great title and estate, suddenly his responsibility; the woman he loved revealed as a heartless, status-seeking flirt, and now she had arrived to inform him he was about to be the father of an illegitimate baby.

'There is nothing to say. We can only be thankful that one complication is removed from this situation. I suggest that you continue to London, as soon as you feel up to it, and I will visit your aunt and uncle in perhaps a week and ask for your hand.'

'My hand?' Hebe knew she was staring stupidly, but his words made no sense.

'In marriage. Hebe, you did not seriously think I would let you go off and bring up this child alone, did you?'

'If you had been married…'

'That, I admit, would have made it more difficult, but whatever the consequences, I would have acknowledged it, made sure you were all right and were not cut off from your family. Now there is no reason why you cannot marry me.'

After weeks of feeling queasy Hebe wondered if now she really was going to be ill. She took another sip of tea. 'I cannot marry you, I told you…'

'You told me you would not tolerate a loveless marriage. Yes, I heard that message clearly enough. But are you so fixed on that resolve that you would bastardise your child? Our child? You told me it changed everything. Are you telling me that you would beg money from me, deceive your family, spend your entire life living a lie, but you will not do the one thing that will ensure that child a future? If it is a boy, he will be the heir to an earldom. If it is a girl, she may marry where she will, have every comfort.'

Hebe watched the tall figure pacing up and down the room as though he suddenly had more energy than could be contained in the space. 'I…if you put it like that… But…' Marry Alex. She was going to marry Alex and have his child. She would have everything in the world she desired, except the thing she had wanted almost from the moment she had begun to know him: his love.

'But,' he echoed. 'But. There is no need to worry, Hebe. I give you my word, I will not lay a finger on you. I will not touch even your hand without your permission. I will never put a foot over the threshold of your bedchamber.'

She had no trouble believing him. She had just heard the bitter words of a man who had discovered how shallow and fickle the woman he had loved was. He was not going to give any part of himself as hostage to another. She could imagine it would disgust him to be reminded of the appalling revelation she had just forced him to listen to. He was not going to forgive himself for what had happened with her, nor, she was certain, was he going to trust his heart to another woman again.

But there was the baby to think of. And he was correct. What right had either of them to consider themselves first? 'Yes, Alex, I will marry you.'

'Thank you. Believe me, I will do everything in my power to ensure you never have cause to regret it.' She looked at him and managed a small smile, not realising how pale and fragile she looked at that moment. 'Circe... No, I must stop calling you that. Hebe, I think I had better have a quiet word with Starling and come up with some explanation as to why his future mistress is visiting here under an assumed name. I do not think you had better spend the night here, but the Dower House, where my aunt Gertrude lives, is only half a mile away.'

'My aunt and uncle are expecting me in London by this evening. They will worry if I do not come. Perhaps if I could just wash my hands and face?'

'Are you certain?' He made as if to take her hand, then remembered and dropped his own. 'I will call the house keeper, Mrs Fitton, to take Anna and you to one of the bedchambers. Ask her for whatever you need.'

Anna was talking to a pleasant-looking woman in the hall. They both looked up as Hebe emerged, followed by Alex. 'Mrs Fitton, please take these ladies to the best guest room and ensure they have everything they need to refresh themselves.' He broke off as the sound of a carriage on the driveway sent the footman to the front door.

'Lawyer Stone, my lord, just arriving, and it looks as though Parson is with him again.'

'Please, you must attend to them,' Hebe said, holding out her hand. After a moment's hesitation Alex took it. 'I am sure Mrs Fitton will look after us wonderfully, and then we must be on our way. I will tell Aunt and Uncle that you will be calling in a week or two: oh, I must give you their direction.' She took a card from her reticule and scribbled on it. 'There. Mr and Mrs Fulgrave, Charles Street. Goodbye my lord, and my apologies again for intruding upon you at such a time.'

Hebe and Anna followed the housekeeper upstairs and into a pleasant bedchamber. The woman tugged the bell-pull. 'I will just get hot water sent up, ma'am. Is there anything else I can get for you?'

'Thank you, no, Mrs Fitton. I am sorry we were forced to intrude upon the earl at such a sad time, but I am afraid I had no choice, I had a very important message. What a terrible blow, so soon after the death of his father.'

'That it is, ma'am.' The housekeeper folded her lips tightly, then suddenly burst out, as though she had been bottling it up and could bear it no longer. 'Two deaths and then that heartless madam! I do not know how poor Mr Alex—his lordship, I should say—I don't know how he keeps such a pleasant way with him. Most men would be impossible, but, no, he looks severe, but otherwise he's as kind a gentleman as ever was. Not a cross word, ever.'

'You know about Lady Clarissa, then?' Hebe ventured, earning a scandalised look from Anna.

'Well, not at first, ma'am, but I was in the room when that letter came. He didn't know I was there, I was bringing in the fruit bowl, quiet like, and he had his back to me.' The housekeeper broke off as a maid came in with a pitcher of water and some towels, then resumed as the door closed. 'He opened it up, and I thought there'd been another death, I did really. He said "Clarissa!" all choked like, then he screwed up the note in his hand and said, "My love, oh, my love", just like that.'

She began to smooth out Hebe's pelisse which was lying on the bed. 'Broken-hearted, that's what, poor gentleman. Of course, we didn't know what had happened at first, but, well, we heard bits here and there.' She gave Hebe a sharp look. 'I'm not one to gossip, ma'am, but we all love the Major—his lordship—and we care about him. And I can tell you are a friend of his. So I just tell you, so's you know. Hope I haven't spoken out of turn, ma'am.'

'No, of course not, Mrs Fitton. You are quite right, as his friends, we all want to help him.'

Back in the chaise and heading for London, Anna burst out, 'Hebe, what has happened? If you do not tell me, I will go mad!'

Hebe realised she had been sitting in silence since they had got into the carriage. 'I am sorry, Anna. Well, Alex is determined to marry me, and now that Lady Clarissa has jilted him, he can.'

'Oh, thank the good Lord and all the saints!' Anna broke into Spanish until she could collect herself. 'Oh, Hebe, *querida*, what a relief! You do not look very happy.'

'How do you think Alex took the news of what had happened—how it had happened?' Hebe asked bitterly. 'And I have to tell him on top of that dreadful family tragedy, and, to crown it all, he finds himself feeling obliged to marry me immediately after the woman he loves has jilted him.'

They fell into a depressed silence. After a few miles Anna ventured, 'But this is better for the baby.'

This received no more than an abstracted nod. After they had passed through Berkhamsted, she tried again. 'Your mama and Sir Richard will be very pleased.'

'Yes, an Earl. Who would have thought it.' Hebe smiled ruefully. 'That was unfair: they are genuinely fond of Alex, I know they will be happy for me.'

The chaise was making good time and had passed though Watford when Hebe gave a little gasp. 'Hebe?' Anna sat up sharply from the light doze she had fallen into. 'What is wrong?'

'My back has been aching all day, but suddenly, a pain.' She put a hand to the small of her back and then gasped again as a cramp lanced though her stomach. 'Oh, Anna, it hurts!'

Anna took one look at her white face and dropped open the window to lean out. 'You! Postilion! Stop!' The man reined in and twisted round in the saddle. 'Quickly, the lady has been taken ill. Drive to the first respectable inn you come to!'

The man whipped the horses up and Anna sat next to Hebe. She touched her forehead, which was clammy with sweat. Through the pain Hebe heard her say, 'Put on my ring, and remember you are Mrs Sersay. Yes?' The warm metal band was slipped on to her finger, then Hebe's hands clenched again.

'Anna, what is it? Is it the baby?'

'I am afraid so, *querida*. Try to hold on to my hand, we will soon be at an inn and we will get a doctor.'

The next half-hour passed in a haze. Hebe was aware of being helped from the chaise and into a house. Strong arms scooped her up and she was being carried and placed on a bed. A strange voice said, 'Put her down here, Joe, gentle now, then go and get Dr Griffin, and hurry.' There was more pain, Anna's voice and that of the strange woman, both kind, both trying to hide fear.

Then a man's voice, elderly, firm, reassuringly confident. 'Give me some room, now. How far pregnant did you say, ma'am? Two months, hmm.'

At some point she must have fallen asleep, for Hebe woke to morning light in a strange bed. She felt as weak as a kitten, but the pain had gone. 'Anna?'

'Here I am, ducky.'

'The baby…'

'I am sorry, my love. The doctor said there was nothing to be done. Sometimes it just happens, as though was never meant to be.'

Never meant to be. My baby. Alex's baby, never meant to be…

'I would have done anything to protect it.'

'I know.' Anna had her in her arms and was gently rocking to and fro.

'But I never felt it was real. Does that make sense?'

'No,' the older woman said, 'but that doesn't matter'

'When can I travel? Aunt and Uncle will be worried'

'Tomorrow, the doctor says, if you rest today. He will come back this afternoon.'

'I will write to them. We are still on the main road are we not? It should catch the mail.'

Anna went for writing paper and a quill and Hebe wrote a brief note explaining that she had been taken sick on the road with an illness she had been suffering from since Gibraltar, but hoped to be with them the next evening. That went off with reassurances that it would be in town by the afternoon and Hebe tried to compose a letter to Alex.

This was far harder. She had to tell him that the need to marry her was gone, but in such a way that if it were read by anyone else it would give no clue as to what was talking about. She hated to break the news in such a way. Surely he would be sad to hear what had happened, even if it spared him the painful necessity of an unwelcome marriage?

After much thought she wrote: *My lord, I feel I must write at the earliest opportunity to thank you for your hospitality when I called yesterday. Your patience and kindness to me at a moment of the deepest grief for your family is not something I will ever forget. Nor will I forget the efforts you made to assist me with the problem that I discussed with you. I regret to tell you that I have been taken ill upon my journey. Although the doctor assures me I may travel tomorrow, the nature of my illness is such that I find all my previous plans have come to nothing and I believe I will spend some time quietly in London with my aunt and uncle and not undertake the journey against which you so strongly advised me. Please accept my sincere condolences upon your sad loss, and for all the other distressing instances that have marked your return home to England. I remain, as ever, your friend, Hebe Carlton.*

Surely he would understand her meaning. Hebe folded the letter and wrote the direction. When Anna came back she gave it to her to seal. 'Please see this is sent to Tasborough Hall, Anna. And that it is put into Alex's hands only.'

The doctor came later that day and expressed himself satisfied with Mrs Sersay's progress. He spoke to her plainly but gently, assuring her it was no fault of hers and that there was no reason at all why she should not bear many healthy children in the future. But not Alex's children, Hebe thought sadly. Nor anyone else's.

* * *

The journey to London was accomplished safely and slowly, and it was with relief that Hebe found herself outside the smart townhouse in Charles Street. Her Aunt Emily, her late mother's younger sister, came running down the steps, cap ribbons flying, as pretty and impetuous as Hebe remembered her from so many years ago.

After one look at Hebe, she summoned a sturdy footman and ordered her niece carried inside and up to her bedchamber immediately. 'Take care, Peter, do! Oh, good day, ma'am, you must be Mrs Wilkins, Hebe's companion? Welcome… Through here, Peter, put Miss Hebe down carefully. No, Joanna, you may not see your cousin, she is not well and needs to rest.' Shutting the door firmly on husband, footman and daughters, Emily Fulgrave leaned against it and regarded Hebe with a warm smile.

'You poor child, you look exhausted. Now, what is this mysterious illness? I must get Sir William Knighton to see you tomorrow.'

Hebe sent Anna a look of desperate entreaty, and she plunged into the breach, taking Mrs Fulgrave by the arm and beginning to whisper confidentially. Eventually Emily came over to the bed and sat down, patting Hebe's hand.

'Poor child. No wonder you do not want to be embarrassed by more male doctors examining you. The advice your own doctor gave you seems perfectly sensible: we must let you have lots of rest and build you up with good food. Plenty of milk and chicken, did you say, Mrs Wilkins?'

'Yes, ma'am. And liver,' Anna added firmly, ignoring Hebe's horrified expression.

'Well, dear, you are here now, and we are all looking forward so much to you feeling yourself again. Joanna wants to show you London and all the sights, little William has promised to lend you any of his toys if you are bored, and Grace and I cannot wait to take you shopping and to parties. Town is a little short of company now, at the start of the summer, but I am sure you will find plenty to entertain you. And I hardly need say that your uncle Hubert is delighted to have his favourite niece to stay.

'Shall I leave you with Mrs Wilkins to get undressed and into bed? You can have a little rest and, if you feel a bit better later, Grace and I will come and have supper up here with you.'

Hebe agreed gratefully to this programme and lay back on the bed as her anxious aunt closed the door quietly behind her. 'What did you say was wrong with me?' she asked Anna, who was lifting clothes out of one of the portmanteaux in search of a nightgown.

'I told her it was a woman's problem and not serious and that your doctor said you would grow out of it, but meanwhile you are very embarrassed at being questioned and examined and I was sure you would soon be feeling much better.'

'Grow out of it? Anna, I am twenty years old!'

Anna shrugged. 'She seemed to accept it. If you rest, I am sure you will soon be feeling much better, and then she will stop worrying about you.' She found the nightgown she was looking for and shook it out. 'This is a nice family, I think. I saw the children: two pretty girls and a handsome little boy, all very worried about their cousin they have not seen for so many years. This will be a good house to grow happy in again.'

'Grow happy again.' Hebe blinked away a tear. 'Yes, if I cannot grow happy here, Anna, I do not know where I would.' Except at Tasborough Hall, with Alex, her heart told her.

Chapter Nineteen

Hebe slept until supper time, then had a wash, put on a wrapper and lay on the daybed with a tray while Aunt Emily and Grace, her newly engaged nineteen-year-old daughter, ate their suppers from a card table Peter the footman carried in.

'You look better already,' Grace said, smiling happily. She was a short, slightly plump blonde with a pretty figure, wide blue eyes and an expression of quiet contentment. 'I am so looking forward to us being able to go around together. I have my wedding clothes to buy and you have your new wardrobe for your come-out. Although that is not quite right, is it? You have already come out in Malta.'

'Yes,' Hebe agreed. 'But, of course, nothing there was as fashionable as London parties and assemblies.'

'I can see no problem at all in securing you vouchers for Almack's, my dear,' her aunt confided. 'And, of course, your presentation at the next possible Drawing Room. Just as soon as we have your court dress ready.'

'But that will be very expensive, will it not?' Hebe enquired anxiously. 'Mama and Sir Richard have made me a very generous allowance, and I am sure that will cover all my other dresses and so on, but not a court dress.'

'I think we can contrive,' Aunt Emily said. 'I have been thinking about it. I have Grace's plumes laid up in silver paper, so that is one big expense spared. Now Grace's gown would not do for you, for you are taller, but we can use the hoops and I have laid by just the fabric.'

The thought of being presented at court was enough to keep Hebe's mind pleasantly occupied for some time, and she was unaware of Anna's relieved smile as she watched her talking to her cousin, her face relaxed and her cheeks just stained with colour.

The next morning Aunt Emily bustled in while Hebe was taking her breakfast. 'How did you sleep, dear? Was the street too noisy for you? You look so much better this morning, what a relief. Now, dear, will you and Mrs Wilkins be all right if you are alone in the house for a while? I am so sorry, but your uncle has to go and speak to his bankers, Grace and Joanna really must go to buy new shoes—what they have done to all their satin slippers I just cannot conceive!—and William, I am sorry to say, is bound for the dentist. He will not go with his tutor, so I am afraid I must drag him there myself.

'We will all be back by lunchtime. If it stays warm, would you like to go for a drive in the barouche with the top down this afternoon?'

'We will be quite all right, Aunt, you must not worry about us,' Hebe assured her. 'Anna wants to continue unpacking and I will lie on the daybed with a book, if there is something I might borrow? And, yes, I would like a drive very much.'

Grace ran up a few minutes later with an armful of

books. 'All novels except…here we are, Byron's poetry. Don't let Papa see, he doesn't approve. Have you read Miss Austen's *Pride and Prejudice*? Do try that if you don't like Byron. Mama says you can come for a drive this afternoon. I am so glad!' She bent and kissed Hebe on the cheek and ran out with a cheerful, 'Goodbye!'

'So much energy, this family,' Anna commented laughing. 'They seem to run everywhere. Would you like to get up now, Hebe? See, I have found this pretty wrapper and given it a press.'

Hebe was glad to get out of bed and curl up on the daybed with *Pride and Prejudice* in her hand. Her body seemed to be recovering with uncanny speed. She supposed it was because she had always been healthy and fit. Her spirits, though, were all over the place. Part of her just wanted to curl up and weep over the baby. Another part was happy to be with her aunt's cheerful, loving family. Her sensible self told her what a good thing it was that she had escaped a loveless marriage; her rebellious, emotional self pined for Alex.

Anna, wandering about the room, folding clothes in drawers and setting out Hebe's brushes on the dressing table, watched the play of emotions on her face and remarked, 'I think you will feel very mixed up for a day or two, Hebe. It happens to women who have had a baby—one minute happy, the next all tears, and I have heard it said that it happens also in cases like yours. I not expect too much too soon.'

There was the sound of the knocker. 'Who can that be?' Hebe said idly. 'They will be disappointed to find all the family out.'

A moment later there was a tap on the door and Peter appeared, somewhat red in the face and studiously averting his eyes from Hebe in her wrapper. 'I beg your p don, Mrs Wilkins, ma'am, but there is a gentleman here asking to see Miss Hebe. I told him she was not at home, so he says he wants to speak to you. I said I didn't think you were home either, ma'am, the mistress not having given me instructions, but he says if you don't come down, he'll come up.

'I don't rightly know what to do, ma'am.' The footman shifted uncomfortably from foot to foot. 'I mean, he's a gentleman and all, and he's big—I don't think he'll take kindly to me shutting the door in his face, and there's only me and Cook and little Dorothy in the house, ma'am.'

He spun round as the sound of steps on the stairs reached them. 'Oh, gawd, begging your pardon, ma'am.'

'Anna! Where the devil are you?' It was Alex, and, by the sound of it, he was in a towering rage.

'Thank you, Peter. I know the gentleman, I will come down.' Anna went out, followed by the footman, who sent Hebe a harassed and apologetic glance as he shut the door.

Alex! Here… She put down her book with fingers that shook slightly and was wondering whether to get up or stay where she was, when the door opened with enough force to send it back against the wall and he stalked into the bedchamber, Anna behind him.

'Major! You cannot go in there!'

He turned to look at the agitated Spanish woman, who was hanging with some determination to his sleeve, and at the footman who was bobbing about on the landing in an agony of indecision. 'Anna, I *am* going in there, and, unless you can find someone other than this unfortunate youth to throw me out, I am not sure how you are going to stop me.' He turned sharply to face them, making them back off as he advanced, and the moment Anna was over the threshold he shut the door, turning the key in the lock with a twist of his wrist.

He stood against the door for a long moment, ignoring the efforts of those outside to turn the handle. Hebe had never seen him look so gentle, and, she realised with a start, so fearful. He walked over until he was beside the daybed, then went down on one knee, close beside her but without making any attempt to touch her.

'My dear girl, I am so sorry.' All the anger that had been in his voice as he had spoken to Anna and Peter was gone, and the tenderness made Hebe blink back tears.

'You understood my letter, then?'

'Yes. I would have come at once, but the funeral was yesterday. I left as soon as I could, rode through the night and got here at dawn. I have been standing in the street until I saw everyone leave. I did not want to have this conversation with your aunt present.' She realised that he was indeed in riding breeches, his boots thick with dust.

'I see you haven't shaved,' she said, her voice shaking as she tried to speak lightly.

'No French spies to notice,' he answered in the same tone. 'How are you? Have you seen a doctor?'

'Yes, I saw a very good one, I think, but not since I got to London. My aunt has no idea what has happened, just that I have been ill since Gibraltar and that the same thing overtook me on the journey here.' She paused, looking down at his hands, lightly clasped on the edge of the daybed beside her. 'I feel much better, I will soon be well.'

'But sad?' he asked gently.

'Yes, sad. Are you sad?'

'I thought I only cared that you were well, but I find

I care about the baby as well. More than I would have thought possible in the circumstances.'

Hebe wondered what would happen if she gave in to her feelings and just turned into his arms and clung to him. Instead she swallowed hard and said, 'There was no need for you to come.' It came out sounding harsher than she intended and he withdrew his hands from the bed and stood up.

'I think there was every need, beside my concern for your health. What did you mean by saying in the letter that all your previous plans had come to nothing?'

'Why, that there was no need for us to marry, of course. I did not want to say anything more specific in case anyone else saw the letter.' Hebe watched him as he stood turning her brushes over and over on the dressing table, apparently engrossed in the play of sunlight on the silver backs.

'And why is that?' He was not looking at her. From the severe, priestlike profile she could read nothing.

'Because, without the baby, there is no necessity.'

At that Alex turned slowly on his booted heel and walked back until he was standing over her, looking down. 'There is every necessity. I have ruined you, I will marry you.'

'Nonsense,' Hebe retorted with more confidence than she was feeling. 'I do not feel in any way ruined. Society might consider me so—I feel perfectly normal and ordinary and I will not be forced into a—'

'Loveless marriage. You would rather have a loveless spinsterhood?'

'I…well, I would have my independence.'

'And no money to enjoy it.'

'I could become involved with charitable work, that would be worthwhile.'

'Why not do so from a position of power and influence and do some real good?'

'There are other things than charitable works.' Hebe was beginning to feel trapped. 'I want to stretch my mind…'

'Then stretch it with a large estate to look after, and a big house to be mistress of. Collect books—' he gestured at the pile that had fallen across the end of the daybed '—collect works of art. Do what you will, I can afford to indulge you.'

'I do not want to be indulged,' Hebe snapped, now thoroughly on the defensive. The thought of marriage to Alex, of Alex indulging her, was painfully seductive.

'Hebe, I warn you, I will not be gainsaid on this. It touches my honour. I will marry you.'

'I do not see why I should marry you because of your sensitive honour,' she protested. 'And I will not. It is not right.'

Alex suddenly hunkered down beside her, his face on a level with hers. 'Then I will do what I have to do to ensure that you do as I say.'

'What can you do? This is not the Middle Ages. Do you intend to ride off with me over your saddle bow?'

'No, nothing so melodramatic. I shall wait here until your aunt and uncle return and then I shall tell them, in detail, exactly why you have to marry me.'

'They cannot make me, I shall refuse.'

'Then I shall write to Sir Richard and to your mother and tell them. Can you imagine how that will make them feel, to know what has happened to you when they are too far away to be with you?'

'That is blackmail!' Hebe protested hotly. 'How could you do that to Mama?'

'Yes, it is blackmail, and I have no intention of doin

anything to cause your mama distress unless you force me to. And ask yourself, what she would prefer to happen now.'

Hebe dropped her eyes from his angry gaze. 'Very well,' she muttered.

'Hebe, I warn you, do not even think about trying to run away. You may think you can outwit Bow Street Runners, but I promise you, you cannot escape from me.' He hesitated, then added, 'Hebe, I need hardly tell you this, I am sure, but believe me when I say that I swear I will not touch you in any way.'

He got stiffly to his feet, and Hebe remembered that he had ridden through the night, and had done so directly after his brother's funeral. She swallowed back a small sob and said, 'I am sorry, Alex. I promise I will not run away.' The import of his last words were lost on her, other than to think it was considerate of him to acknowledge that she was unwell. 'What will you do now?'

'Go to the Clarendon Hotel, where I keep some clothes in case I have to come up to Town unexpectedly. I will sleep for a few hours, change and call upon your uncle this afternoon.'

He unlocked the door with a suddenness that propelled Anna into the room. She ran to Hebe's side. 'Hebe, *querida*, are you all right?'

'I have not ravished her, Anna, if that is what you mean,' Alex said savagely, striding out on to the landing where Peter was waiting. 'Come along, lad, you can throw me out now.'

Hebe indulged in a good weep on Anna's shoulder and then lay trying to think what to say about Alex to her aunt and uncle. What on earth would Peter say to them about the incident when they got home?

Finally she got up, bathed in the slipper bath that Anna

nagged a panting boot boy to lug up from the basement, and got dressed. Slowly she went downstairs and found the front salon where she sat and waited for the family's return.

They arrived within minutes of each other. Firstly the girls, delighted to find their cousin up and dressed, Joanna excitedly pulling all her new pairs of slippers out of their boxes to show Hebe. Then Uncle Hubert, beaming with pleasure, stooping to kiss her and remaining by her side, patting her hand and telling her how worried he had been about her. And finally Aunt Emily with William in tow. William, the tear streaks on his apple cheeks now disregarded, was inclined to be boastful about his courage in the face of the dreaded dentist and sent his sisters screaming from the room by producing a gory molar from his pocket to show off.

His nice new cousin, however, was made of sterner stuff, and even invited him to open his mouth and show her the gaping hole—surely the largest any boy had ever had—from whence the tooth had been wrenched. Aunt Emily soon packed him off to get his books ready for when his tutor called that afternoon. His voice could be heard vanishing in the direction of the green baize door. 'Peter, I say, Peter, look at my tooth…'

'Wretched boy,' Emily said fondly, turning back to her niece. 'You look so much better, my dear. You have colour in your cheeks.'

Hebe decided she had better tell her uncle and aunt something of the morning's excitements before Peter did so. 'I am afraid I had a caller this morning, Aunt Emily.'

'Afraid? Why, my dear, any of your friends may call at any time, you must treat this house as your own.'

'It was the Earl of Tasborough, Aunt, and I am afraid

he upset Peter.' They were looking at her blankly, so she stumbled on. 'You know the old Earl died in a carriage accident?' They nodded. 'He was succeeded by his elder son, but he too had been hurt in the accident and died suddenly four days ago. He was succeeded by Major Beresford, the younger son, who was a friend of ours on Malta.

'I had intended to call on my way back from Portsmouth, but when I did I found that the new Earl had just died, and obviously I left as soon as I could. But then I was ill on the road, and mentioned it in my letter of condolence to Major...I mean, to the Earl. And he was very anxious about me and called this morning, and when Peter denied me, I am afraid he...well, he forced his way in.'

'Goodness,' Aunt Emily said faintly after absorbing her niece's tumble of words. 'The Earl of Tasborough, so anxious about you that he visits London especially to see you, despite a death in the family, and then forces his way in when you are denied?'

Hebe, blushing rosily, nodded.

'Exactly what are his intentions, my dear?' Uncle Hubert enquired seriously.

'Marriage,' Hebe whispered, going redder. 'He is going to call this afternoon, Uncle, in order to speak to you.'

'But I am not your guardian! What will your mama expect me to say to the man?'

'Erm...Mr Fulgrave, my dear.' Aunt Emily put a hand on his sleeve. 'Do you not recall the letters from dear Sara?'

'You mean he is *that* young man?'

'Which young man?' Hebe demanded, thoroughly confused.

'Your mama wrote of a Major Beresford in several

letters, saying what hopes she had that he would make you an offer. Then she said she had been disappointed in him because he was engaged to another young lady.'

'That was a mistake,' Hebe said, trying not to feel resentful that her love life was apparently the subject of a lengthy family correspondence. 'Lady Cl…I mean, the young lady in question, realised they would not suit and called it off.'

'Well, in that case, I see no reason why I cannot act *in loco parentis*.' Mr Fulgrave looked earnestly at Hebe. 'What do you want me to say to him, my dear?'

'Yes,' Hebe said bluntly.

'It is wonderful news, dearest,' Emily said, still sounding faintly stunned. 'And I am so happy for you, only I cannot help feeling selfishly sorry that I will not have the pleasure of bringing you out.'

'But, Mrs Fulgrave, consider, the Earl is in mourning. Surely the betrothal cannot be announced yet. If it were to be, Hebe would have to go into mourning, too. As it is, I would imagine no announcement will be made for at least six months, if not longer, so Hebe will be able to enjoy at least part of her first Season.'

'Why, yes!' Aunt Emily brightened up. 'The best of both worlds, indeed.'

This aspect of the matter had not occurred to Hebe. With no official announcement for six months, surely she would find some way to turn Alex from a course which, despite her heart, her head told her was bound for disaster?

Aunt Emily, Grace and Hebe spent the early part of the afternoon in a state of high tension, sitting in the front salon in their best afternoon gowns, attempting severally to read *Pride and Prejudice*, write to a series of aged

aunts and sew a ribbon on a new bonnet. Anna, confess-
ing to an attack of nerves about the whole thing, went to
her room, and Mr Fulgrave retired to his study to digest
his luncheon and to get himself into a paternal mood for
the expected interview.

At last, at the very correct hour of three o'clock, the
knocker sounded and all three ladies jumped. Hebe heard
a familiar, cool, deep voice in the hall and Peter's nervous tones answering him. Then the visitor was led away
in the direction of Uncle Hubert's study and the ladies
sat back again.

'He has a wonderful voice,' Grace remarked. 'So…
masterful. It sends shivers down my spine.'

'Grace!' her mother reproved. 'What would Sir
Frederick say? Sir Frederick Willington is Grace's fiancé,' she explained to Hebe. 'I am planning a little dinner party soon so you can meet him.'

Hebe began to ask Grace about Sir Frederick, who
sounded nice, but somewhat dull. She was surprised that
the vivacious Grace would be attracted to a man of such
uniform temperament and stolid virtues as Sir Frederick
appeared to be, but perhaps it was an attraction of op-
posites. She smiled wryly. Here she was, plain, ordinary
Hebe, attracted to a man who was handsome, dashing,
sardonic and who lived a life of adventure.

As nothing was heard from the study, tension began to
mount again until finally there was the sound of voices
outside. All three ladies returned to their occupations
with an unconvincing air of preoccupation and all pretended surprise when Mr Fulgrave opened the door.

'We have a visitor, my dear.' They stood up, setting
down bonnet, quill and book, and both the young ladies
bobbed curtsies in response to the Earl's bow. Mrs
Fulgrave inclined her head graciously. 'My lord, please,

allow me to introduce you to my elder daughter Grac
I believe you know my niece, Miss Carlton.'

'Mrs Fulgrave, Miss Fulgrave, Miss Carlton. Good a
ternoon. I am happy to see you are a little recovere
Miss Carlton.'

'Thank you, my lord, yes.'

'Please, do sit down, my lord.' Mrs Fulgrave had
intention of leaving her niece unchaperoned yet. 'I b
lieve I must express my deepest condolences on yo
recent very tragic loss. It has been a most sad homecoi
ing for you after what I believe has been a long peri
on duty abroad.'

'Thank you, ma'am. Your sympathy is much app
ciated. Yes, it has come as a great loss, and also a co
siderable change in my circumstances. While I am
London I will have to go to Horse Guards and arrai
to sell out.'

'And you have seen much service in the Mediter
nean, I believe?'

'Yes, ma'am. Greece, Malta, Spain. Occasionall
have set foot in France.'

Mrs Fulgrave kept the conversation going along rigi
conventional lines until, after ten minutes, she caught
husband's eye. He rose to his feet, announcing, 'I n
bid you goodbye, my lord, for the present. I have
appointment at Brooks's. Grace, did you not wish m
drop you off at your friend Miss James's house?'

Alex rose politely as they left, then sat again, with
air of a man prepared to endure polite chitchat for
requisite half-hour and then depart. However, Aunt E
had obviously decided she had done enough to estab
her watchful chaperonage and she too got to her fee
have just remembered I have to send a message...I I
you will excuse me for a few moments, my lord.'

bowed graciously and swept out to the hall where Anna was waiting anxiously.

'What has happened, ma'am?'

'Nothing yet, Mrs Wilkins. Oh dear, I feel all of a flutter. Let us go and sit in the breakfast parlour for ten minutes.'

Hebe, left alone with Alex, regarded her hands studiously. Now she had had time to consider the question of mourning and the consequent delay she felt more relaxed, less under pressure.

'You know why I called, Hebe.' It was not a question.

'Yes.'

'Your uncle has given me his permission to address you.'

'Yes?'

'Damn it, Hebe, will you look at me!'

It was a very fierce saint indeed who was glaring at her. Hebe tried to suppress the memory of Maria's apposite description and failed. The corner of her mouth must have twitched for Alex's brows drew together thunderously.

'What are you laughing about?'

'I was remembering my maid Maria, who said that you looked like a beautiful, fierce saint. You are looking very fierce now.'

'Do I understand from that remark that you are feeling somewhat better?'

'Yes, thank you. My spirits are uneven, but I am sure will improve with time,' Hebe responded tranquilly, realising that her very composure was aggravating him, nd somehow not caring that this was so.

'Hebe: will you do me the honour of becoming my wife?'

It was the least lover-like of declarations. Hebe looked

into his face and said, 'Yes, I will.' There was relief, and some other emotion she could not read, in his eyes, but that soon vanished as she added, 'I do appreciate that in your present state of deep mourning an announcement cannot be made for at least six months.'

'Oh, no, Hebe, that was a very good try, but I told you, you could not run away from me.' Alex walked up to her and stood very close, looking down into her face. 'Because I am in mourning there will indeed be no announcements before the event. We will be married, very quietly, by special licence in St George's, Hanover Square, tomorrow, and we will return in the afternoon to Tasborough Hall.'

Chapter Twenty

'No!' Hebe gasped, just as the door opened and her aunt returned, attempting not to look as though she had fully expected to find the young lovers clasped in each other's arms.

'No?' Emily echoed. 'You mean you have turned his lordship down?' She looked from one set face to the other, her large grey eyes wide with distress.

'I have accepted his lordship's proposal, Aunt,' Hebe said, managing to smile in what she hoped was a suitably happy but modest manner. 'But he wishes us to be married by special licence tomorrow.'

'Out of the question,' Mrs Fulgrave responded robustly. 'My lord, your eagerness to marry my dear niece is understandable, and I quite appreciate that in your present state of distress the thought of her being by your side must be something you greatly desire, but consider Hebe's position. To marry her now, out of hand, will mean that she too is plunged into mourning when her mama has entrusted her to me for the purpose of bringing her out into Society.'

'I appreciate your concern, ma'am,' Alex responded politely with the air of a man who had not the slightest intention of listening to arguments. 'However, Miss Carlton can have her introduction to Society as my wife in a few months. I am sure she will value your support and guidance then, as I have no close female relatives.'

'All the more reason, my lord, to postpone the wedding.' Aunt Emily was not going to give up that easily 'Hebe has not the slightest idea how to run a big house To find herself a countess, and under such circumstances with no one to tell her how to go on…'

'I shall tell her.' Alex, unused to the sort of opposition he was getting from the ladies of this household, was looking more and more like a functionary of the Spanish Inquisition. If he had realised it, he might have attempted to soften his expression, for Hebe could see it was making her aunt even more determined to put off the wedding.

'A man is not the same,' Aunt Emily retorted robustly

Not the hint of a smile touched Alex's lips as he returned a slight bow as acknowledgement of this truism

'Then that is settled,' she said, subsiding into a chair looking, as Hebe told her afterwards, like a dove with ruffled feathers, settling in its nest after an alarm.

'By no means, ma'am. Reluctant as I am to contradict a lady, I fully intend to marry Hebe tomorrow.'

Fascinated by this duel of wills, Hebe watched quietly from the corner of the sofa where she was perched. was her own future, her own happiness, that was being discussed, but she could not help but admire the fixity purpose in Alex's manner. He was fighting this most polite of duels with one hand tied behind his back, for must retain his polite manner to his hostess at all times But Hebe knew for him this was deadly serious: not only did he believe that he must do his duty by her, but believed his own honour to be at stake here. Having re

of, and seen, the things gentlemen felt obliged to do in
the name of 'Honour', Hebe had a sinking feeling she
knew which was the most important.

Anna slipped quietly into the room, obviously expecting to be able to congratulate the happy couple. Mrs
Fulgrave turned to this stalwart female supporter. 'Mrs
Wilkins, please help me convince the Earl that he simply
cannot marry Hebe out of hand tomorrow!'

'Tomorrow?' Anna shot Alex a look that should have
withered a less strong-willed man. 'Impossible. Hebe is
not well.' She stared meaningfully at Mrs Fulgrave, who
suddenly looked extremely thoughtful.

'Yes, of course, thank you for reminding me, Mrs
Wilkins. Yes, my lord. Hebe is still unwell, despite her
being recovered enough to receive you this afternoon.
She cannot possibly be married tomorrow.'

Despite the hideous embarrassments of the situation,
Hebe was hard pressed not to laugh, however bitterly.
Alex knew exactly why she was indisposed, but could
not reveal that he knew and had already promised not to
insist on his marital rights while Hebe was recovering.
Anna knew that he knew, but could not tell Mrs Fulgrave,
and Aunt Emily thought she knew that Hebe was suffering from exactly the sort of female indisposition that one
did not want on one's wedding night. But, of course, she
could not possibly explain that to a man!

How are you going to deal with this, my lord? Hebe
mused, watching the flicker of frustration in Alex's eyes.
Then a cold shiver went down her spine. The frustration
was replaced by a look she had come to know very well
on that nightmare walk over the mountains: sheer determination.

'It may be, ma'am, that Miss Carlton has not explained
to you the history of our courtship,' he said evenly. 'I

am sure if she had done so you would understand ho
deeply I feel about this. Perhaps I should tell you every
thing.' He did not once look at her, but Hebe knew
was a direct threat: give in, or I will tell your aunt abo
the night in the shepherd's hut and what followed.

'Perhaps three months?' Hebe suggested hastily. Sh
should have known that an officer would have master
the art of strategic retreat.

'That is certainly more acceptable, but still too lon
Ten days.'

'A month,' Aunt Emily insisted, then, at a slight cou
from Anna, thought better of that particular piece of ti
ing and said, 'No, six weeks.'

'A fortnight,' Alex countered. Hebe wondered son
what hysterically if a sheep at market being haggled o
felt quite so unimportant to the negotiators as she w
feeling now.

'If I might say what I want?' she ventured, manag
to look meek and sound furious simultaneously. The c
ers turned to look at her as if they had forgotten
existence.

'Yes, of course, my dear,' her aunt said hastily,
eyes on the Earl. He was proving alarmingly force
she did hope Hebe knew what she was about accepr
him, whatever Lady Latham had said in his praise.

'I think three weeks would allow me to recover an
purchase my bride clothes—or, at least, my mournin;
would also, my lord,' she added tartly, 'allow me to er
the company of my aunt and her family, which I am :
you would not wish to deprive me of.'

Without appearing wholly insensitive and heartless
had no way of refusing this compromise. With a l
that promised he would have something to say abo
when they were alone, Alex surrendered gracefully.

'That would be very satisfactory, ma'am, if you are agreeable?' Aunt Emily nodded, somewhat dazed. She had experienced none of these problems when dealing with Sir Frederick's entirely proper proposal to Grace! 'It will allow me time to have Hebe's rooms made ready for her: the suite of the lady of the house has not been occupied for many years. I will return to Tasborough Hall, then; we can finalise arrangements by letter, I imagine.'

Aunt Emily was having some difficulty reconciling this cool approach to the violently suppressed passion that she had to assume lay behind the urgency of his proposal. 'Yes, indeed, I am sure, with such a very quiet affair, it can be organised by letter. We can hold the wedding breakfast here—how many guests would you intend to invite my lord?'

'Just Major Gregory, a friend of mine who fortunately is home on furlough. I will ask him to be my groomsman.'

He appeared to be making ready to leave without as much as kissing Hebe's hand. Aunt Emily said hastily, 'Please, on such a happy occasion, I am sure there is not the slightest objection to you bidding Hebe farewell by...er...'

Hebe got to her feet, her eyes on Alex's face as he turned to her. Not to kiss her would cause her aunt to doubt that this really was a love match. She read the question in his eyes and nodded slightly, extending both her hands to him. He took them and she was shocked at how cold his were. He stooped and pressed his lips to her cheek: they were warm, gentle and lingered a moment. How long was it since he had touched her?

She racked her brains and remembered that formal handshake on the balcony in Gibraltar. Alex freed her hands and stepped back. Hebe looked at him and saw again the tiredness that shadowed his eyes. Without thinking she put up one tentative hand and touched the taut skin over his right cheekbone. His skin was losing its deep tan, and with it one of the ways he could disguise fatigue from her. 'You will not travel back today, surely?' she asked softly. 'You will exhaust yourself.'

He stepped back abruptly, leaving her with her hand raised. 'There is much to do, I must go. I will write: take care of yourself, my dear.' He bowed to Mrs Fulgrave and Anna, and was gone.

'Well!' Aunt Emily said, dropping back into her chair. 'What a very determined young man—and so intense. Hebe, my dear, if you are not sure about this, now is the time to say so. He is undoubtedly highly eligible, but are you sure you want to marry a man who is quite so forceful?' She watched Hebe's averted face. 'Do you love him, dear?'

'Oh, yes, indeed I do, Aunt.' The warmth of her niece's instant response reassured her.

'I suppose you are both very shy of each other: on top of strong feeling that can make anyone act strangely.' She broke off as both Grace and Joanna put their heads around the door.

'May we come in, Mama?' Grace rushed over and took Hebe's hands. 'I couldn't bear to go out, so I went up to Joanna's room. Oh, Hebe, he is *so* handsome, and he looks so masterful. Why, if I were not in love with dear Frederick, I declare I would be swooning over him myself.'

'He is the most beautiful man in London,' Joanna declared. At seventeen she was taking a lively interest in young men and her mama had a sinking feeling she would prove to be both a flirt and a handful when she came out.

'Joanna!' she reproved.

'Well,' Hebe said with a smile, 'he was certainly the most handsome man on Malta, although he would not thank you for saying so. My maid told me he looked like a "beautiful, fierce saint" and I made the mistake of repeating it to him.'

Grace giggled. 'What did he say?'

'He professed himself mortified,' Hebe said. 'We were in a boat in the Grand Harbour at the time and it literally took the wind out of his sails.'

'It is good that he is not set up in a high opinion of himself,' Aunt Emily said thoughtfully. 'He is indeed a handsome man, although, until he smiles, I find him quite severe.'

'Yes,' Hebe agreed. It was wonderful to be able to talk about Alex like this, to enjoy a little feminine gossip. Indulgent, but wonderful. 'When I first saw him I took an instant dislike to him, for he looked so severe and priestlike. And when he senses danger he resembles a fierce bird of prey.'

'Ooh!' Joanna regarded her with saucer eyes. 'You were shipwrecked with him, were you not? It must have been a wonderful adventure. Did the Earl have to protect you from many dangerous Frenchmen?'

That was far too near the knuckle for comfort. Anna intervened. 'Fortunately the Major—I cannot think of Major Alex as my lord yet—was soon able to get Hebe to my village.'

Grace was far less interested in exotic adventure, and much more concerned with romance. 'But when did you decide you did not dislike him?'

'When I realised that he was not severe at all, merely

exhausted, for he had just returned from a long and dangerous mission. He does not like showing weakness: few men do, I should imagine. However, I saw through his pretence and we soon became friends.'

'Just friends?' Grace questioned.

'At first. We shared a mutual interest in Greek mythology.' Hebe ignored Anna, who had cast up her eyes in mingled amusement and disapproval.

'Goodness.' Grace was obviously finding it difficult to reconcile the Earl's good looks, his dashing military background and an interest in mythology. 'So, when will the wedding be announced? And when can we go shopping for your bride clothes? You will not have to wear mourning if it has not been announced, will you?'

'The wedding will be in three weeks' time,' her mother told her, managing to conceal her own feelings on the matter. 'Because of the family bereavement it will not be announced beforehand and will just be a simple ceremony at St George's. Which means,' she added with a sigh, 'we have a great deal of shopping to be done in a very short time. And a considerable amount of mourning-wear to obtain.'

'Hebe will not have to be *married* in black, surely, Mama?'

Aunt Emily pondered. 'No, I do not think so, as it is a private, family affair. Nothing too light, of course—perhaps a dusky rose pink? That would suit you, dear But immediately after the wedding breakfast you wil need to change into blacks: it would not do to arrive at your new home in colours.

'I think you should go back to bed and rest for the remainder of the day, Hebe, while Grace and I make lists We can consult tomorrow morning and then, if you fee well enough, we will go shopping. We will take the ba rouche, and Peter, so we will have to do no walking or carrying parcels. Now, up you go, dear.'

Hebe found herself ruthlessly tucked up in bed by Anna who demanded, *'Qué pasa?'* the moment she was sure they were alone. 'The Major cannot surely want to snatch you away from your family so quickly, and in your condition?'

'I think he is afraid I will manage to escape him somehow, and it touches his honour that he has ruined me,' Hebe said wearily. 'He has assured me that he would not dream of touching me.'

'Until you are well,' Anna said.

'Why, yes, I assume so,' Hebe replied, startled. 'I mean, I know he is in love with Lady Clarissa, or whatever she is called now, but he *is* a man, after all. And beside anything else, he must want heirs.'

'And this you do not mind?' Anna asked.

'Of course I mind,' Hebe said sadly. 'Do you think I like the idea that my husband is in love with another woman and only making love to me because he has to, or because I am…handy?'

'Handy?' Anna worked the expression out. 'Oh, I see, you are to hand. But you are in love with him, so you would like him to make love to you? *No?*'

'Of course.' Hebe was trying not to blush.

'And you are not afraid of him? After what happened? It cannot have been a pleasant experience.'

'No, I am not afraid of him, and, yes, it was not *pleasant*. But you know, Anna, because it was Alex, and I love him, there was something…' She broke off, the blush getting the better of her.

'Ah ha! I thought so,' the older woman said with a smile. 'It will be all right, *querida*, you let him make love to you as soon as possible, and he will soon forget that other silly woman.' She added something crisply in her own language.

Hebe smiled. 'You are very Spanish this afternoon, Anna.'

'That is because we are planning a wedding. It brings out the *duenna* in me.'

Hebe suddenly thought of something that she had not considered. 'Anna, you will come to Tasborough Hall with me, will you not?'

'But surely, Hebe, you do not want me there? You will just be married…what will the Major say?'

'I am to be a Countess,' Hebe said firmly, ignoring an hysterical desire to laugh at such a ridiculous thought. 'And I imagine no one would think it odd that I have a lady companion. I must find a maid, and I expect Aunt will say I should have a dresser as well, but I don't think I want to deal with one of *those* very superior servants just yet.'

'I will remind Señora Fulgrave, then. Are there places in London where one can find maids?'

'Yes, Registry Offices. Would you be very kind and remind Aunt Emily that we need to put that on the list?'

Anna went out and Hebe fell into a doze, too worn out to lie awake worrying about what was happening to her

Dusk had fallen before she woke to find her aunt sitting beside the bed, a chamber candle lit, waiting for her to wake.

'Oh, I am sorry, Aunt Emily, have you been there long?'

'Twenty minutes or so, dear. I just wanted to make sure you were all right after all the excitements of the day.'

'Yes, thank you.' Hebe sat up against the pillows. She did, indeed, feel much better: less tired, with no discomfort and even the sharp attacks of misery that had kept piercing her when she least expected it had settled into a quiet melancholy regret at the back of her thoughts. The events since she had landed at Portsmouth were beginning to take on the aspect of a dream.

She realised that her aunt was looking uncomfortable and said, 'Is anything wrong, Aunt Emily?'

'No, dearest. It is just that with your mother not being here—' She broke off, then said more firmly, 'Is there anything you would like to ask me, dear? About men and…er…marriage?'

'Oh. Oh, I see.' Hebe smiled reassuringly at her aunt. 'Thank you, but I…I mean, before I left Gibraltar…'

Her aunt leapt immediately to the conclusion she had hoped. 'Of course, your mama took the opportunity to have a little talk. Well, if there is anything else you would like to ask me, you must not hesitate.'

She left a short while afterwards, reassured. Hebe closed her eyes and wondered what her aunt's reaction would be to the news that her well-brought-up niece needed no instruction at all as to what happened between a man and a woman.

Chapter Twenty-One

The ladies set out the next day with a list that filled an entire book of tablets, a resigned-looking footman sitting up beside the coachman and a warning to Mr Fulgrave that he must expect to eat his luncheon in company with his two younger children or at his club, whichever he pleased. He was left in no doubt that his wife intended to devote herself entirely to his niece's needs for as long as it took to achieve a creditable, although sombre, trousseau.

An amiable man with a strong sense of family, he raised no objection to this desertion, instead pressing a roll of banknotes into his wife's hand with a whispered injunction to 'buy something special for little Hebe'. It was not every day that a connection of the Fulgraves allied herself to an Earl. His dear Grace had done very well for herself, but what might Joanna achieve with her cousin's new influence when she came out next year?

'Where are we going first, Mama?' Grace enquired conning the lists, which were long enough to give ever such a dedicated shopper as herself a faint feeling o exhaustion.

'Madame de Montaigne,' her mother declared. 'W

have no time to spare in having Hebe's wedding dress and one good evening gown made. Perhaps a walking dress, as well. I would not normally think of a riding habit as you will be in mourning, but, in the country, it may be necessary. She has such a good figure that we may be able to get away with other things made up by Miss Bennett if we obtain fabrics and patterns today.'

She turned to Hebe, who was dividing her attention between the bustling street and her aunt. 'Miss Bennett makes all our day-to-day things my dear—such a clever seamstress, why, show her a fashion plate and she will contrive excellent results. Her sisters work with her, so I have every confidence she will be able to produce, let me see, four day dresses, two afternoon gowns...' She began to rattle off a list that appeared to Hebe, who had grown up believing that three new dresses in a year was wanton extravagance, to be outside all possibility of need.

'But, Aunt—' she began, but was silenced with a wave of her aunt's hand.

'You are about to become a Countess, dear, that changes everything.'

'But the money,' Hebe interjected. 'I am not a Countess yet!'

'Your uncle has given me a little present for you, which will pay for your evening gown, and while he was with your uncle, Lord Tasborough arranged for funds for you, quite appreciating the position you might find your-self in.' She smiled complacently, as happy for her niece as she would have been for one of her own daughters. 'We need not stint on the smallest item.'

Madame de Montaigne, who might, or then again, might not, have been the aristocratic *émigrée* she pur-ported to be, threw herself into the task confronting her with enthusiasm. She knew that to betray by so much as

a whisper the news that there was about to be a new
Countess upon the social scene would be to lose her
every hope of ever dressing this prestigious new client
again. But once the announcement was made and smart
ladies learned that the charming Lady Tasborough was
dressed at de Montaigne's, she would be able to pick and
chose her clientele.

'But, of course, Madame Fulgrave! A dusky rose
would be of the most charming for *mademoiselle*: so
pretty, yet so suitable under the circumstances. It so hap
pens that I have a gown of just that colour—not a suitable
style, but if *mademoiselle* cares to try it on to see the
shade…'

Hebe found herself dressed in an evening gown of
great elegance and far lower cut than she had ever worn.
She hardly dared breathe lest what felt like an entirely
inadequate bodice allowed her breasts to escape. There
were puff sleeves attached to the slimmest possible shoulders and the skirts fell from immediately below her
bosom to her ankle bone.

The colour was exquisite, Hebe thought, looking
down: the shade of raspberries mixed with cream. The
Madame turned her around and she found herself confronting a stranger in the long pier glass. The shiny
brown hair was hers, but her face was suddenly finer, her
eyes bigger, her mouth fuller in contrast to the high cheek
bones. It was as if every vestige of youthful plumpness
had gone, leaving a young lady of haunting and unusual
looks.

'Enchanting!' Madame sighed.

'Yes,' Aunt Emily agreed, looking at her niece
though for the first time. 'Enchanting is exactly the
word.'

'Now, this colour is exactly right for the wedd

gown, and this style, but in black of course, for the evening gown.'

'But, Aunt Emily, this is much too low,' Hebe gasped.

'Not for a married lady of fashion,' Madame assured her. 'Now, what do you think of this silk, with a gauze overskirt of embroidered net? I have a net here with the work all concentrated at the bottom—wreaths of leaves, which would be most appropriate.'

The evening gown settled, they turned their attention to a design for the wedding dress. To Hebe's huge relief the neckline was more modest, trimmed with satin ribbons in an unusual twisting edging that was reflected in the hem and in undulating bands of trim which circled the skirt.

'With roses in the hair and at the bosom and pearls, do you not think, Madame?' Aunt Emily enquired.

By the time they emerged with a gratifyingly large number of garments crossed off Mrs Fulgrave's list, Hebe was feeling decidedly light-headed and made no resistance at all to being steered into Gunther's. A cup of hot chocolate and a delicious ice with almond biscuits had a reviving effect and she was able to contemplate an afternoon at the silk warehouses with some enthusiasm.

'Millard's East India Warehouse might have the best prices,' Aunt Emily mused while the coachman sat stolidly ignoring the curses of carters until she had made up her mind where to send him. 'But do we really want to go as far as Cheapside? No, I think Shears. Henrietta Street, Grimes!'

Shears's of Bedford House certainly had the most staggering display of mourning fabrics one might hope to view. Hebe allowed herself to be seated by the counter while assistants brought bombazines, crepes, Italian nets,

silks, gauzes and Gros de Naples for her approval. She
was overwhelmed and simply said, 'Whatever you think,
Aunt,' at regular intervals as pelisses and gloves, trimmings and beadings followed the fabrics.

'Stagg and Mantle's for linens,' was the next decree,
once Peter, sweating freely from trying to fit the numerous parcels into the carriage, had finally climbed back on
to the box, mopping his brow.

Once they found the linen drapers, Grace whispered
'Do all Hebe's underthings have to be mourning too?'
She was already beginning to embroider daringly flimsy
unmentionable items for her own trousseau.

'I really do not think so,' her mother answered. 'This
is, after all, a wedding outfit.'

If Hebe had blushed at the neckline of the evening
gown, she was reduced to silence by the items which the,
fortunately female, assistant brought for her inspection.
Cotton petticoats and camisoles for day wear were modest enough, if made in the finest fabric she had ever worn
and with exquisite tucks and lace trims. But some of the
underwear made from Indian lawns, and all of the night-
wear, was, to her innocent eyes, utterly immodest.

'Aunt, I cannot wear that, why, it is transparent!' she
protested on seeing the most fragile nightgown and its
accompanying peignoir.

'My dear,' her aunt whispered, 'this is for your wedding night.'

Only the thought that Alex was not going to be seeing
any of this outrageous underwear—not at least, for some
time—calmed Hebe's hectic colour.

The next day her aunt declared she must stay at home
and rest while Miss Bennett and her younger sister
tended her. The new fabrics were spread all over the

on while the long-suffering Mr Fulgrave was forbidden
he house, William was banished to the park with his
utor and Joanna was instructed to sit in the corner and
ot touch anything.

Hebe had not imagined that black was such a variable
olour. The fabrics, each with their own texture—from
ne sensual softness of the silks, through the imposing
heen of the satins to the dull glow of the bombazines or
ne ridges of the twills—made blacks the colour of a
nagpie's wing, of a thunderous sky, of the gloomiest
nadow and the sparkling dark fire of jet.

Contrasting was the crispness of a white ruff or edge
f cotton lace; the softness of a fine lawn fichu or the
erest peep of a white rouleaux edging against a neck-
ne. Grace and Hebe bent their heads over sheaves of
shion plates, the Misses Bennett and Mrs Fulgrave
aped fabrics, held up trimmings, disagreed politely
out the exact fullness of a skirt or the length of a cuff,
d all thoroughly enjoyed themselves.

When the post arrived in mid-afternoon Hebe seemed
wake from a dream back to reality. None of this lux-
ous preparation really seemed anything to do with her,
ore an enjoyable game, but the post brought two letters
m Alex, one for Mrs Fulgrave, one for Hebe.

Her aunt handed her the letter saying, 'I really do not
l I need to read your letters, dear, now you are about
be married.' When she opened it, Hebe was profoundly
eved at this indulgence.

Are you still so sad? it began without preamble, as
ugh he were speaking aloud to her. *I wish I could find
rds to comfort you, but I do not think there are any,
y time. I know you think me overbearing and unkind
orce you to this marriage, but believe me, Hebe, it is*

*the right thing to do. I want you to be happy here: I think
you will enjoy the countryside, the fresh air, the change.
And, as you feel ready for it, there is much I would like
your help with, in the house and on the estate. I mean
what I said, there is no need to fear that I will make any
demands upon you. Alex.*

Hebe read and reread the short note. Surely he did no
mean 'no demands' *ever*? Of course not, she was being
foolish. Giving herself a little shake, she waited whil
Aunt Emily read her own letter, which she handed ove
for Hebe to see.

Obliging and reasonable in every word, it left th
Fulgraves to arrange matters exactly as they saw fit, co
firmed the name and direction of his only guest an
groomsman, and requested politely that the weddin
breakfast be finished by two o'clock so that he cou
ensure Hebe did not arrive at her new home too late th
night. If there was any matter in which he could assis
he would be only too happy and remained their mo
obedient servant, etc., etc.

The three weeks sped by, marked only by the dai
delivery of completed garments or parcels arriving fro
the shops that Emily and Grace visited for yet more e
sentials. Hebe's toothbrush would never do; had she
more than a dozen lawn handkerchiefs? How many fa
had she? No black ones? That would have to be rem
died, with two black and one purple one. Gloves, stoc
ings, toothpowder, sponges, veils, shawls and hairbrush
heaped up in the spare bedroom and new luggage had
be bought. Hats of the utmost elegance from Mada
Phanie jostled in their boxes next to silver paper packag
containing lace and artificial flowers.

* * *

Finally, the day before the ceremony, Aunt Emily declared herself satisfied and gazed wearily, but triumphantly at her niece and daughters. She, Grace and Joanna had used the opportunity to extract new gowns and hats from the indulgent Mr Fulgrave and all the ladies felt that however quiet the ceremony, at least the splendour of their outfits would lend it distinction.

Major Gregory, Alex's friend, called as he had done almost every day since hearing the news that he was groomsman, to enquire if there were any ways in which he might make himself useful. He had, without in any way putting himself forward, become an instant friend of the family. 'What a thoroughly *nice* young man,' Mrs Fulgrave commented, observing the patient way he allowed William to bombard him with questions about the war.

She did wish he did not look quite so dashing in his scarlet coat, though; Joanna had taken to slipping into the room the moment he arrived, and her mama had a feeling it was not to listen to tales of *piquet* duty and camp life. Oh, well, doubtless she would fall for many a young man before her affections were settled; it would do her no harm to indulge in a little puppy love with this one.

Giles Gregory appeared to treat her as a slightly older version of her little brother, which, as she looked such a schoolroom miss still, was not surprising. Hebe, when her aunt had discussed Joanna with her, had made the perceptive observation that she was growing into her looks. Looking with fresh eyes at her daughter's straight black hair, her big hazel eyes and emphatic dark brows she thought her niece was probably right.

Then it was the day itself, dawning bright and clear and with a promise of warmth and light winds. Hebe was ordered to stay in bed, her face white under Mrs Fulgrave's favourite skin cream for at least an hour while the other ladies hastened about, their hair still in curl papers hidden under turbans. The servants spent the time sighing heavily as they received one contradictory order after another, the limits of Cook's patience being reached when *that Spanish lady*—not that she isn't very nice, mind, but she is foreign—instructed her to accommodate in the pantry all the buckets of fresh flowers that Miss Grace was about to arrange as the yard was too hot for them.

Somehow by ten o'clock it was all done: the flowers arranged, the table laid, the ladies in their gowns, Mr Bruning the coiffeur administering the last tweak to Hebe's hair before Charity, her new maid, pinned a spray of roses in it and Mr Fulgrave left with nothing to do but to ensure his son and heir kept his new suit clean and under no circumstances brought a frog, spider or interesting toadstool to the church.

The carriages arrived at half past the hour: two closed barouches, for there was no desire to call attention to what was afoot. Mr Fulgrave assisted Grace and Hebe into one while his wife, Joanna, Anna and William took the other.

'You look lovely, my dear,' he said with affection, for he had grown very fond of his niece in the past three weeks. And he spoke only the truth, for Hebe's new gown was a triumph, the colour glowing against her creamy skin. Her hair was piled and twisted into an elaborate mass with one long ringlet lying on her shoulder and little curls around her temples and forehead, the only place she had allowed Mr Bruning to cut it.

Cream roses nestled at her breast and in her hair and

her simple pearl earrings and necklace were her only jewels, except for the ring that glowed on her left hand. Captain Gregory had brought it the day before, expressing himself deeply relieved to have discharged his errand and safely delivered it from Rundell and Bridge where it had been to be cleaned and have its settings checked.

With it had been a simple note: *This was my mother's, A.* The single large diamond surrounded by rubies had slipped on to her finger as though it had been made for it and now Hebe kept touching it as she fiddled nervously with the ribbons of her bouquet of cream and pink roses.

Grace touched her hand and smiled reassuringly as the carriage moved off and Hebe took a deep breath. *My wedding day.* How strange it seemed to be saying it. That day in the garden in Malta, when she had been sure Alex was going to make a declaration, seemed a hundred years ago when she had been an innocent, sheltered girl. Now she was indeed marrying him, not because he loved her, but because duty compelled them to it.

Would Mama and Sir Richard have received her letters yet? How happy they would be at the news, how unsuspecting of what lay behind what must seem to them a simple love story.

The carriage turned into Hanover Square and drew up before the pillared portico. Aunt Emily, Anna, Joanna and William went up the steps into the church, then Peter came and let down the steps to help Grace out. Before an interested crowd of passers-by she smoothed Hebe's skirts, twitched the ribbons of her bouquet, cast a harassed glance over the set of her father's coat and finally gave a satisfied nod.

Feeling as though she had drunk too much champagne, Hebe took Uncle Hubert's arm and slowly they began to climb the steps, Grace following. The church was cool and shadowy, echoing because so few people were in it. She could see the Fulgraves in the front left-hand pew and the scarlet of Captain Gregory's uniform on the right-hand side at the altar rail.

Then they began to walk down the aisle and through her veil Hebe could see Alex in immaculate black coat and cream pantaloons, his shirt the whitest thing in the church, his hair ruthlessly cropped, his face as pale as she thought hers must be.

As she got closer she saw his face, but could not read the look in his eyes. Was he imagining the lovely Lady Clarissa with her dark chestnut hair walking towards him in a church full of well-wishers?

He turned to face the altar as she drew level with him and the clergyman stepped in front of them and began to read. 'We are gathered here together... Who givest this woman?' Uncle Hubert transferred her hand from his to Alex's cool fingers, which tightened momentarily on hers. '...speak now or forever... With my body...' A blush sprang to her cheeks: she did not dare glance at Alex. And finally, 'I now declare you man and wife. You may kiss the bride.'

She turned and looked up at Alex as he lifted the veil, carefully placing it back over her hair. His blue eyes suddenly blazed as he saw her face for the first time that day and, as though he could not help himself, he whispered 'Circe!' Then he bent and kissed her, very lightly, on the lips.

Hebe shivered violently at the touch, so light, so restrained. She wanted to throw her arms around his neck, force him to kiss her hard and deeply, but he seemed to register the shiver, for he withdrew at once, formally offering her his arm to guide her to the vestry to sign the register. As he handed her the quill, she sensed the care

with which he avoided touching her hand and Hebe wondered if it were possible to feel any colder than she did
at that moment, carefully inscribing *Hebe Annabel
Eleanor Beresford* for the first time.

Chapter Twenty-Two

The wedding breakfast passed to Mrs Fulgrave's entire satisfaction. Whilst she could not suppress an entirely worldly disappointment that such a prestigious event should be witnessed by only the family and Major Gregory, she still felt that she had contrived an entertainment fit for an Earl.

The Earl in question also behaved to her complete satisfaction. There was no sign of the imperious, severe man she had confronted such a short time ago. Alex, as he begged she would call him, was amiable, co-operative and entirely charming.

'I do hope he remains so,' she whispered to Mr Fulgrave on her way up to help Hebe change from her wedding dress into the black walking outfit she was wearing for the journey to her new home. 'I am sure he will be a wonderful husband unless crossed, but I really would not wish Hebe to risk crossing him in any way.'

The bride herself was all too aware of her new husband's forbearance and wished fervently she could find some way of undermining it. She was quite sure that if she set out to seduce him, she could do so, despite her lack of experience. But what was she about, to want to seduce a husband who was in love with another woman? He might desire her body, but she wanted more than that. Still, she consoled herself, surely after a few months he would begin to forget Clarissa, or at least become accustomed to her loss and would turn to Hebe.

It was not a very cheerful prospect though, to be 'turned to' as second-best. Her sigh as she thought it made her aunt look at her sharply. 'Are you all right, my dear? You are not too tired? I do wish you did not have to make a journey this afternoon.'

'I am perfectly fine, Aunt Emily.' Hebe smiled. 'It is all just rather overwhelming and this…' she gestured at the unrelieved black of her skirts '…this is somewhat lowering to the spirits.'

'Never mind, dear,' her aunt replied with what Hebe could only interpret as a wicked twinkle. 'Think of the nightgowns.'

Hebe was positively shocked by the realisation that she was now counted as a married woman and such things might be said. If only Aunt Emily knew that the only person likely to be seeing those filmy garments or the exquisite lingerie was her new maid, Charity, who was self-importantly guarding Hebe's somewhat unimpressive jewellery box. Charity was already jealous of Anna, who she was sure would want to take responsibility for such matters, and was not looking forward to a journey with the formidable Spanish lady.

They all trooped downstairs to find the carriages drawn up. The first one for Hebe and Alex, the second, laden with Hebe's trousseau, for Anna and Charity. Mrs Fulgrave shed a tear, Grace and Joanna kissed Hebe, Alex, and, in Joanna's case, a startled Major Gregory, who returned the salutation with interest, sending Joanna into blushing confusion. Mr Fulgrave vanished into a large pocket handkerchief with an unconvincing mutter of 'Something in my eye, dear,' and, before Hebe could catch her breath, they were off.

Warily she eyed her new husband, who was watching her with some amusement. This was a relief, for she was afraid he would become distant once they were alone. 'Well, Circe, how does it feel to be a Countess?' he enquired.

So, he was calling her Circe again. Hebe clung to this pet name with what she knew was probably the self-deluding hope that it meant more than simple affection. 'Very strange,' she said lightly. 'I have not the slightest idea how to go on in a big household, you know. Mrs Fitton will despise me, Starling will look superior and the staff will think their master has run mad.'

'Nonsense. Mrs Fitton will adore you. Starling looks superior about everyone, including me, so I do not know how you will tell what he thinks about you.'

'And the staff?'

'Well, they definitely think I have run mad already, for I am not at all their idea of an Earl. I am relying upon you to re-establish my credit.'

If their journey was to be confined to a discussion about the household, then it would be far less trying than Hebe had feared. 'But how?' she persisted. 'I have never had to do more than cope with three maids at a time—and then Mama was really running things anyway.'

'It struck me,' Alex remarked, 'fairly early on in our acquaintance, that you were born to be mistress of a great estate. In fact, I can recall thinking it was a pity that my brother William had not met you, for you would be just the one for Tasborough Hall.'

Oh. Hebe digested this. So he had wanted to marry he

off to his brother, did he? Unable to decide just how that did make her feel she persisted, 'But why?'

'Because you are interested in people. I can see how it will be: within weeks you will know every servant, every tenant. You will know about their families, their illnesses, their hopes and dreams, weaknesses and failings. And they will all be enchanted by you, except for the rogues who will rightly be afraid of you.'

'*Afraid of me?*' Hebe laughed out loud. 'I cannot imagine anyone being afraid of me.'

'You terrify me,' Alex said. His voice was dry, but Hebe, who was beginning to be able to hear every nuance of his speech, even when she could not read it aright, could sense some other meaning behind the teasing words.

'You must tell me all about the servants,' she said firmly. 'Then I will make a good start with them. And everything you can about the house and estate.'

'I know very little,' Alex said with a shrug. 'I did not grow up there as a boy, for my father inherited from his grandfather, not his own father. They were not close and we rarely visited. I am having to learn very rapidly myself, which is why I will value your help.'

Hebe turned a glowing smile on him. 'Of course, I will do everything I can. It is such a pleasure to know there is something I *can* do. I was afraid you would feel that nothing might be touched or changed—not that I would without asking your permission, of course—and I would find myself having to live up to doing everything as it had been done before.'

He smiled at her enthusiasm. 'You may do as you wish. I am only glad you look forward to being busy.'

They fell silent as the miles slipped by. Hebe let her head fall back on the squabs and closed her eyes.

* * *

She must have dozed, for she awoke with a start as the
carriage wheels rumbled over cobbles and out of her window she saw the King's Arms in Berkhamsted go by.

'I am so sorry,' she said apologetically. 'I have been
poor company.'

'Not at all. You were tired.' Alex watched her for a
while then said, 'Have you not been sleeping?'

'Not well,' Hebe admitted. 'I keep dreaming.'

'About the child?' he asked gently.

'No,' Hebe said slowly. 'Wherever he or she is, they
are safe, I feel that. No, I dream of…other things.' *Of
you in my arms, of the scent of you, the strength of you,
how much I long to show you I love you. That is what I
dream about, and that is what I cannot tell you.*

Alex reached out a hand as if to comfort her and Hebe
flinched away, frantically aware that in her present state
of mind he would only have to touch her and all her
defences would be down and she would throw herself
into his arms. It would be bitterly humiliating to see his
embarrassment. Bad enough to be jilted, then to find
yourself married to satisfy considerations of honour. But
how did a man cope with an unwanted wife who wept
in his arms and begged to be loved?

Hebe was well aware that demonstrations of strong
affection between husband and wife were considered bad
form, even in the case of the few admitted love matches
in Society. She had never seen her parents, nor her aunt
and uncle, display more than the most restrained affection
in public, and she had every reason to suppose theirs
were warm and loving relationships. And she was a
Countess now: it behoved her to behave with restraint
and dignity.

After a moment Alex said, 'I am sorry, I did not think.
Perhaps now is a good time to repeat what I said before

n case you were unsure that I meant it. Ours is a strange
narriage, Hebe, one neither of us looked for. I want to
eassure you that it will be a marriage in form only and
ou need never fear that I will…trouble you in any way.
 give you my word I will not enter your bedchamber.'

Hebe looked at him, her gaze wide and troubled. 'Not
ver?'

He was as expressionless as she had ever seen him,
is eyes cast into shadow. 'Never, you have my word.'

Somehow her pride came to her rescue. 'Thank you
r being so frank. It is as well to know where we stand,
it not? I am relieved you feel able to speak to me about
'

It was perhaps as well that the carriage passed through
e gates of Tasborough Hall at that moment, for Hebe
ubted whether she could maintain this calm pose for
ch longer. The groom up on the box blew a long blast
 his horn, and by the time they drew up in front of the
ors the servants were already assembled on the drive-
y, the maids hastily patting their hair down and
aightening the long ribbons that streamed from their
s.

Alex helped Hebe down, offered her his arm, and be-
 to walk her down the ranks of staff, introducing each
urn.

or many a young bride, unused to such splendour as
 numbers drawn up to greet them signified, this would
e been a terrifying experience. For Hebe it was a mer-
l relief. Here were people: new faces, new characters,
of whom would form part of her new life. She would
e to learn to manage them, to be mistress of the
sehold, but she knew as she looked at the line of
ing, newly-scrubbed faces that these strangers would
 become part of the family.

She shook hands warmly with Starling, much to his surprise and that of his underlings. 'Good afternoon Starling! How glad I am to see a familiar face to welcome me. And Mrs Fitton, of course: we must have a long talk and you will tell me how to go on here at Tasborough Hall.' She did not miss the look of shock on the housekeeper's face at the realisation that she had been so incredibly indiscreet about his lordship's lost love to the lady he had now married.

'You have already been such a help to me, Mrs Fitton, I know I can rely on you,' she added, much to that good woman's relief.

As the housekeeper said to Starling much later in the privacy of her sitting room when they were indulging in a much-needed bumper of his lordship's brandy, 'I could have sunk through the floor, Mr Starling, when I saw her sweet face and I recall what I said about that Lady Clarissa, cruel flirt that she must be.'

'Well, he has married this lady now, hasn't he, Mrs Fitton, so you can't have done much damage. Old friend of the family, his lordship told me, with an important message from the fleet in the Mediterranean—them not knowing that the Major was now an Earl, you see. That's why she had a false name, and came while he was in mourning.'

'Ohh!' Mrs Fitton was enjoyably titillated by the glimpse into the war against the Corsican Monster, as she always liked to think of Napoleon. 'Well, he's made the right choice, I say: a nicer young lady you could not hope to meet.'

Mrs Fitton had bustled after her new mistress and was soon showing her to her room, then escorting the pair to where the new countess's lady companion would be installed. Anna gravely approved her new suite, but the

he first opportunity to hiss in Hebe's ear, 'I am very
ired and will not, of course, be dining anywhere but in
ny chamber tonight.'

Hebe whispered back, 'Thank you, Anna, but you may
have no fear of interrupting the slightest intimacy.'

Anna raised her eyebrows at Alex's retreating back and
ighed. She had not thought the Major so blind. She was
ravely tempted to presume on past friendship and tell
im exactly how his new bride felt about him and what
e was throwing away by clinging to the memory of one
eautiful, but faithless, woman. But Hebe had confided
 her, trusted in her, and all Anna felt she could do was
 help and advise the English girl whom she had grown
 love like a sister.

So it was that the new Countess sat down to dinner
at night at one end of what seemed an endless expanse
 Jamaican mahogany and warily eyed the only other
cupant of the dining room—besides, that is, three foot-
en and an expressionless butler.

The first remove consisted of what would have gen-
usly fed the entire servants' hall with some to spare
 luncheon the next day. Hebe pecked at a slice of
ached chicken in white wine sauce, crumbled a bread
l and nibbled a single spear of asparagus. Her lord
de a rather better attempt upon the dishes spread be-
e him, but even so, it took some time for the footmen
clear the remains before resetting the table with the
ond remove.

Hebe made a decision. Either this house was going to
 her or she was going to be mistress of it. 'Starling.'

Yes, my lady?'

Please present my compliments to Mrs Dexter upon
xcellent dinner and convey my apologies for not hav-
done it justice. We have had a long day.'

'Indeed, my lady.'

'Please ask Mrs Dexter to attend me at ten o'clock tomorrow so that we may discuss the week's menus.'

'Certainly, my lady.'

'And, Starling—'

'Yes, my lady?'

'When my lord and I dine alone, or with Mrs Wilkins we will only require the presence of yourself and on footman.'

'Certainly, my lady. May I help your ladyship to som salmon?'

'Thank you, Starling. And, Starling, unless we are en tertaining twenty or more, please remove that epergn and three of the leaves from the table.'

The meal wound on its interminable way until Het decided enough was enough and rose gracefully from h seat, remembering just in time the length of train on h second-best dinner gown. 'I will leave you to your po my lord,' she said, acknowledging with an inclination her head Alex rising from his place.

'Ma'am. I will join you very shortly in the Panell Room.'

'Which is the Panelled Room?' Hebe hissed to Starli as he opened the door for her. 'And please do not say is the one with the panelling, they all have that in t part of the house.'

She had surprised the glimmer of a smile from butler. 'The door on your right, my lady. It has m panelling than any of the others.'

Hebe had to agree that the room certainly had a perabundance of panelling. She felt confident that could identify linen-fold style, plain panelling and so thing which appeared to be Gothic in its inspirati

Alex, arriving half an hour later—more, he ruefully felt,
to comply with the expectations of his butler than any
desire to linger over his port—found his bride standing
on a chair and inspecting the carvings over the fireplace.

'Looking for dust?' he enquired casually.

Hebe jumped at the sound of his voice, but said reprovingly, 'Certainly not. Mrs Fitton is an admirable
housekeeper. I am looking for the boss which opens the
secret panel, of course.'

'The what?' Alex strolled into the room, pleasantly
flushed with a good dinner, wine and port and ready to
be entertained by the Countess's explorations.

'The secret panel,' Hebe repeated, regarding him from
her superior height. 'Please do not tell me there are no
secret panels, priest holes, skeletons in cupboards or
headless ghouls.' She had a sneaking suspicion that she
had had rather too much wine at dinner, but Alex appeared merely amused, so her light-headedness could not
have been apparent.

'I am very sorry to disappoint you,' he said, coming
to stand by the chair, his head tipped back. 'This house
was never a monastic building—so no headless monks or
walled-up nuns, and we have been a Protestant family
since the Reformation, so no priests' holes either.'

'Oh,' Hebe said flatly. 'Never mind. I shall not repine.'
She made to jump down, slipped and found herself being
lifted safely down to the floor. For one long moment she
was back in a small boat in the Grand Harbour, the sun
beating down and the strong arms of this man encircling
her waist. Hebe inhaled deeply, filling her nostrils with
the scent of citrus and sandalwood, before she was sat
firmly on the hard chair with her husband already settling
himself in a wing chair by the fire.

She got up and took the chair opposite, still quivering slightly with the memory his touch had evoked.

Alex picked up a newspaper, but left it unfolded in his lap. 'What would you care to do tomorrow, my dear?'

'I think I had better spend my time with the female upper servants,' Hebe decided. 'If that is agreeable to you.'

'Certainly. I hope I do not have to say again, Hebe, that whatever changes you wish to make to any aspect of this establishment and its running, you must do. There is no need to refer to me.'

'Thank you, my lord.' That sounded uncomfortably like a pleasant rebuke for having taken such a firm line with Starling at dinner.

Alex regarded her with a smile twitching the corner his lips. 'Hebe, when you call me "my lord" in that manner, I have the gravest misgivings that you are up to no good.'

Hebe twinkled back, suddenly at ease. 'Me, my lord? Good Heavens, no. I think, if you do not mind, I will to bed. I find I am very tired.'

She was surprised that he got to his feet and walk with her to the foot of the stairs. 'Can you find your way amidst all this panelling?' Hebe shot him a suspicious look. 'No, no, Starling did not say anything, but I have uncommonly sharp hearing.'

'Yes, I can find my way,' Hebe said. 'Goodnight.' The stairs seemed endless, but the corridors were well lit with candles and she found her way easily to her room. Wearily she tugged the bellpull, and when Charity came sat quietly while the maid unpinned her hair and put away her simple jet jewellery.

When she turned from the basin, however, she taken aback to find the girl had laid out the flimsy night

own and negligée. It seemed ridiculous to put them on,
nd she almost said so, then caught herself in the nick of
me. On top of everything else, she was going to have
) pretend to the servants that she and their master were
njoying a perfectly normal married life.

Finally, clean, powdered, beribboned and dressed in
er finery, she dismissed Charity and began to explore
er new suite. The bedroom was vast with a half-tester
ed and looming furniture. Well, if Alex said she could
dulge herself with the house, this was where she was
)ing to start.

Through a jib door hidden in the panelling was her
essing room, with its clothes presses and the luxury of
earth closet behind a further door. Hebe had read
out new, water-flushing closets: that too was an indul-
nce she was ready to try.

The final door, when she twisted the handle, was
:ked. She looked at it perplexed for a moment, then
lised what it was—the door that led through to Alex's
ssing room and bedchamber.

With a soft sigh Hebe discarded the exquisite negligée
d went to bed, remembering to crumple the sheets on
far side of the bed and burrow her head into the
ows until it looked as though it had been occupied all
ht by two people.

he lay for a long time staring sightlessly into the dark-
;, but she did not hear Alex pass her door or enter his
room, and no key turned in the dressing-room lock
night.

Chapter Twenty-Three

Days at Tasborough Hall began to fall into a pleasa[nt]
pattern during that first week. They would breakfast t[o]
gether, sometimes joined by Anna, sometimes not. The[n]
Alex would vanish to consult with his steward or he[s]
gamekeeper and Hebe and Anna would explore t[he]
house, talk to Mrs Fitton and Mrs Dexter, the formidab[le]
cook, or ride out around the estate visiting tenants.

Usually Alex joined them for luncheon. On the fi[rst]
day Hebe decreed that the sunny parlour on the so[uth]
face of the house would from now on be the Sm[all]
Dining Room, whatever Starling said about the cavern[ous]
chamber that had previously carried that appellation. S[he]
tried to imagine the occasion when the Large Din[ing]
Room might be pressed into service, but only a State v[isit]
seemed appropriate. The butler was rapidly getting [the]
measure of his new mistress and noted her list of ord[ers]
about drapery, furniture and paintings with a perfe[ctly]
straight face.

'I am not prepared,' Hebe said firmly, 'to eat my l[un]
cheon facing a gentleman who appears to be in the [habit]
of casting me into hellfire.' She gestured towards an [ex]
ceedingly large and gloomy portrait of a gentleman [in]

in severe dress in the style of the preceding century. He
clasped a large volume in one hand and had the other
raised, apparently for the chastisement of all before him.

'Ah, Grandfather Bellingham,' Alex observed, strolling in at that moment. Hebe was within an ace of saying
'So that's where you get the look from' when she remembered the presence of the butler and bit her tongue.
Alex's expression showed he had read her mind with
tolerable accuracy. Hebe twinkled at him and received a
wink in return.

'And what would your ladyship wish to be placed there
instead?' Starling enquired, managing to ignore the byplay with the superb aloofness of the superior upper servant.

Later, over their evening glass of brandy, he relaxed
his guard with Mrs Fitton. *'Anything you like, Starling,*
he said, *just so long as it is cheerful.* Cheerful! I ask
you, Mrs Fitton, where am I going to find something
cheerful in this house? Mind you, she's a real lady, I will
say that for her.' And the housekeeper had nodded in
solemn agreement.

The ladies stayed in until three o'clock for the first few
days in case of visitors, but they received none. Most of
the local gentry wrote letters of felicitation following the
discreet announcement in the newspapers, but, respecting
the early days of mourning, stayed away and no invitations were issued.

Hebe consulted Starling on when they might expect
callers and was told that it would be perhaps three weeks
before their isolation was broken. She could only be glad,
for it would give her a breathing space to become accustomed to her new role before she had to play the
countess to a no doubt inquisitive and possibly critical

audience. After that they decided to use the sunny after-
noons more profitably and either rode or drove out to
visit all the tenants on the list which Glossop, the steward, gave Hebe.

The days were pleasantly full of new experiences, new
lessons and new people to meet. Hebe felt busy and useful and enjoyed Anna's company. Even dinnertime was
less of a strain with a more modest menu, a small table
and fewer hovering servants. At Hebe's request Anna
joined them, but she refused to do so on more than al-
ternate evenings. 'You have to grow accustomed to being
alone with him, ducky,' she said, patting Hebe's cheek
'You feel safe with him, do you not?'

Hebe felt like retorting that she felt all too safe, bu
said nothing. She lived in fear that Anna would decide
that enough was enough and she was going to lectur
Alex on his husbandly duties. The thought made Heb
cringe with embarrassment, so she did her best to mak
Anna believe that she was content.

But the evenings were another matter. Hebe felt a coi
stant tension, however relaxed and charming Alex wa
He always made time to sit and talk about her day, te
her about his and he was full of praise for her effor
with staff and tenants. Already he was giving Mr Glossc
instructions based on Hebe's observations about bad
thatched roofs on cottages, or holes in hedges.

Yet, despite his praise and his consideration, she w
acutely conscious of how he kept his distance from h
and of a constraint that entered his voice whenever s
strayed into too personal a topic.

At first Hebe could not account for it, then she beg
to wonder if it was the effect on a healthy, virile you
man of leading a celibate life. She could not believe
had a mistress in the country and he was certainly r

the sort of landlord who would prey on the daughters of his tenants for sport. In London, of course, even Hebe knew there would be ample opportunity for a man to find congenial and obliging female companionship, and for all she knew, Alex already had a mistress established.

She wondered if she should encourage him to go up to Town, although quite how to do so without betraying her motives eluded her, and much as she loved him and wanted what was best for him, she could not quite bring herself to plot stratagems to deliver him into the hands of some willing barque of frailty.

Eventually she confided in Anna, who raised her eyebrows somewhat at her young friend's earnest enquiries about the deleterious effects of self-denial on men, but answered her willingly enough.

'Well, priests and monks do it for life, of course. At least, they should,' she amended carefully. 'But they have strong reason for doing so and are supported by their vows and the discipline of their faith. For ordinary men, I would say it often makes them, what is the word? Grumped? No, grumpy and short-tempered, and it is not comfortable for them to desire it but not to be able to consummate it.' She eyed Hebe's face as she sat there unconsciously nibbling the end of one finger in thought. 'You know, it is not of such meaning for a man as for a woman. For women, except of course those who sell their favours, it is important to feel an attachment, at the very last, for the man. Men do not have that need, they can separate love and lusting.'

All Hebe said was, 'Oh. Thank you for explaining, Anna,' but her friend had given her much to think about. Alex could separate one from the other, then he could make love to Hebe while still loving Clarissa. In fact, she realised, looking back with as much composure as she could, that was what had happened. In his delirium he had spoken of Clarissa, but had felt a strong enough physical attraction for her for it to overcome his fever and weakness when she lay in his arms.

So, she reasoned carefully as she wandered up and down the brick paths of the flourishing herb garden on the south side of the house, his restraint now stemmed only from the fact that he did not want to shock her or frighten her after what had happened in France, and because he did not love her he had no driving reason to attempt to seduce her out of what he interpreted as her revulsion. *So*, she continued, *if I try, I can probably lure him into my bed.* But at that point she stopped. No, she could not do it. What she had told him was true, it had to be a love match for her, anything else was not right.

She had reached this conclusion when Anna appeared around the side of the house, her broad straw hat swinging from its deep grey ribbons, her quietly elegant walking dress showing off her striking figure. Far better than Hebe, Anna could wear black to advantage for it suited her dark, dramatic looks to perfection.

'Are you ready for our drive?' she asked. 'The gig is at the front. I have spoken to Mr Glossop and he has told me how to find those last three farms we have not visited.' She conned the list in her hand. 'Bourne Farm, that is Mr Peterson, then there is Cold Furlong: Mr Grayson and finally, he suggested we call at Flint Acre on our way back. A Mr Thorne.'

They duly made their calls. Mr Peterson was elderly and supported by three stalwart sons, each with a wife and brood of children, spilling out of the cottages that hugged the farmhouse close. Mr Grayson was jovial with an equally cheerful wife and they were invited in for plum cake and a glass of his cowslip wine and a comprehensive account of all the doings at Cold Furlong.

Taking the reins afterwards, Hebe confided, 'I think I am a trifle tipsy, goodness knows what he puts in that wine.'

'Indeed, yes,' Anna agreed, tying on her hat more firmly. 'Now, let me think, first left here and another mile, Mr Glossop said. This Mr Thorne is a widower with no children.'

The farm came in sight, a rambling brick and flint dwelling that appeared to have grown over the years, like a humble version of the Hall. The farmyard was well kept and busy and the men stopped their work to touch their hats and take the pony's reins. The master was in, they confirmed, if the ladies would just like to step round there into the garden.

He was indeed tending a magnificent cottage garden in the best traditional style. As he saw them approach he straightened up, brushing the soil off his hands: a tall, well-built man of about forty with an open expression and a shock of blond hair. Around him the beds were a riot of flowers, close packed and all blooming in abundance. In between were rows of vegetables, in some cases they were even mixed, and Hebe saw beans growing through roses and onions rearing up through the geraniums.

'Oh how lovely!' she exclaimed, breathing in the scent of delight. 'Oh Anna, look, there are beehives as well.'

But her companion was silent. Hebe glanced at her and realised that not only was the farmer staring at Anna with the air of a man who had been struck dumb, but the Spanish woman was meeting his gaze with equal intensity. How long they might have stood there if she had

not spoken, Hebe had no idea, but she coughed and Mr
Thorne started out of his trance and came towards them.

'Good afternoon, ladies. May I be of service?' His
voice had the slight West Hertfordshire burr, and close
to Hebe saw he had blue eyes and laughter lines around
his eyes. She liked him on sight.

'I am Lady Tasborough,' she said, holding out her
hand and laughingly ignoring his protest that he had been
gardening and was all earthy. 'And this is my companion,
Mrs Wilkins.' To her amusement Anna was now formi-
dably in control of herself and inclined her head with fine
Spanish dignity. 'We are visiting all the farms on the
estate to meet everyone: I do hope this is not an incon-
venient moment?'

'Oh, no, my lady,' he assured her. 'Might I offer you
some refreshment?'

Hebe refused, explaining that they had just sampled
Mr Grayson's cowslip wine and were feeling somewhat
over-refreshed.

'Ah, yes, Jimmy Grayson's peggle wine is notorious
hereabouts, my lady, you did well to refuse a second
glass.'

Hebe, looking sideways at Anna, who was feigning
complete indifference to the farmer, said, 'Might we look
around your lovely garden?' and set off down a path
leaving Anna and Mr Thorne perforce to fall in together
behind her.

'This is very beautiful, Mr Thorne,' she continued.
'You must have green fingers.'

'Green fingers?' Anna asked.

'Have you not heard the expression, ma'am? Lady
Tasborough wishes to compliment me on being able to
make things grow.'

'Ah,' Anna said. 'I had not heard it. My late husband was a man of the towns, you understand.'

Oh, well done, Anna, Hebe smiled inwardly. *How neatly you have let him know you are a widow.*

The Spanish woman scanned the garden and remarked, 'But you do not have the green finger for the 'erbs, Mr Thorne.' Indeed, the herb patch was a sorry sight, sparse and straggly with several plants run to seed. 'You should have planted them more in the sun.'

He listened meekly to the criticism. 'They are poor, I do acknowledge, ma'am. My late wife always grew the pot herbs, and since she died six years ago, I haven't really had the heart to struggle with them.'

So, now you both know the other is free, Hebe chuckled to herself. *Who is going to make the next move?*

'There is a fine 'erb garden at the Hall,' Anna mused. 'If Lady Tasborough does not object, I could bring you some plants from there if I pass this way again. But you must plant them in the sun, and mix some little stones—'

'Grit, ma'am.'

'Ah? Grit, then, with the earth.'

'Perhaps you will be good enough to direct me? I will dig over a bed, ready, and lay in some grit. Would that patch there do?'

Quite forgotten, Hebe perched on a bench and stroked the ginger cat who was sunning himself on it while Anna lectured Mr Thorne. At last they remembered her and hurried back, he looking flushed and self-conscious, she with an air of having put right a problem to her entire satisfaction.

Hebe was itching to say something as they drove back, and knew Anna was waiting for her to do so, but wickedly she launched into a lengthy monologue on the delightful Peterson family, wondering if their cottages were big enough, whether a second well should be dug and speculating about the quality of the village school, if one existed. She had a good idea that her lack of interest would perversely send Anna off with her basket of herbs far sooner than she would have done if teased and encouraged.

Back at the Hall, she left Anna eying the herb garden and hurried in. 'Where is his lordship, Starling?'

'The Long Gallery, my lady. I mentioned a nasty crack in the plaster, I believe his lordship has gone to look at it.'

Hebe whisked up the stairs into the Jacobean part of the house where a long gallery, built to provide indoor exercise when it was too inclement outside for the ladies to walk, remained the principle hanging space for the family portraits. She had not given them much attention before, waiting to ask Alex to show them to her, and now she ran past them without a second glance to where he was standing, head back, looking up at the ceiling.

The sound of her running feet caught his attention at once and he swung round, his face anxious. 'Hebe?'

'Oh, nothing is wrong. Goodness, what a nasty crack Oh, Alex, the most famous thing!' She perched on the edge of a heavily carved table and beamed at him.

'Do you want me to guess?' He came and stood before her, smiling at the pleasure on her face. It was the closest he had been to her for days, and Hebe tried not to let affect her visibly.

'You never will guess,' she said, 'Anna is in love!'

'In love? That is very quick, is it not? With whom?'

'Mr Thorne, one of your tenant farmers. We were visiting today: he seems such a nice man, and he has the most beautiful garden. He and Anna just took one loo at each other, and I think if I had not coughed, they would be standing there still, eye-fast.'

'Love at first sight?' Alex sounded dubious. 'Do you believe in such nonsense?'

'It is not nonsense,' Hebe averred stoutly. 'I have just seen it happen before my very eyes. I think it is lovely, but I want you to ask Mr Glossop about Mr Thorne. It would be dreadful if he proved to have beaten his late wife, or has a fatal tendency to drink or some such thing.'

'I will do as you ask, although I have a sinking feeling that if we do discover something to Thorne's discredit, you are going to expect me to warn him off.' There was something in Alex's expression that chilled Hebe suddenly. He still appeared perfectly pleasant, yet when he asked, 'So, love at first sight, a *coup de foudre*, is your ideal, is it?' she felt she had erred very badly in blurting out her enthusiasm. Alex had always remarked sardonically on her desire for a love match: did he think now he was comparing her own marriage unfavourably with Anna's new affection?

'Good heavens, no!' she said as lightly as she could, sliding down from the table. 'Why, it is almost a fairy tale: one certainly could not wish for it.'

'Not like an ordinary love match, then?' she thought he said under his breath, but when she looked at him he showed no sign of having spoken. They began to walk back along the Gallery, stepping in and out of the checkers of sunlight cast by the lead-paned windows on the polished boards. Hebe racked her brains for some less sensitive subject of conversation.

'Will that crack in the plaster be a problem?' she asked at last.

'I am not sure, I will get Glossop to have it investigated whilst I am away.'

'You are going away?'

'Yes, I must go up to London for a few days, I am sorry, I meant to mention it at breakfast.'

'Oh, good,' Hebe said, relieved that he would be able to visit his mistress, or some other lady of the night, and relieve his enforced celibacy.

'Good?' Understandably Alex sounded surprised.

'Oh, I mean…that is, I am sure you will find the change is good for you,' she babbled. 'With no visitors at the moment, and so many memories in this house…oh and you will be able to visit Aunt and Uncle Fulgrave, would be glad if you could take letters…' She ground to a halt in the face of his sceptical expression.

'I do hope you too have not acquired a lover in the short time you have been here,' he said lightly.

'No! I wish you would not tease me, Alex,' Hebe said vehemently. 'What if someone had overheard and took you seriously?'

'And what makes you think I am not serious?' he asked with a lift of his dark brows that left her entirely at a loss to know whether he was teasing her or warning her. 'You must excuse me, I have to talk to Glossop.'

Hebe was left at the end of the Long Gallery, staring after her husband with a sick feeling in the pit of her stomach. That conversation had gone incredibly badly, she knew. It was as though the careful pretence of a normal life that they had constructed had suddenly cracked open: not wide enough to bring the structure tumbling down, but enough to make her deeply uneasy at what might lie beneath.

Just like that crack in the ceiling, she thought, wandering back down the Gallery for want of anything else to do. Then her attention was caught by the portraits the walls and, more for something to think about at first, then with increasing absorption, she began to study them.

They had not been hung in any sort of chronological order, so it became a game to try and sort them out. There was a small, very dark charcoal sketch that she thought might be Tudor, some very stilted Jacobean ladies and gentlemen, none of whom looked as though they resembled real life and suddenly a number of what she felt were true portraits.

Living, breathing people stared out at her from the eighteenth-century canvases. In their best clothes, adopting postures of dignity and solemnity to be sure, but real faces for all that. She began to find resemblances to Alex, mainly in the line of the jaw and the shape of the eye. Then she found a more recent picture, a charming, almost informal family group, and she realised she had found the source of Alex's incredible looks.

The scene was a picnic under a spreading tree. A gentleman stood leaning against the trunk. His wife, her wide brocade skirts flaring about her, sat on a rug on the grass, clasping a small boy—Alex—to her. His taller brother stood beside his mother, his father's hand on his shoulder.

The woman was undoubtedly Alex's mother—her raven head gleamed beside the identical locks of the little boy in her arms and two pairs of deep blue eyes regarded Hebe seriously across the years. The older boy was more like his father, lighter in colouring, stockier, with the same jawline as Alex, but with less refinement in his face.

Fascinated, Hebe stood studying the portrait group for a long time before she turned and walked slowly out of the Long Gallery. The import of those generations of similar Beresfords hit her with the force of a blow. Son had succeeded father down the years and the pride of that lineage showed on every face. What Alex had sworn to by promising never to touch her was to deny himself those heirs, those succeeding, unknown generations.

Had that occurred to him yet, or was he still too distressed by the deaths of his father and brother and by the revelation of what had happened between Hebe and himself to consider it? Or had being in the Gallery just now recalled it to him and was that why he had been so abrasive?

And what, in the face of his intransigence, should she do about it?

Chapter Twenty-Four

Dinner that night was a difficult meal. Anna, who still appeared to be in a daze, absently made her excuses and did not appear. Hebe felt she was in disgrace in some way, but could not account for it other than that Alex was still displeased by her unguarded enthusiasm for his trip to London.

She tried to think of ways to raise the subject, but realised that any mention of it would be protesting too much and could make him even more suspicious.

Alex was scrupulously polite, making conversation about the events of the day and ensuring she had exactly what she wanted to eat, that her glass was filled and that the salt cellar was instantly at her hand the moment she looked for it. Hebe would have been even more mortified if she realised what Starling was saying to the footman when he managed to draw him outside the dining room for a moment.

'His lordship's in a rare taking tonight, so just you be careful, my lad! No dropping plates, no slopping soup. Do nothing to draw his attention to you or aggravate his nerves.'

'But he seems very pleasant tonight, Mr Starling,' the

young footman whispered back. 'Never a cross word, so attentive to her ladyship.'

The butler rolled his eyes at such innocence. 'Don't you believe it, lad,' he unbent so far as to advise. 'Just watch his eyes.'

So the junior footman took the opportunity to do just that when he was pouring his lordship's wine and nearly dropped the bottle when he got the full force of the cold blue gaze. *Gawd*, he thought, backing away to stand by the panelled wall. *I wouldn't want to be in her ladyship' shoes tonight.*

Unaware of the silent sympathy of her staff, Heb struggled through the meal, politely responding to eac' question or observation. She was so relieved when it wa time for her to withdraw that she could almost hav thrown herself on to Starling's fatherly chest and sobbe when he opened the door for her with a sudden smi' that instantly vanished again behind his mask of profe: sional impassivity.

The small salon was pleasantly lit by numerou branches of candles and a fire that flickered cheerfull although the evening was warm enough for it not to ! necessary. Starling had realised that his mistress miss the sunnier southern climes and had ordered fires lit the evening in the hope she would find them comfortin

Hebe shivered, out of nerves rather than any chill, a picked up her embroidery. She had set herself the ta of replacing all the dining-room chair-seat covers. As s had not yet managed to ascertain exactly how ma chairs there were in the set, she had a sinking feeling t was an over-ambitious project for a reluctant need woman. Starling, on being questioned, thought th might be twenty-four in various rooms: she could o hope he was wrong.

Part of her hoped that Alex would not come in. The braver part told her that she could not just let him go off tomorrow to Town with whatever was between them unresolved. But when he did join her, Hebe found no words at all.

'What did you do for the rest of the afternoon?' Alex enquired at length, having flicked through the news sheet in silence, trimmed the wick on a guttering candle and picked up a skein of silk from the floor.

Hebe jumped guiltily as though he had demanded the name of her lover and said, 'I was looking at the portraits in the Long Gallery.'

'Indeed? What did you make of them?'

'Some I thought were very fine as pictures, but the ones I liked best were those where you could see the real person there.' She hesitated. 'I liked the one of you with your parents and brother very much.' He said nothing. 'Your mother was so beautiful.'

'Yes. She died soon after that was painted. Some sudden inflammation of the lungs. I do not think my father was ever quite the same again after that.'

'It must have been terrible for you and your brother,' Hebe said, her voice trembling at the thought of the effect on those two little boys all those years ago.

He nodded, apparently unwilling to speak of it, and Hebe had no intention of pressing him. Then he suddenly remarked, 'It taught me to conceal my feelings. Perhaps too well.' It seemed to her that his face softened, the hard lines relaxing until she could see the hurt and the anger beneath the skin.

What devil prompted Hebe to speak she had no idea. It was as though the question left her lips without any thought passing through her head at all. 'Alex, do you want children of your own? Do you not want heirs?'

His head came up and he looked at her with all the furious arrogance of the bird of prey she had likened him to in Malta. 'I have heirs.'

'You have?' she faltered.

'My father had two younger brothers. They have three surviving sons between them and I have lost count of the male grandsons: six, I think, at the last count. I have no need of heirs, Hebe. Believe me, the Beresford name is quite safe.'

'I am sorry,' she stammered, unsure what she was apologising for. 'Will you excuse me? I feel rather tired. I will go to bed.' She was aware of him getting to his feet, but she tossed her embroidery hoop on to the chair and walked swiftly from the room. Alex did not follow.

Once in her room she rang for Charity and went through the process of undressing and preparing for bed as though in a dream. Not until the maid had slipped her nightgown over her head did Hebe realise it was the exquisite bridal nightgown, just returned from laundering and fragrant with rose scent.

Somehow she got the girl out of the room before she gave way to tears. They were the first she had shed since marrying Alex, for she had resolved to find happiness where she could in this strange alliance and not to repine. But now, certain that he must be bitterly regretting ever having tied himself to this loveless, sterile, marriage, she turned her face into the soft lawn of her pillow and wept bitterly, without inhibition.

How long the tears lasted she had no idea, but she finally sat up, scrubbing at her wet face with the back of her hand and finding her mind clearer. And with the clarity came a growing sense of guilt as she thought back over the past few weeks.

Alex had offered her everything, including his absolute

promise not to press on her demands he was certain would be repulsive to her. The only thing he had not given her was love. But how could he, if he had given it to someone else? *How would I feel,* this new, clear-headed Hebe wondered, *if I knew Alex was lost to me entirely? Would I lightly tell someone else that I loved them? Of course not!*

But she had demanded a love match and had made it clear that he had forced her to accept him because he could not offer her that. Hebe wrapped her arms around her bent knees and stared ahead into the candlelight.

Anna had told her that men did not have to love the woman they lay with. Why could she not put her high flights of sensibility behind her and go to Alex? She need not tell him she loved him and so make him feel sorry for her, she could simply let him see she craved his affection and nearness. If it made him feel better to make love to her, and if he knew she was not repulsed or frightened by him, surely they could only grow closer? And if she became pregnant again, however many nephews he had, surely he would be happy to have his own family?

Before she could explore this terrifying train of thought any more and lose her nerve Hebe threw back the covers and ran on bare feet to the door. She pulled it open abruptly and took a step back with a gasp as her action almost propelled Alex into the room.

Hebe realised he must have been standing close against the heavy panels, his hands pressed against them. With the reflexes of a cat he regained his balance on the threshold and stood, his hands either side on the door frame, his eyes dark and intense on her tearstained face.

'Alex! What are you doing here?'

'I heard you crying.'

'But I stopped crying quite ten minutes ago.'

'I know.' He had been standing there, she realised, prevented by his promise from entering her room, yet unable to leave her weeping alone. Hebe saw he was wearing a long silk dressing gown, his feet bare on the boards.

Alex followed her eyes and said simply, 'I heard you crying as I went past to my room. I started to go to bed, but I had to come back and then I found I could not leave.' Hebe was so touched that she could not speak. After a moment he added, 'Where were you going?'

Hebe swallowed. Now, if ever, was the time to have courage and follow her heart. 'To your room.'

'*My room?* But why?'

'Because…because—' Hebe broke off, feeling the blush rising steadily up her throat to stain her face. 'Because I wanted to go to your bed, Alex.' There, she had said it.

The shuttered look had come down over his face again. Hebe could have wept. 'Why?' he asked harshly. 'Because you feel guilty about not giving me an heir?'

'No! Not guilty, but sad about that. And sad too that I should have driven you from my bed because of my nonsense about love matches and the fact that I did not have the courage to tell you that I am not afraid of…of you.'

Alex stared into her face with the look of a man trying to unravel a deep and mysterious riddle. 'You are not afraid? After what happened in France? After I raped you? After I have seen you recoil every time I tried to touch you?' He sounded incredulous.

'You did not rape me,' Hebe retorted, furiously. 'And I did not want you to touch me because if you had would have found myself in your arms and I knew yo did not love me.' She had lost her temper now, wit herself or with him she could not tell, but it made saying all this much easier. 'I was such a fool, I said those things about love matches and I told myself I could not possibly be a proper wife to you because you loved Clarissa. I should have been happy with what I could have...'

'*I? Love Clarissa?*' His voice cut across her tumble of words, silencing her.

'Why, yes. You proposed to her. You were amazed and delighted when she wrote to accept you. You stopped flirting with me. Mrs Fitton said that when you got her second letter you...you... She said you groaned Clarissa's name, then said "my love, my love" as though your heart was breaking.'

'How the devil did she know that? And what was she about, to tell you of it?'

'She told me she came into the room quietly, not realising you were there, just when you opened the letter. She told me the first day I came here because she thought I was an old friend of the family and I had expressed anxiety about how you must feel with your double bereavement. She meant it for the best, Alex: she was furious with Clarissa and thought I might be able to help you if I knew, I think.'

'No wonder you were so difficult to convince when I came to London. Hebe, once and for all, I do not love Clarissa and I do not think I ever did.'

'But you proposed to her!' Hebe's feet were growing colder by the minute but she was quite unaware of them, or of the cold draughts playing over her exposed skin in the fragile gown.

'I had been on the receiving end of yet another lecture from my father on getting married and starting a family. Clarissa was beautiful. It was the fashion to believe one was in love with her. I proposed, she laughed at me and sent me on my way. I wonder now if I asked her because I knew she would say no, and at least I could show my father I was trying to put his advice into practice.'

'Then when she accepted you, you had no choice but to pretend to be happy about it,' Hebe said, with a wave of joyful comprehension running through her. 'It would have been dishonourable to tell anyone of your true feelings, let alone jilt her.' Her courage was building with every passing moment. Dare she… 'Alex, that day in the garden, before her letter came…were you going to say anything to me?'

Still he did not touch her, his hands clenched so that the knuckles showed white as he stayed framed in the doorway. 'I was going to ask you to marry me, Hebe.'

'I thought so,' she breathed. 'Why?'

'Because I love you,' Alex said, finally uttering the words she had dreamed of for so long. 'What would you have said?'

'I would have said yes, Alex, because I love you.'

For the longest moment he stayed still, his eyes reading her face as though he could not quite believe her words, then his arms came down and round her and she was crushed against his chest. Hebe thought he was going to kiss her, but he held her away so he could look into her face.

'When I knew I was no longer tied to Clarissa I had no idea where you were—on the Rock being flirted with by half the officers of the Mediterranean fleet for all I knew. I could not leave home because of my father and my brother, but I wanted to find you so badly. It was you I was speaking of when Mrs Fitton heard me, only you my darling, enchanting, lost Circe.

'Like a dream, as I was reeling from William's death you walked into my house. I could not believe it wa possible to be so happy. Then you tell me that I raped you, that I had hurt you and that I had made you pregnant. It was as though I had despoiled the most precious thing in the world. I dared not touch you, all I could do was to try, somehow, to make some small amends. And then—' his voice broke '—then you were…ill.'

'Oh, Alex, darling, how can I convince you that there is nothing to forgive?'

As though he feared his dream might shatter, Alex bent his head and found her lips, his mouth gentle. Yet the kiss was not tentative: Hebe felt utterly cherished, sheltered by his love. Shyly she kissed him back, her lips moving sweetly under his, parting to the urging of his, until she gasped at the invasion of his tongue and the heat of longing and desire lanced through her.

Without knowing it, her fingers dug into his back through the thick silk and she sensed the change in his body as he realised she was truly not afraid and that she wanted him.

Suddenly there was the sound of footsteps and an exclamation. Alex swung round and, peeping below his sheltering arm, Hebe could see Starling, improbably clad in heavy flannel nightrobe, slippers on his feet and a nightcap on his head. He had a bunch of keys in one hand and a candle snuffer in the other.

'My lord! I beg you pardon, I was doing my rounds and extinguishing the candles, as you see. Is everything all right, my lord? I did not look to find you here in the corridor…' His voice trailed away in the face of a situation beyond the experience of the most superior butler.

'Everything is quite all right, I thank you, Starling. I was merely kissing my wife.'

Hebe, torn between blushes and giggles, tugged at Alex's arm, but he stood firm while Starling gathered his wits and bowed slightly. 'Goodnight, my lord. Good-night, my lady. It is, if I may say so, my lord, somewhat chilly for her ladyship to be out in this draughty corridor at this hour.'

'Thank you, Starling, I believe you are right.'

Hebe watched as the butler vanished around the corner. 'Oh, poor Starling! Alex, you must apologise to him in the morning, it is way and beyond what any butler might be expected to have to deal with.'

Alex looked down with laughter brimming in his eyes. 'Nonsense, do him good: he might go and flirt with Mrs Fitton as a result. But he is right about the cold, my darling, you are frozen.'

'So are you, Alex, come in and shut the door.'

He hesitated, 'I promised I would not…'

'Then I end the promise!' Hebe tugged his arm and shut the door firmly before his scruples could persuade him to retreat again. She curved her arms around his neck and gazed up into his face. 'Please, Alex, make love to me.'

He stooped and she found herself lifted high in his arms and the next moment she was lying on the bed, her hair fanning the pillows, the fine fabric of the nightgown lightly veiling her body. Alex closed his eyes, one hand clenched on the bedpost. 'You are so lovely. I cannot believe that you can trust me after what happened.'

Hebe sat up, curled her legs under her and reached out to tug at his arm. 'Alex, listen to me! I cannot pretend that was how I wanted to lose my virginity. I cannot pretend it did not hurt, because it did. But, Alex, none of that mattered, because it was *you*. Can you not understand? I loved you then, I love you now.'

He sat on the bed beside her, taking her hands in his 'Do you really mean that, Hebe? Oh, my love, if you w let me I will show you how it ought to be, and I promise I will not hurt you.'

Hebe smiled trustingly back at him. 'I knew that must be the case. I expect it would always hurt the first time, and, after all, you hardly had your mind on the matter. Nor, I hope, do you have much experience with virgins.' Alex gave a muffled snort of laughter and dropped his face into his hands. Hebe could see his ears turning red. 'Oh, dear, I am sorry, that was a most improper thing to say.'

Alex opened his hands, revealing his face alight with laughter and something else that made Hebe's stomach contract sharply with a strange sensation which made her breathless. 'My innocent Circe: we are married now, it is almost compulsory to have improper conversations. Whilst we are being so frank, would you care to tell me why you were so pleased at the news that I was going to London tomorrow?'

'Oh, dear. That really is *extremely* improper. Must I tell you?'

She realised with a start that Alex was trailing one long finger up and down her right ankle. It made it extraordinarily difficult to think. 'Yes, you must.'

'Very well, I thought you would be going to visit your mistress.'

'My what? Hebe, let me assure you, I do not have a mistress, and if I did, it passes my comprehension that you should be pleased about it.'

'Well, you were not sleeping with me, and I was sure you would not behave towards the local girls in any improper way, so I thought you must be feeling…well, Anna said it made men grumpy. I thought if you went to London you could find one of the muslin company and that would make you feel better.'

'The only thing that was making me grumpy, as Anna so charmingly puts it, was the fact that I was burning to make endless, passionate, highly improper love to my wife. What other helpful advice did my good friend Mrs Wilkins give you?'

'Only that men do not need to be in love with the lady they are making love to. That is what made me think that perhaps you would not repulse me if I came to your bed tonight.'

Alex looked at her grimly. 'Tomorrow I am not going to London. I am going down to see Thomas Thorne and tell him that if he does not marry that woman by special licence within the week and remove her from this household I will tear up his tenancy.'

Hebe snorted. 'What nonsense. Anna did not interfere, she simply answered my questions when I asked her things. I have not been discussing you with her, I promise. I would just ask her for general information.'

'Then, Madam Wife, allow me to give you one very particular piece of information. I love you. I will never want to make love to another woman for as long as you are mine, and I fully intend for that to be for the rest of our lives. Is that quite clear?'

'Yes, my lord,' Hebe said meekly, then, 'Alex if you do not make love to me very quickly and stop doing whatever it is you are doing to my ankle I think I will have strong hysterics.'

'The last thing I intend to do is to make love to you quickly, Circe. I intend to be very, very slow.' He reached out and started to untie the ribbon bows that formed the shoulder straps of Hebe's nightgown. 'This a very fetching piece of nonsense. Just exactly how does it come off…ah, yes. And then down here, just so.' Wi

he last bow untied the gown slid from Hebe's body like
a retreating wavelet over warm sand.

Alex stared down at the smooth, pale skin, trembling
lightly with shyness under his gaze. 'Did I tell you once
that you were not beautiful, Circe? I was so very wrong.'

Hebe reached out and tugged at the belt of his robe.
'Ah, yes,' Alex said as he shrugged it off his shoulders.
'You have the advantage of me, having washed, prodded,
bandaged and bullied my unfortunate and unconscious
naked body in the past.' His eyes twinkled wickedly.
'Still no fig leaf, despite your studies of the classical
nude.' He saw her eyes widen as she took in the fact that
he was very aroused. 'It will be all right…'

'I know,' Hebe said firmly. 'It was…I mean, in the
dark I did not quite realise.'

'Stop being brave, my love, just kiss me and trust me.'
Hebe was borne back on to the bed, Alex's long form
stretched beside her, his mouth tantalising hers until all
she could think about was the feel of his lips, the warmth
of his mouth, the taste of him.

He began to caress her, his hands running gently over
her body until she was moaning and twisting with the
teasing, unrelenting sensation. Only then did he lift his
mouth from hers and catch one peaking nipple between
his teeth. Hebe sobbed and arched towards the incredible
sensation that seemed to reach deep inside her. While his
mouth and lips continued to tease her aching breasts, his
hand moved lightly down, never stopping its subtle ca-
resses until she suddenly gasped with mingled shock and
exquisite erotic torment as he touched the most intimate
place.

Without hesitation he shifted his weight over her and
before Hebe realised what was happening he had possessed her. This time there was no pain, nothing but a

soaring, aching, building crescendo of feeling. She was
unaware of her mouth feverishly seeking and finding his
only to break off to kiss the hot smooth skin of his shoul
der above her, unaware of her nails in the hard muscl
of his back as he arched over her. All she was aware o
was the agonising, wonderful torment of their mutua
passion and, as her body strained against his, of the soar
ing release of utter ecstasy that racked her even as Ale
cried out above her.

Hebe opened her eyes to find Alex's face close abov
hers, his gaze wide and dark as he watched her. Ther
was a look of such possessive tenderness and awe in h
eyes that she trembled and tears sprang to the corners
her eyes.

'Hebe, darling.' He was all concern, rolling off h
body and cradling her against his chest. 'Darling lov
what is wrong?'

'Nothing,' Hebe murmured against his chest, rubbi
her cheek against the dark hair. 'Nothing at all. I am j
so very happy.' She felt, rather than heard, his sigh
relief, snuggling down against him as he pulled the co
erlet over their hot, relaxed bodies.

'Go to sleep now, Circe.' Alex's voice was husky
he nuzzled the angle where her neck met the smo
slope of her shoulder.

'Must I? Cannot we make love again?'

Alex rolled over on to his back, pulling her with I
so that she lay on top of him. 'One of the things wh
your invaluable Anna obviously did not tell you is
men require a while between bouts of passion. Howe
if you lie there and continue wriggling in just that
voking and outrageous manner I can promise you tha
wait will be short.'

Hebe twinkled wickedly. 'Really? Like this?' She

rewarded with a slap on her behind, which made her giggle.

'Are you going to prove to be a wanton wife, Madam?' Alex enquired severely, not quite managing to disguise how ragged his breathing was becoming.

'Would you like that?' Hebe enquired, seeing the answer very plainly on his face. She suddenly laughed with pure happiness. 'Oh, Alex, I know I am only a very ordinary enchantress, but I do have some powers after all. I have turned you into a husband!'

'More than that,' he whispered, pulling her hard against him. 'You have turned me into the happiest of men. I never realised that part of me was missing until I found you, my Circe. I told you that you were dangerous, for the void did not hurt until I realised it was there: then it ached unbearably. But now I am complete, whole, and I'll never cease to love you for it.'

And Hebe, in her new wisdom, did not seek to answer Alex with words, only with her lips as they sought and found his and spoke silently of her love for him.

* * * * *

THE ELLIOTTS

Mixing Business with Pleasure

The saga continues with

The Forbidden Twin

by

SUSAN CROSBY

(SD #1717)

Scarlet Elliott's secret crush is finally unveiled
as she takes the plunge and seduces her twin
sister's ex-fiancé. The relationship is forbidden,
the attraction…undeniable.

On Sale April 2006

*Available at your
favorite retail outlet.*